Praise for Dorien Kelly

"Warmly appealing, thanks to its assured prose and deft
characterizations."
—*Publishers Weekly* on *Hot Nights in Ballymuir*

"Smartly written, the characters are entertaining, with
dialog zinging between Jenna and Dev.... Kelly is an
author who delivers first-rate reads."
—*Oakland Press* on *Hot Nights in Ballymuir*

"Warm and captivating, *Hot Nights in Ballymuir* is a
charmer from the talented Kelly."
—*Romantic Times BOOKclub*

"...an upbeat, bright bit of romance sure to whet readers'
appetites for more."
—*Oakland Press* on *Designs on Jake*

"Ms. Kelly has a rare talent for writing amusing and
realistic dialogue."
—*Romantic Times BOOKclub* on *Designs on Jake*

"Strong plot...a touching novel.... Lovers of Irish romance
will definitely look forward to the next installment."
—*Romantic Times BOOKclub* on
The Last Bride in Ballymuir

"Readers will not believe that *The Last Bride in Ballymuir*
is Dorien Kelly's debut novel and will be looking
forward to more novels from this series of contemporary
romances featuring foreign locations."
—*Midwest Book Review*

Dorien Kelly

Dorien Kelly is a former attorney who is much happier as an author. In addition to her years practicing business law, at one point or another she has also been a waitress, a law school teaching assistant and a professional chauffeur to her three children.

When Dorien isn't writing or driving her kids to after-school activities, she loves to travel, dabble in gourmet cooking and avoid doing the laundry. A RITA® Award nominee, she is also the winner of the Romance Writers of America's Golden Heart Award and the Georgia Romance Writers' Maggie Award. Dorien lives in Michigan with her husband, children and two incredibly spoiled West Highland white terriers named Ceili and Seamus.

DORIEN KELLY

Off the Map

OFF THE MAP

copyright © 2006 Dorien Kelly

isbn 0373880812

TheNextNovel.com

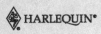 HARLEQUIN®

PRINTED IN U.S.A.

To Rod and Martha Westergaard,
for two wonderful words: Costa Rica.

CHAPTER 1

In the grand scheme of things, Tessa Wright considered herself a relatively uncrazy person. She was Prozac- and Xanax-free and required only the occasional tune-up from her therapist. Yet she sensed vultures circling outside her office door. She said as much to her friend and fellow banker, Kate.

"That's paranoia talking," replied Kate, no mincer of words.

Tessa supposed her unrest might be chemically induced, rising with the glue fumes from her new carpeting. More likely, though, it was a spot-on assessment of her prospects for continued employment.

"Be logical," Kate said as she lounged in the one guest chair that fit in Tessa's small space. "We're both members of the streamlining team. They wouldn't have asked us to join the group if they plan to terminate us. This place has always been about teamwork, and no one's done it better than us."

True, to a point. They had met at Midwest National Bank as fledgling credit analysts seventeen years earlier. To Tessa, that first heart-pounding, new-suit, hopes-abounding day seemed in some ways recent and in others ancient history. She and Kate had been anomalies, staying on instead of job-hopping in Detroit's volatile financial services industry. In those years together, they had formed an alliance. Kate was the balls-out tough member of the team, and Tessa was the charm and diplomacy department.

Ultimately they'd been rewarded, too—though Kate more so. She was a first vice president in charge of the asset-based lending group, and since that promotion, also Tessa's boss. For friendship's sake, Tessa had managed to swallow her jealousy with only the occasional hiccup.

"Teamwork? Absolutely," she said. "Teamwork's key, right up until the moment you're summoned upstairs and terminated. We all die alone."

"Relax, Tessa. Morbid doesn't suit you," Kate replied.

Tessa knew it didn't, but the events of the past several weeks—the former coworkers departing with their boxes of personal effects, the falsely jocular farewell parties where too much was drunk and too much said—had taken their toll. She'd developed a taste for gallows humor and an alarming fondness for the acid bitterness that had begun to leach into her heart.

"I think I'm wearing morbid rather well."

Kate's smile was tinged with the sense of impending doom they all carried these days. "You're wearing it as well as any of us are wearing our armor."

Which wasn't saying much. Kate was edgier than usual, and Tessa nearly out of ways to smooth the turbulent atmosphere. Still, they would survive. She and Kate had weathered changes in management, changes in economy, fashion crises, men crises and some all-around botching-up of their lives. And as essentially different as they were, they'd stuck it out together.

Kate stood. "I need a cigarette and you need to clear out of here for a few minutes. Come on, let's go walk the fitness trail."

The heavily treed path winding through the headquarters' suburban campus was most often used by smokers seeking sanctuary from smoke-free laws. Kate, a chain-smoker, was now incredibly and ironically fit. Tessa, who had never smoked, could hardly keep up. In this instance, she preferred to blame her penchant for high heels rather than her avoidance of exercise in any form. Still, it was a balmy—by Michigan standards—seventy-degree, mid-October day. She would walk and pretend to enjoy it.

They were nearly to the elevators when Kate's secretary stopped them. "Kate, Simon Pearson wants to see you in his office."

Pearson, the corporate angel of death. Since the firings had begun, silence and averted gazes had become his harbingers in the hallways. A mention of his name killed conversation. To be summoned meant career annihilation.

Tessa's reaction to Kate's summons wasn't her finest moment. She briefly closed her eyes and tried to quell her mental celebration, but it was a losing battle. She sent one selfish and heartfelt thought out into the universe: *Thank God the vultures weren't mine.*

When she again focused on Kate, her friend had lost much of the color beneath her fading tan. Tessa was sure that even gutsy Kate sometimes bolted awake at four in the morning, cold with panic because her job could be going away. In Tessa's experience, exhaustion and the human mind's resilience were generally enough to lull one past those moments—but when faced with the reality…?

"Shit," Kate said.

Kate's secretary had already moved two steps back, as though retreating from the creeping grasp of failure. "I'll, uh, just…"

"Go on," Kate told her, calmer now. "You might as well start finding me a couple of boxes for my things."

Tessa scrambled for poise, folding her hands together. She was startled to find them shaking, but shouldn't have been, considering the metallic taste of fear heavy in her mouth.

"Do you want me to come up there and wait for you?" The offer had been impetuous and, she suddenly realized, impolitic.

Kate shook her head and punched the elevator's up button. "No. As you said, we all die alone."

After Kate had stepped into the elevator, Tessa considered making a weak joke about Kate's trip to a better place, but found she didn't have the stomach for it. Gallows humor was losing its gloss.

She returned to her mini-office, pausing briefly outside her door to look at the charcoal-colored placard with her name imprinted in neat white letters. As her circumstances had changed, she had slid that particular bit of plastic—and before, one like it bearing her maiden name—in and out of any number of holders. She thought of Kate, soon to tuck her nameplate into a box and depart, and knew yet another unbecoming moment of relief. This was the first time she would willingly cede the role of trailblazer to Kate Murkowski.

Tessa sat, elbows braced on her desk, head bowed with thumbs pressed to her cheekbones and fingers following the arch of her widow's peak—her customary pose for corporate meditation. She had customers to call and, thanks to a dearth of credit analysts to handle grunt work, financial reporting to input into the bank's tracking system. Both could wait. So many tasks had fallen onto the wait list since she'd become aware that the bank wasn't staying its course.

Dinner with one of her husband Jack's customers? Not in the past eight months. She couldn't, and she'd be poor company, anyway.

Sneak away midafternoon for some rare "together time"? Impossible. She needed to be seen at her desk, just for appearances, if not to actually function.

For months now, she'd been awaiting her fate. In some small way Kate had been the lucky one today. Not that Tessa planned to share the sentiment with her.

Eyes closed, Tessa listened to the ebb and flow of conversation as people passed by her door to linger in front of Kate's. She didn't bother straining for the words, for most would be spoken with insincerity. Seeing the mighty tumble had a way of bringing quiet glee. As she well knew.

The unsentimental truth was that someone would have to replace Kate, though not at Kate's salary level, which Tessa knew was loftier than her own. It wasn't as though the bank could extract itself from the business of asset-based lending. Around industrial Detroit, machinery and equipment were the coin of the realm. They were a gritty form of collateral, and worth a fraction of their original purchase price when liquidated, but unavoidable.

It was wrong, almost like corpse-robbing, but already Tessa considered the comforts of Kate's full-size office. One with a window, two guest chairs and space for files. As the bank had begun to pare down, it had packed more employees into the headquarters building. In this process Tessa's office—and a number of others—had been subdivided. Kate had said not to take it personally; the facilities department had told her that it had been a matter of Tessa's location. And at least she had new carpet.

The quietly selfish voice that Tessa seldom let slip out had whispered that Kate was just next door. Why had she been immune? Now regret nipped at Tessa for both her prior and present selfishness.

"Napping again?"

Tessa looked up to see Kate in the doorway. She'd regained a measure of her color, though the set of her jaw remained tense.

"The deed's done," she said.

"And how was it?" Tessa asked, uncertain of what else one said to the newly terminated. Unlike some in the building, she'd shied away from the firing postmortems.

Kate shrugged. "Clinical. I have two days to wrap up matters and give final reports to Hank," she said, referring to her direct superior. "Really, it was painless."

Kate had never lied well, always giving herself away with a subtle roll of the shoulders, as though the fit of her clothing had grown too tight. This time was no different.

"I'm sorry," Tessa said. Those, at least, were the appropriate words.

"I'll be okay. It's no big deal."

Tessa noted the shifting of shoulders that marked yet another lie. She wanted to be able to fix this for Kate, to give some assurance that everything would indeed be okay, but that particular well had run dry.

Kate glanced over her shoulder at the small group clustered on the outer boundary of the cubicle maze behind her. "I *really* need that cigarette now. In fact, I need the hell out of here." She paused and shook her head, perhaps recalling that her wish had just been permanently granted.

"Why don't you head over to Dante's?" Tessa suggested. "I'll meet you when I'm done here."

Dante's was a bistro not far from both Kate's and Tessa's homes. Over the years, it had become their official Friday evening cocktail/appetizer/gripe session location.

Kate nodded and was gone. Tessa rose and closed her office door. Better to be trapped in an airless closet, adrift on the buzz of glue fumes, than to witness the whispers, e-mails and gossip now rippling out from the epicenter of the latest firing.

After a few minutes, Kate's side of a phone conversation came through the wall to Tessa. She couldn't pick up the particulars, but the hostile tone was obvious, as was the hard ricochet of the receiver being slammed into its base. Following that was the louder slam of Kate's door. And thus a new era began.

Tessa debated calling Jack just to share the morning's heartache, but knew that even if she reached him, he wouldn't have time to deal with her issues. It would be yet another of the "Yeah, babe, life's a bitch all the way around these days. Did you get a minute to pick up the dry cleaning?" calls she'd lately come to expect. And accept. It hadn't always been this way, and Tessa hated that it was, now.

Any time for the blues on that count, too, was cut short by the phone ringing. She cleared her throat and attempted a greeting that made her sound engaged instead of fume-addled.

"Tessa Wright," she said, wincing at the way she'd tripped over her own tongue.

"Tessa, this is Simon Pearson. Could you come up to my office?"

There had been moments in Tessa's life when time seemed to go as thick and slow as amber forming—the Halloween night her mother called to tell her that her father had died, the humid June morning at the top of Chicago's Navy Pier Ferris wheel when Jack had proposed, and, it seemed, *now*....

First vice president? She'd had only a brief moment of imagined glory, but that made the downward death spiral no less dizzying.

"Of course." Devoid of any emotion but shock, she hung up and tried out Kate's favorite word. "Shit." Tessa seldom swore, but at the moment she could appreciate its appeal. She repeated the word, this time with more gusto. Her blood began to move again, sluggishly at first, and then with enough force that she could breathe. One last time she said it, a furious indictment of Midwest National. *Shit* was undeniably a one-size-fits-all word for her day. And the sewage had just begun to flow downhill.

Midwest National's executive floor was what one would expect in an age marked by terrorist threats and corporate overcompensation: posh, clubby paradise under prison lockdown. After she'd cleared the bulletproof-glass-encased security screening area, Tessa took her time walking to Pearson's office. In the end, though, there was no delaying her fate. Simon's secretary efficiently escorted her those last few feet.

Pearson's office was appointed as though he had tried to create an aura of old money—deep greens and paisleys that also smacked vaguely of hotel furnishings. Simon, too, was slightly skewed. The man's well-rehearsed smile shone eerily white, his teeth so bleached that they appeared to be false. Not at all the look he was going for, Tessa was quite sure.

He extended his hand. Out of rote politeness and with no remorse for her clammy palm, she shook it. Once they'd exchanged brief greetings, she noted another occupant in the room.

"Tessa, this is Marta Reynolds from legal," Pearson said. "She'll be sitting in with us."

Marta, whom Tessa had seen in the cafeteria a few times, nodded, then took a seat in one of the two fat club chairs opposite Simon's desk. Tessa knew the woman's purpose. She was a silent observer, a set of corporate eyes should Tessa later bring a claim regarding her firing. Tessa sat in the chair next to the lawyer. Pearson circled to his side of the desk. "This has been a difficult time, Tessa," he said as he settled in.

Did he actually think she'd feel sorry for him? She withheld comment, as airing the thought "you pompous bleached bastard" wouldn't help on the reference front.

"To improve the bank's performance, we've had to make some adjustments. We've instituted a hiring freeze for all but entry level positions and—"

"I'm aware of all this. I'm on the streamlining team," she said automatically.

He glanced down at some paperwork on his desk. "Oh, that's right."

Marta the Silent shifted slightly, her impatience with him obvious. Tessa stung under the knowledge that she hadn't been worth more time in Pearson's day.

He leaned forward, resting his palms either side of the file he'd not quite read. Some distant part of Tessa, a cool spectator, noted his calculated effort to create a connection with her. She preferred her executioners impersonal, thanks.

"Tessa, yours is among the positions that we're forced to eliminate. It's sheer economics at play and certainly no reflection on your performance."

On the way upstairs, she'd tried to prepare herself, to tell herself that the nonsense about "a better place" that she'd spared Kate was really true. She'd tried, but evidently not quite hard enough. The illusion of detachment wavered and then vanished as she watched her life fall into two distinct halves: Successful Bank Executive and Unemployed Nearly-Forty No One.

"It's no reflection? Odd how it feels that way, then. I'll agree that my portfolio's performance is slipping, but what would you expect when my customers are automotive suppliers? The industry is gasping for air. If senior management weren't so anxious to sell the bank, this wouldn't..."

She trailed off, realizing that Simon Pearson was somewhere past uninterested in her career crisis, and worse, a member of the senior management who would grow very rich if the bank sold. There was no talking her way around this. As the daughter of a man who'd been one heck of a lawyer, she was genetically predisposed to detest the thought of words being insufficient.

"Look," she said, "I know you have no idea what I do every day, any more than I know what you do...except fire people."

"You're not being fired, Tessa. You're being streamlined."

Fancy that. "I'd have settled for a little liposuction." Tessa's breath hitched. Her internal editor—a creature she'd trained too damn well—had slacked off shockingly.

The corner of Pearson's mouth twitched, but held fast against a smile. She supposed that was about as much as she could expect in the way of genuine response from a hatchet man.

Her anger receded and, like Kate before her, she simply wanted out. "Why don't you just tell me the terms?"

Now that she'd gone back to script, her executioner relaxed. "You'll find our separation agreement generous," he said, extracting a thin document from the "Let's Streamline Tessa" file. "You'll receive six months' severance, job placement services and continuation of your health insurance for the same term. We'll also compensate you for any accrued vacation or sick days." He slid the document across his desk. "Take this and review it. Once it's signed, we'll get you in process."

Six months was more than the gossiped-about "week of pay for each year of employment" that she'd dreaded.

"I'll want time to have my lawyer look at it, too," she said, thinking that now she'd also have to find an attorney who specialized in employment law.

"Of course," he said. "Though you should know that we make it a practice not to negotiate these agreements. Once you're comfortable with the terms, just drop the signed document with my secretary." He gave a subtle glance toward the door, and followed that with a more obvious one at his watch. Tessa guessed that the meter was running on sham solicitude.

"Take care, Tessa," he said.

As she stood, the separation agreement slipped from her fingertips. With a muttered expletive, she picked it up, then left.

When she returned to her office, the flock of vultures lurked a few cubicles away in the maze, as though biding their time to be sure she was well and truly dead. Judging by the chill that had worked into her bones, they didn't have long to wait. Ignoring the avid glances cast her way, she closed her door and called Jack.

"Be there," she said, but even when life had been at its best, he'd never been a man of impeccable timing. She got his voice mail, and in exchange he received the word of the day.

Tessa rose, opened her door a fraction and peeked out. The vultures hadn't completely dispersed, and she lacked the luxury of a secretary to find her packing boxes.

A voice rose from a nearby cubicle. "You know the deal. She has to confirm it before the pool pays out."

Jesus. They'd started a firing pool? She'd enjoyed a bit of betting on babies and basketball, but this made her sick. With no thought other than finding sanctuary, Tessa grabbed her car keys and fled. She hurried though the parking lot, unlocked her car and threw her purse onto the passenger seat. Hand shaking, she jammed the key into the ignition. And as Midwest National disappeared behind her, Tessa finally cried.

So much for being in a better place.

CHAPTER 2

The interior rooms of Dante's were dimly lit, which Tessa viewed as her first flat-out blessing of the day. Lunchtime was fifteen minutes off, but she knew that if she looked around, she'd happen across acquaintances. Head down, she took a direct line to the bar. Both her throat and emotions were too raw for a brief hello, save the inevitable cheery small talk that would ensue.

Relieved to have skirted conversation, Tessa slipped her purse's strap over the ladder-backed beech stool next to Kate's.

"Hey," she said in greeting before awkwardly settling in. She remained convinced that tall stools were created to strip the dignity from short women.

"Hey, yourself," Kate said. "I wasn't expecting you for another couple of hours."

Tessa wasn't quite sure where to start, so she began with a thought that had struck her on the drive to the bistro. "I should have gone to art school."

Kate tilted her head. "Okay, I think I see where this is going, but I'm game for a story…. Go on."

"When I was sixteen, I told my parents I wanted to go to

art school and work on my painting skills. I had always been the artsy type, and even had a couple of awards by then. My dad was all for it." Which was exactly why she'd adored her father. "But Mom took me aside and told me that the biggest mistake she'd ever made was not having any money-making job skills she could fall back on. She begged me not to do the same thing."

"She made good sense," Kate said.

"Yesterday, I would have agreed. And back then, that conversation changed the way I looked at her…always wondering if she stayed with my dad because she didn't know what else to do. I decided I'd save myself that grief and paint as a hobby."

"And so you got a business degree?"

Tessa nodded. "A lot of good it did me. Seventeen years of hard work shot to hell. So…I should have gone to art school."

"Bastards." Kate shot her a wry sidelong glance. "And I had myself convinced that you'd have my job before the close of business. I suppose you'd been thinking the same thing."

Ouch. The truth definitely hurt. Tessa didn't answer and instead dug through her purse in search of cash.

"We've got another victim here, Mark," Kate called to the bartender. She looked again at Tessa. "What can I get you? Decaf iced tea? Mineral water with a wedge of lime?"

Kate's benign offerings were Tessa's standard fare. It was

no secret that she and Jack had been trying for a baby for the past handful of years. With Jack's cheerful atta-girl urging, Tessa's body was part plump temple, part science project. Right now, though, she simply didn't care about her folic acid intake, sushi avoidance, or the rest of her endless litany of pre-pregnancy rules. All she wanted was an alcohol delivery device.

"A martini," she said, then hedged on her bravado. "Apple."

"Really?" Kate paused to light a cigarette. "What's Jack going to say?"

"What can he? Pregnancy and job hunts are mutually exclusive events." Even Jack, with his ardent—nearly fanatical—pursuit of fatherhood, would have to understand that. It wasn't as though their "trying" ever showed signs of success, anyway.

Kate nodded. "You've got a good point. Apple martini, Mark."

Tessa slipped a cocktail napkin from the stack at the bar's inner edge and began to fold it into tighter and tighter squares. Now that the initial rush of emotion had passed, leaving her dry and empty, she didn't want to think of Jack. And she'd sooner eat Kate's cigarette butts than call him again.

She needed time to construct a subtle means to break the news of her firing...one that wouldn't elicit his standard first response in all Tessa-created crises—angry lecturing, as though she were a child.

They were in this together, and they were in trouble. They would never cover their massive mortgage payments on his income alone. Last year, when they'd bought their new house in lovely and socially ambitious Birmingham, the possibility of unemployment hadn't even entered into the equation. Now that she had absorbed the day's full weight, panic began to stir. Tessa shoved aside the napkin and sought a new distraction.

"I don't think I've been in a bar before noon in ten years at least," she said to Kate.

"Not even poolside on vacation?"

"Never. You know Jack...supercompetitor to the end. Even on vacation, he's up at the crack of dawn, parasailing or rock climbing or whatever. I figure it's my duty to keep balance in the universe, so I sleep in."

"Tough job, but someone's gotta do it," Kate agreed.

The bartender set a martini glass garnished with a thin wedge of Granny Smith apple in front of Tessa. She supposed an argument could be made that the drink wasn't entirely unhealthful. A sip of the chill, pale green liquid told her that it was also going to knock her on her rear.

Kate slid a small silver dish of roasted nuts her way. "So, should we ask for our farewell party to be held here?"

Tessa's heart lurched. "I don't want a party. I just want to…I don't know…slink off, I guess."

"No party? That's about the only half-decent thing coming out of this mess."

"I'd rather just lick my wounds and then move on." In an effort to chase away the bitterness, she took another swallow of her martini. The only drawback she could find in the drink was its small size.

"Lick away," Kate said. "I plan to sit back and relax on Midwest National's dime for a while. Speaking of which…" She dug into the large purse she used in lieu of a briefcase. "Have you read this piece of work yet?"

Tessa glanced over. It appeared to be the same agreement that Simon Pearson had pushed across the desk at her. "No." She would delay that depressing task for as long as possible.

"It's a real treat," Kate said as she paged through the document. "We're waiving claims of any sort that we might have against the bank, including age and sexual discrimination. And if we don't sign…no severance. I've signed already. Good thing I can be bought as easily as I can be screwed over, isn't it?"

Tessa absently nodded.

Age discrimination. She took another swig of her drink. Jesus, was she already that old?

Oh, she knew on a rational level that the language was likely in every arrogantly onerous agreement that the bank had dealt out, but still it stung. Kate didn't seem to care, though. Then again, she didn't feel the press of years in the horribly personal way that Tessa did. Kate dated, but hadn't had a long-term relationship since splitting with her fiancé five years earlier.

Tessa measured each passing month with yet another failure to conceive. For a while she'd held out hope in herself, then hope in science. Now she mostly hoped that Jack would give it up and agree to adoption. He'd become skilled at evading any real discussion, and she'd decided to back off the issue until he seemed more receptive.

With no solace to be found in that topic, she reached for the nuts and began picking through them for her favorites. As she nibbled the cashews, she watched Kate and Mark the bartender flirt with an ease she'd once had. The only time she joined in the chat was to ask Mark for a refill on the martini.

Time drifted by, clouded with Kate's cigarette smoke and passed in desultory conversation with the older man who'd sat on the other side of Tessa for a quick meal. Once the second drink was down, Tessa's life began to look better. A bit blurred, perhaps, but nothing she couldn't face…tomorrow. Today was all about surviving until then.

She and Kate ordered a late lunch. Tessa opted for pasta to soak up the vodka sloshing in her stomach. She could have used a trip to the ladies' room, but she knew she'd be none too steady on her feet.

"So I'm thinking maybe Jamaica," Kate said.

"Jamaica?" Tessa echoed. She seemed to have lost her conversational bearings along with her balance.

"Sure. A week at one of those all-inclusive resorts where all I have to worry about is sunblock and condoms. And not in that order," she added with a smile. "Want to come along?"

"Assuming we can find the money, I'll still have to ask Jack about his vacation schedule."

Kate looked as though she were about to choke on the wine she'd just sipped. "I was hoping for more of a girls' week," she said after clearing her throat.

"I'm not sure if—" Tessa paused. Kate's cell phone, which sat on the bar next to her cigarettes, had begun to vibrate, the sound as low and angry as a hornet's wings.

"Sorry," Kate said, then read the caller ID, swore and flipped open the phone. "Do you have something else you want to say?" she asked the caller in the same tone that Tessa reserved for only the lowest of telephone solicitors.

Kate faced away from Tessa, which of course made her all the more curious about the call. Still, to keep up the pretense of lack of interest, she motioned Mark over for a third and final drink.

Tessa started a bit when Kate made a scoffing sound.

"Like that helps. You're just digging yourself in deeper." Whatever the caller offered next also failed to appease. She sat up arrow straight. "Get screwed, Hank," Kate said with enough volume to carry from the bar to the dining rooms beyond. "And not by me anymore."

Hank?

Tessa ventured for possible Hanks, and only one came to mind—their boss. It was, she was sure, just her brain's attempt to give familiarity to an unfamiliar turn of events. Imperious and often hostile Hank Kyle wasn't the sort of man one spoke to that way...or screwed. Along with his various unpleasant character quirks, he was also married.

Kate snapped her phone shut, then drained the last of the wine from her glass.

"Want me to pretend I didn't hear that call?" Tessa asked.

Kate hooked a lock of hair behind her ear, then shook her head. "Thanks for the offer, but there's not much point."

"In that case... Hank, as in Hank Kyle?"

"Hank, as in total duplicitous shit Kyle."

"What do you mean?"

"He knew I was getting fired. He knew and did nothing about it." Kate paused long enough to nod her thanks to Mark, who'd placed a salad in front of her and pasta in front of Tessa. "Four years of perfunctory sex on every third Tuesday of the month. Four years wasted believing that, yes, Rita had been unfaithful before he'd given in to his attraction to me, and that—on his mother's grave, yet—he was going to leave Rita as soon as she was stable enough to support herself. All that believing on my part, and he couldn't even give me a heads-up in exchange. God, I'll bet his mother's not even dead."

Tessa pushed past the rather nasty moral issues, seizing the thought that at least Hank and Rita Kyle had no children. Unfortunately, she was then snagged by an uncomfortable mental image of Kate and Hank and perfunctory sex. It was a stubborn little portrait, requiring a large swallow of martini number three before it would be excised.

"Well," Tessa said to Kate once she'd regained control over her imagination, "you're better off rid of him."

"To the extent I ever had him at all…agreed. But it still hurts. Stupid, huh?"

Just as stupid as it was for Tessa to be hurt that Kate had hidden this.

"Hey, don't get that look," Kate said.

"Which one?" Tessa asked, though she knew.

"The supremely disappointed one," Kate replied. "I couldn't tell you, Tessa. I knew you'd have problems with the being-with-a-married-guy idea, and I didn't want to drag you into the bank's antifraternization policy. It was one thing to risk my job because I thought I loved the dolt, but to leave you with the knowledge that if you were going to live up to your moral high road, you'd have to report me? I couldn't do that to us."

Tessa was too weary to fight. "One less drink in me and I'd be really hurt. But as it is, I'm just going to let it roll on over me and save the ache for morning."

"I am sorry, Tessa. Really. To the bottom of whatever soul bankers might have. Which circle of hell are we supposed to be in, anyway?"

Tessa smiled in spite of herself. "Fourth or seventh, depending on the interest rate we charge."

When they'd first stopped at Dante's all those years ago, it had been out of a sense of aptness. As most of their bitch sessions consisted of consigning Midwest National's more galling souls to their appropriate circle of hell, a restaurant named for *Inferno*'s author had been too perfect.

"Good, you're softening," Kate said. She waved Mark back over. "How about two shots of Cuervo Gold, up," she said.

He looked at them closely, his expression borderline dubious. "For the public good, your car keys first. Both of you. And a promise you'll actually eat your food."

Cuervo? Tessa kept the tequila stocked for Jack and a few of his buddies, but she'd never tried it. Or felt particularly inclined to, until today.

Kate's keys hit the counter with a loud *clank*. Tessa dug through her purse, then tossed her key ring atop Kate's. Jack was going to kill her, but she'd deal with that later. After the tequila.

"To finally seeking our goddamn bliss," Kate said. "We have to grab it, Tessa."

"To bliss," Tessa replied, though to the extent she thought of bliss, she had pretty relaxed expectations.

The Cuervo sat well in her mouth and slipped down her throat painlessly, but then her stomach lodged a wrenching complaint.

"Another?" Kate asked, after exhaling with a satisfied hiss.

"Don't think so," Tessa said once she'd tamed her gag reflex. "It's pasta time."

Though her meal had reached room temperature and her appetite had fled, she did a fair job of self-defensive eating. She hadn't been this buzzed in forever, and she was sliding south into naptime. As Tessa ate, Kate upped her flirtation campaign with Mark. Tessa supposed she couldn't blame her. She'd want a memory to write over that of bad sex with Hank Kyle. Just as Tessa wanted to be able once again to make love with Jack, instead of having optimally timed sex.

As she nudged the last bit of fettuccine around its shallow, broad-rimmed bowl, the muffled ring tone of her cell phone slowly came to her. Numb fingers did not make for good purse mining. The phone had stopped ringing by the time she'd dredged it out. She checked the number.

"Jack," she said aloud, feeling a mix of relief and, oddly enough, guilt.

Kate exhaled a thin stream of smoke from her latest cigarette, then gave her a teasing "uh-oh."

Tessa frowned at the phone.

"Gonna call him back?" Kate asked.

"I'll have to, sooner or later."

She set her phone on the bar next to Kate's. Not much later, the phone rang again.

"Jack again, right?" Kate asked, blond brows arched.

Tessa nodded. Recently, patience had become something Jack demanded be bestowed upon him, but seldom gave in return.

"Hello?" she said.

"Where are you, babe? I've been calling for the past hour." He sounded rushed, which was nothing new. "Dante's," Tessa replied.

"Christ—and with Kate, no doubt." Even though Kate had introduced them to each other back in the dark ages, he was no fan of hers.

"Yes."

"I give you your Fridays. Isn't that enough?"

Tessa bit back a cynical laugh. She could now sit here Monday on through, steeped in apple martinis, Cuervo and self-pity.

"Think you can tear yourself away and come home?" Jack asked. "I've been waiting for you."

"What time is it?" she blurted while trying to twist her watch around so she could read its face without moving the phone from her ear.

"Six," he replied, saving her the effort. "I came home early. I thought maybe after your one-word message on my voice mail, we should have dinner together."

"Sorry," she said.

"So, will you come home?"

She glanced at the cash register now holding her keys. "Uh...I can't."

"*Can't?*"

"Mark took my car keys."

"Mark?"

"Bartender Mark. Before a shot of Cuervo. Sneaky stuff."

She half waited for Jack to launch a rant about her drinking and half watched Mark flirt some more with Kate.

"I don't know what the hell's going on, but I'll come get you," Jack said.

Even Tessa's dulled state didn't soften her surprise at Jack's tirade-free response. She chalked it up to the fact that, other than her lack of efficiency in reproduction, she'd done nothing to move him off his aggressively charted life course. All that compliance should buy a woman a one-day pass for irresponsibility. Maybe Jack had finally grasped that. Or maybe he was just saving it up.

Jack arrived, and Tessa's heart sped as it did every time he walked into a room. He possessed a classic handsomeness that would always turn women's heads. She, on the other hand, was what her mother had once cheerily described as "almost unusual." Tessa, who preferred to think of her deep olive skin and dark brown hair prone to tight, unmanageable curls as exotic, hadn't bothered to act flattered.

"Ready?" Jack asked, tight-faced and not quite meeting her eyes.

Tessa privately thought of this as Jack's shunning act. Since she was lapsed Catholic and not Amish, it had never particularly rattled her.

"Sure," she replied.

She stood and teetered on her heels as he settled the bill and collected her keys from Mark. Tessa gave Kate a hug as Jack impatiently waited.

"I'll call you in the morning," she said to Kate.

"Make it the afternoon," her friend replied.

Tessa held fast to Jack's arm as he led her to the parking lot. She looked around and failed to see his beloved blue Mercedes. "Where's your car?"

"I had someone from the office drop me here."

Tessa frowned. She could swear he'd called from home earlier, not the office, but her brain was too soggy with drink for her to be sure of much of anything.

"So, want to tell me why you're drunk?" Jack asked.

"Cuervo. Definitely the Cuervo and not the martinis."

"Funny, babe. Now, why the Cuervo?" he asked as he opened the front passenger door to her well-used Taurus—a car she'd kept for matters of economy, but resented nonetheless.

She should have skipped the damn tequila and worked on that diplomatic explanation. As it was, all she had was a rebelling stomach and words of few syllables.

"I lost my job," she announced as her bottom hit the upholstery.

Jack hesitated, then said, "You *what?*"

A cloying heat wave climbed her body, and Tessa groped for the seat heater controls, until she recalled that the car wasn't that fancy. Her surroundings began to spin. Tessa braced her hand on the dashboard.

"Lost my job. Let's talk at home."

The door closed with the force of a gunshot, and Tessa suspected that she was about to be very, very ill.

The red glow of the digital alarm clock on Tessa's nightstand made out a fuzzy 5:14 a.m. She assumed she wasn't dead, though that might have been a preferable state. She usually slept spooned to Jack. She loved the way her heartbeat seemed timed with his. She'd always held this synchronicity as evidence that they were meant to be together—even when life distracted them from that essential truth. Last night, though, she'd clung to the outside of the bed simply to shorten her trip to the bathroom, should she be sick again. She was officially swearing off both tequila and terminations.

Tessa rolled onto her side and reached for Jack, but the bed was empty. The linens were rumpled and the pillow bore the indentation where his head had rested, so at least she hadn't forced him to flee to the guest bedroom. She rose slowly and made her way to the bath, where she showered, brushed her teeth twice over and pulled on her favorite gold-colored silken robe. She had amends to make and explanations to give. While she'd managed to get out the bare facts before going facedown into her pillow, she hadn't gotten to the saving grace of six months' severance.

Tessa switched on the hallway light and padded downstairs. Jack would likely be in the basement with his workout equipment. The basement door was open, but no lights shone from below.

"Jack?" she called softly toward the kitchen, not fully ready to break the peace of the predawn hour.

He didn't answer, but from the direction of the den at the back of the house, she picked up the muted sound of his voice. Tessa walked the unlit hallway, truly knowing this place even with eyes closed. On moving in, the den was the first room for which they'd bought new furniture, making it into a home office for the two of them.

Jack sat at the desk, his back to her and phone to his ear as he faced the large picture window opening onto their backyard. It was dark enough that the small brass desk lamp left him in a circle of light, and the window gave her a ghostly reflection of his face.

"Jack?"

He swiveled around in the sleek leather chair they'd chosen together. Tessa watched as his expression altered from relaxed to guarded. She tugged the lapels of her robe tighter about her chest, then came closer.

"I'll talk to you later," he said to whomever he'd been speaking with, then hung up the phone. "Feeling better?" he asked her.

Tessa pushed her fingertips through her hair, which was wild of its own wavy accord and from her sleep of the dead.

"Nothing a gallon of water and a few aspirin won't fix. Couldn't you sleep?" she asked, evading the question that really begged delivery.

His gaze darted from item to item on the desk between them, before finally settling on her face. "Sophie's pregnant."

"Sophie, the sales rep at your office?" she asked once she'd caught up with the leap in topic.

He nodded.

Tessa didn't recall Sophie being married, but she'd never paid much attention to those sorts of details. Actually, she'd never even met Sophie. All she knew was that Sophie and Jack had been working together for the past several months to wrap up a lucrative parts order for car dashboards.

"It shouldn't affect closing the GM deal, should it?" she asked.

"No. But, Tessa…"

It was as though Tessa's heart grasped what Jack was trying to say before her mind would let in the meaning. Her pulse raced rabbit-fast as she spoke. "I know it's tough every time someone comes up pregnant before us, but we can handle it."

Her comment was met by a silence that made her feel even sicker than the tequila had. "Jack, what is it?"

"Sophie's pregnant...and I'm the father."

Tessa braced her hands on the desk, trying to absorb the blow. Jack shifted slightly, and she glanced at their wavering reflection in the window in front of her. *Scene from the End of a Marriage*, she'd call the tableau.

He scrubbed his hand over his face, and for the first time in the eleven years she'd known him, Jack cried. "Christ, Tessa, I'm so sorry. I didn't want to break it to you like this, but I promised Sophie I'd tell you last night."

Tessa felt it happening as it had the night her dad had died—panic, horror and fury bubbling inside her chest until her heart no longer followed any set rhythm. When she'd let go that Halloween night, she'd begun a spiral down to hell...drinking, driving, accident and addiction. Terrified to let it start again, she frantically pushed back the words and emotions, but was only partially victorious.

The decade she'd spent walling away impulsive Tessa Di-Paulo and nurturing reasoned Tessa Wright crumbled to ash and cinders.

"Fuck Sophie." She clenched her hands so tightly that her nails cut into the flesh of her palms. "Oh, wait...that's right. You already have."

"Babe..."

God, how she hated being called that. The double-edged word smacked of condescension and stood as an indictment of what she could never provide.

"Don't call me babe." She delivered each word in a low, lethal tone that didn't begin to ease the pain slicing through her. She wouldn't be able to hold it together much longer. "I want you to get out."

"But it's not even daylight."

"And your point is?"

"Tessa, be reasonable. We need to talk about what we do next."

"*We?*"

Tessa picked up the first thing her hand brushed—the Orrefors crystal teddy bear figurine he'd given her for Sweetest Day, last year. She'd hated the faceless, saccharine thing. It was cool and heavy in her grip and flew hard and fast when she flung it at his face. Her aim was poor, and Jack dodged to the side. The figurine hit the picture window. Awed, Tessa watched as the thick glass grew a weblike pattern of cracks and then shattered, releasing some of the terrible pressure building inside her.

Slack-jawed, Jack swung around and looked at the window, then back at her. Feeling as though she were channeling Nicholson's brand of lunacy in *The Shining*, she smiled.

"Ready to talk now, Jack?"

Apparently, the moment had passed. Muttering something she couldn't quite catch, he stood and left the room. Not long after, she heard the kitchen door close, the garage door open, and Jack drive away.

In the silence that followed, it occurred to Tessa that maybe yesterday hadn't been that horrible, after all.

CHAPTER 3

Kate's doorbell had shorted out two years ago. She would have had it repaired, except first she'd have to care if someone was at her door, and generally, she didn't appreciate that loss of control. After a childhood spent in a teeming pack of siblings, she liked life better when visitors arrived on her terms. If she wanted someone in her home, she'd tell them in advance. No doorbell needed.

Case in point: Mark the bartender, currently tunneled beneath the covers and doing a damn fine job of waking her up this semihungover morning. Violator of rule: whoever the hell was banging on her front door. It wasn't even seven, an ungodly early hour for the employed, let alone someone in her new and luxuriously lazy state of unemployment.

Mark moved up her body, his blanket-covered head appearing between her breasts.

"You know someone's knocking at your door, right?"

"Low priority," she said.

Nice boy, athletic, determined, but a little too young for

her. He made her realize that her boobs were moving south, and that, fun as it had been, one night with him wasn't going to cure what ailed her. Of course, she'd be willing to see if more than one night might do the trick. Let no one say that Kate Murkowski wasn't fair. Hell, she'd given Hank four years.

The phone at her bedside began to ring.

"Uh…now your phone's ringing," Mark pointed out.

Observant boy, too.

"The answering machine will pick up," she said, rocking her hips to let him know where the real action was supposed to be. The machine did its job, Mark took the hint, and Kate settled back and enjoyed—until the phone rang again.

"Dammit." Tangled with Mark, she rolled to her side and reached for it. "This had better be good," she said to her very favorite bartender, who had slipped away and was now kneeling at the foot of the bed, leaving no camouflage for her past-perky boobs. She grabbed a corner of the sheet, yanked it upward, then picked up the phone. Mark rolled from the bed and ambled toward the bathroom.

"Hello?" Kate said.

"Kate?"

The caller was female and suffering from either very late seasonal allergies or a crying jag. "Yes, it's Kate. Who is this?"

"It's—it's Tessa. I'm downstairs. Do you think you could let me in?"

Tessa? This woman sounded no more like Tessa than Kate did Mary Poppins. "You're downstairs? *Here* downstairs?"

"On your front porch…"

"Holy—" She stood and began wrapping the sheet around herself. "You're joking, right?" She walked to her front bedroom window and pulled aside the drape enough to look out. There in the dim October dawn was Tessa's senior-citizen car, parked in front of her house. "Shit," she murmured.

"Kate, I'm sorry. I know it's early, but—" Whatever Tessa said was lost in a phlegmy sob.

Okay, she could tell Tessa to come back later—like late afternoon or sundown—but curiosity was conquering the knowledge that she couldn't deal with another crisis. She was full to the top herself.

But never Tessa, with her preternatural calm. Tessa had grown so measured over the years, so frighteningly careful. The sobbing wreck on Kate's stoop was as foreign an event as having bartender boy between her sheets…and other locations.

"Hang on. I'll be down in a minute," Kate said, then hung up. She dug through the pile of clothing on the batik-upholstered bench at the end of her bed, extracting a Michigan State sweatshirt and some inside-out black yoga pants. She winced as she pulled on the clothes over skin in need of a shower—preferably with her pet bartender—and then made her way to the bathroom.

Mark was just where she wanted to be, with hot water pelting him and the scent of her rosemary-and-menthol shampoo sharp in the air. She pulled aside the shower curtain and took a moment to appreciate the view, including the scorpion tattoo on his muscled left butt cheek. Maybe *she* wanted a tattoo…or maybe she'd just enjoy his. Less pain and permanence that way.

"Tessa's downstairs," she said. "I need to talk with her. Would you mind too much being really, really quiet?" She worked up her best "I'll make it good for you" tone. "Please?"

She knew the question was demeaning to her guest, but she simply wasn't in the mood to give Tessa any more grounds for disapproval after the Hank-confession yesterday. Kate loved Tessa, one hundred percent, but Tessa had a way of making her feel like a reclamation project. And that upset Kate, because she knew better than most that even Tessa wasn't perfect.

Mark slicked back his hair—nearly black when wet instead of sleek mink brown—and turned off the shower. "Maybe I should just get going. I'll call my roommate and get a ride home."

Fate owed her a morning orgasm, at the very least. "No, really, this shouldn't take long." She stepped over the tub's rim and kissed him. "Promise."

His hands settled on her butt, giving her the uplift that nature, an evil wench, was slowly stealing. "I'll wait."

As Kate made her way downstairs, she noted that her MSU sweatshirt had gone from Spartan green to forest green in a big blotch down the front. With luck, Tessa would be too involved in her crisis to notice some water-spotting.

She opened the front door. Tessa was sitting on the first step, arms circled around her knees and her head tipped down.

"Isn't your butt cold?" Kate asked.

Tessa stood and came inside. "Didn't notice."

Kate spotted Mark's jacket on the living room couch. "Come on into the kitchen," she said to Tessa, feeling a jolt of panic. "I'll get you some water...or something."

Tessa listlessly followed.

Kate flipped on the kitchen light. If she'd had more sleep and less sex, she probably could have been more diplomatic. As it was, she couldn't even fight back her gasp. Tessa's eyes were so swollen she looked as though she'd been on the seriously losing end of a karate match.

"How the hell long have you been crying?" Kate asked.

"Since five-twenty, give or take a minute."

"All over a *job?*" Midwest National had been worth a few tears shed over the slap to her pride, but not this.

"No. Jack."

Ah, smilin' Jack, the biggest jerk ever. "He's not sick, is he?" *I hope.*

Tessa shook her head. "No. He...he got a woman at work pregnant, and I think he wants to leave me for her."

Kate took a second to absorb the news. It wasn't all that difficult to swallow, actually. "And you don't want him gone?"

"Yes…no." Tessa rubbed at a tear. "God, I don't know."

"I'm voting for yes." Of course, she'd also have castrated him by now, while Tessa had apparently just wept.

"I tried to kill him with a crystal teddy bear," Tessa announced.

Now there was something a person didn't hear every day. "And did it work?"

"No. I took out the picture window in the den instead."

Kate's respect increased tenfold. "Damn, Tessa."

An unwilling smile tugged at her mouth. "I was angry."

Kate smiled back. "Just a little, huh?"

Tessa started to cry in earnest, and Kate wished she'd checked her empathy at the door. She was simply no good at handling emotion, which was why dry Hank had so appealed. Besides, Tessa as a wretched mess rattled her. She grabbed a roll of paper towels and unfurled a couple.

"Here… Now do you want that water, or…" Or what? She had no idea what to offer.

Tessa took the paper towels and blew her nose. "What am I going to do?" she asked when she was done.

"You could start with the usual—hire a lawyer, put the screws to Jack, and—"

"I couldn't. Okay, I still want him tortured and then very slowly killed, but this was my fault, too. I've been so distracted by the situation at work. I should have been more aware of Jack's needs… I should have understood how much he wanted a baby."

Kate offered the only comforting thought that came to mind. "I could be wrong here, but I don't think this was a baby derby. I'm betting it was more of an 'oops, the condom slipped.'" Which was obviously the wrong thing to say, as Tessa's sobbing amplified.

"Kate?" asked a male voice.

Shit.

She wheeled around to the doorway. Mark was dressed and had his jacket in hand. She turned to Tessa.

"I'll be right back," she promised.

"No, stay," Mark said. "You've got…" He waved his hand in that uncomfortable way males did—and that she did, too—when faced with tears. "You've got stuff to deal with. I'll call you, though."

"Okay," she said, noting he'd omitted *when* he'd call. *Double shit.*

Mark was gone, and Tessa had somehow managed to go wide-eyed in spite of her overall puffiness.

Kate tipped her head toward the now-empty doorway. "I decided I wanted a little late dessert last night."

"Right. I'd sort of forgotten," Tessa replied. "Jack knocking up a slut tends to do that to me, I guess."

"And I feel compelled to point out that the slut label could extend to Jack."

Tessa blew her nose again. "I'm not feeling very PC. And I don't want to go back to the house alone. Would you come with me?"

Hell, now that Mark had fled, she had nothing else to do. And there was always the off chance she could get lucky and castrate Jack, who had no right to screw up Tessa's life when he'd already done it to Kate years ago, too. But to think of that event was to violate Kate's Cardinal Rule of Survival: No looking back. *Ever*.

"Of course I can come with you," she said to Tessa. "And let's stop by headquarters and drop off our signed separation agreements afterward."

"Separation. God." Tessa's tears started again.

Triple shit. Would she never learn to be sensitive? Kate handed Tessa the roll of paper towels and settled in for the storm.

Three weeks later...

Like the Ramones, Tessa's "damn the man" musical group of choice, Tessa wanted to be sedated.

The twenty-one days she'd been living in Kate's house had been sloppy and self-indulgent. She'd called her mom and wept copious tears over the dual failures of her marriage and career. She'd eaten whatever she craved, kept the guest-room television constantly running, left half-drunk cans of Dr. Pepper—some spiked with vodka—on nearly every flat surface, and fought the sure knowledge that a big, cruel world waited to finish her off. And between the phone calls from Jack's and her friends (mostly Jack's in the end, as there had been an inescapable "have a good life" tenor to their exchanges), she'd slept hours on end…none of them restful.

The sad, soon-to-be-suit-clad truth was that she could hide from Jack no longer. Two weeks ago, she'd served him a lovely Divorce Complaint, and settlement time was upon them. In less than an hour, she was due at her lawyer's office for her first face-to-face meeting with Jack since the attempted murder by teddy bear. She'd managed to shower, don her bathrobe and eat some dry toast, but the thought of pulling on panty hose was so exhausting that she wanted a nap.

Tessa went to the CD player in the living room's entertainment center and switched off Joey and the crew. More sedation would have to wait. Maybe…

Kate, who last week had bought an expensive bicycle as part of her new bliss-seizing campaign, had left for her morning flirtation with Woodward Avenue traffic. Really, no one would be the wiser if Tessa crawled back in bed. Except Jack and the lawyers, and it wasn't as though she courted their good opinions.

Tessa was slinking upstairs to the guest room and its lumpy futon, when the phone rang. She paused halfway up the steps, halted by her conscience. Kate had asked her to pick up any calls while she was out, as she was expecting word from a headhunter about an afternoon interview. Tessa let out her breath in an annoyed huff and padded down to the phone.

"Murkowski residence," she said, raising her voice's pitch and pulling a mock British accent in case her attorney was cagey enough to give her a reminder call.

"Is Tessa Wright there?"

Though the question was tentatively put, the woman's voice sounded familiar. Still, Tessa played on. "Who's calling, please?"

"This is Vee Silverman. I'm a friend of hers."

If Tessa had had more energy, she would have smiled. Glamorous Vee had been not only her friend, but also her idol and apartment-mate during their junior and senior years of college. They both had been princesses—Tessa, the bright, indulged child of her successful father, and Vee, the possessor of a bone-deep grace and confidence that never crossed the line into arrogance.

After college, Tessa had been uncertain she was ready to follow in her father's large footsteps as a civil rights lawyer, so instead decided to conquer the world of finance. Vee had jetted off to California and taken a job as an assistant to an assistant at a movie studio. Irv, a real estate magnate and film investor, had met and married her within six weeks. To say that Vee had become rich was like saying that Jack had developed a slight issue with fidelity. Tessa and Vee had stayed in touch and still managed to see each other a couple of times a year.

Tessa let her voice slide back to normal. "Vee? It's Tessa."

"Thank God for that. I thought the Queen Mum had risen from the dead. Where are you? I just called your house, and Jack gave me this number."

"I'm staying with a friend." She hesitated long enough to brace for the wave of embarrassment that arrived every time she had to give the news. "Jack and I are getting divorced."

"His choice? Yours? Mutual?"

Before Tessa could answer, Vee barreled on. "It doesn't matter. All that does is how you're doing. So how *are* you doing?"

Tessa thought of the panty hose awaiting her upstairs—a miserable prelude to more torture. "Great. Considering..."

Vee made a sound of disbelief. "*Great?* Sure. Tell you what, I was calling to say that I'll be in town today. I'm flying in to see Gram at her nursing home. Can I pick you up at two, your time? I'll make sure the limo's stocked with booze."

"Thanks, but I've had enough lately," Tessa replied.

"So what can I ply you with?"

"Your company."

"You're getting easy in your old age," Vee said. "Promise you won't stand me up?"

"Promise." Vee and her private jets and limos would be a fitting counterpoint to a morning spent unraveling finances with ten years' worth of tangles. She gave Vee directions to Kate's house, then said, "See you at two."

Tessa had approached the meeting with Jack the same way she had all of the other uncomfortably intimate procedures she'd braved during her marriage: with a blank mind and heartfelt prayers for amnesia. The only time she'd been tempted to engage was when Jack said that he and Sophie wanted to buy out her share of the house. Reason conquered the urge to kill, though. This wouldn't be an amicable divorce, but it could be civil. If he and his fertility goddess had the cash, she'd be free of him all the more quickly than if the house went on the market.

Otherwise, it had been what she expected was the standard gut-wrenching, lawyer-brokered admission that a relationship had tanked. Jack had looked as though the collar to his button-down was a tad tight, with an unattractive flush rising from his neck to his face. He'd scarcely spoken to her. And since her only question—*why cheat?*—was one she lacked the courage to hear answered, she had taken the surface route through the emotions thick in the room. It was over, though. Scant solace, but she held tight to it.

Now Tessa considered freedom from Jack as she sat in Vee's hired limo, waiting for Vee to exit the nursing home.

Vee's grandmother became agitated around strangers, but Tessa was quite okay with some solo recovery time after updating Vee. Postmortems stunk, but they also appeared to be inevitable.

Was it truly possible to be free of Jack?

Certainly she had instructed her attorney to petition the court to return to her maiden name, but that Wright-to-DiPaulo switch was nothing more than window dressing. How did one surgically slice away fifty percent of one's life?

They had been Jack-and-Tessa for so many years that sometimes she forgot where he left off and she began. Tessa leaned back against the pale gray leather upholstery and recalled those pre-Jack days. With the exception of a dark and reckless stretch after her father's death eleven years ago—a time she preferred not to think about—she'd been happy enough. Still, the details had melded with the fiction inherent in fading memories. That old Tessa was more rosy-hued watercolor than reality.

Tessa sat upright as the car door swung open and Vee slid in.

"Okay," Vee said. "Gram's present and accounted for…except for that scary loss of short-term memory." She shook her head. "She's got 1949 down pat, though. Or at least well enough that she has me fooled, since it's before my time. But she's content."

"Content is good," Tessa said, not speaking from recent experience.

Vee stretched out her long legs. "So what do you feel like doing...a little shopping? Somerset, maybe?" she suggested, referring to a local high-end mall.

Tessa shook her head. "Sorry. Shopping only cheers up skinny people." And God knew that her recent Kettle Chips and Dr. Pepper diet had eliminated all hope on that front. "Why don't we head to Birmingham and grab a coffee?"

"Sounds good. And we can take our time. I don't have to be back to the airport until six."

During the brief drive south on Woodward from Bloomfield Hills to Birmingham, Vee and Tessa chatted about Vee's teenaged guy-killer daughter and Vee's recent travels. Irv Silverman collected vacation homes in a way Tessa would have found slightly nuts, if she weren't so envious. Vee had the pleasure of decorating each home, so she was in no rush to dissuade her husband.

As they reached Birmingham's small downtown, the limo slowed. Tessa pointed to her favorite coffee house. "Have the driver stop up there at the corner," she said.

Back before life had grown so disjointed, when she was part of that inseparable Jack-and-Tessa, each Saturday afternoon at about this time they would stop at Club Café for a sweet and some coffee and talk. If she could take only one good memory from her marriage, this place would be it.

"Come on," Tessa said to Vee as she slid out of the limo.

"It's time you stood in line with the common folk. It's worth it for the double-espresso brownies alone."

The small confines of the café smelled of rich coffee, and the jazz playing over the sound system tugged harder on Tessa's growing sense of nostalgia. As they waited in the short line, she could almost pretend that this was another Saturday and Jack would be joining her once he'd grabbed a newspaper.

Almost.

Vee nudged her elbow. "Hey, anybody in there?"

"Sorry." Tessa shook off the blues. "I was just time traveling with your gram."

They ordered their coffees, and as they waited at the far end of the bar for Tessa's chocolate-covered cherry mocha, Tessa read the daily horoscope taped to the counter. She would become a true believer if it said, *Capricorn, you are doomed.* But no, it was the same semioptimistic vague pap as always.

Beside her, she felt Vee grow restless, shifting her purse from one hand to the other.

"Just a second more," Tessa said, glancing at the barista. "You can't rush perfection."

"It's not that," Vee replied. "I think we have a bit of a problem, here. Look who just came in."

Tessa turned her gaze to the door. "Oh, God," she said at the same time the barista was calling out her drink.

Jack-and-Tessa had become Jack-and-Sophie.

"Is there another door?" Vee asked.

"No, and I can handle this." She took her paper cup from the counter, automatically slid a cardboard sleeve onto it, then walked toward the couple, who'd seen her, too.

"Jack," she said, though really, she was more interested in checking out Sophie. She'd never seen her before, not at any of the dinners or the Lions' game day gatherings that she'd attended with Jack. At least now she understood why that particular meeting had never occurred. It would have been unsporting to have both wife and mistress at the same event. And Jack was nothing if not sporting.

"Tessa," he replied. She noted a hint of nervousness in his blue eyes. She liked having that effect on him.

Tessa scrutinized Sophie, who clung to Jack's hand. The opposition was older than she had pictured…certainly no dewy ingenue. In fact, she could see a few gray strands mixing with Sophie's nondescript brown.

This, Tessa didn't like. If she was going to lose her husband to the other woman, at least the other woman could have pneumatic boobs, a tiny waist and be no more than thirty, to go with all that free and easy fertility. She'd been dumped for a frump.

She directed her fury at Jack. "It's Thursday," she said.

He blinked. "What?"

"I said it's Thursday. If you're going to swap this—this

uterus into your life like some sort of replacement part, at least get it right. It's Saturday, Jack, not goddamned Thursday that you're supposed to be here with her."

Vee gently closed her hand over Tessa's wrist. "Let's go."

Jack-and-Sophie took advantage of the interruption and retreated a few steps. Tessa tried to close the gap, but Vee didn't want to let the hell go. Though Tessa had her friend beat in sheer pounds, she wasn't up to dragging her along.

"Now, Tessa," Vee said.

Something was missing…

Tessa glanced at her mocha, then back to the counter. "Hang on. I forgot to order my brownie."

"C'mon, let's skip the brownie, okay?"

Skip the brownie? Did Vee fail to understand the importance of the brownie?

"Listen," Tessa said. "I'm walking away from my home, losing my favorite coffee stop to Jack-and-Uterus, over there, but I can control one friggin' thing. I want my brownie. Now."

"I'll buy you a whole factory," Vee said. "Just come on."

"No."

The barista who'd made Tessa's drink suddenly appeared in front of her, napkin-wrapped brownie in hand.

"It's on the house," he said, thrusting it at her.

Briefly mollified, Tessa accepted the offering and pocketed it.

"Thank you," she replied, pleased with her show of manners.

Vee hauled her out the door, leaving Tessa no time to say anything more to Jack and the usurper. When they were on the curb, and the limo was pulling up, somehow sensing their arrival, Vee said, "You were screaming in there."

"Bull," Tessa replied. "I don't scream." She clutched her mocha with both shaking hands to stop it from slopping out of the slot in its drink cover.

Vee snorted. "Trust me, you do."

As they returned to Kate's house, Tessa ate her brownie without offering Vee a crumb. She'd earned the damn thing, after all.

Once inside, Tessa reintroduced Kate to Vee, whom Kate had met a few years back at the annual Jack-and-Tessa holiday bash. While they chatted, Tessa dumped her mocha, then escaped upstairs to rid herself of her panty hose and pull herself together.

In the bathroom, she stared blankly at her reflection in the mirror. She looked to be the same old Tessa—olive skin, brown eyes, Roman nose and wide mouth.

She'd screamed? Impossible.

Of course, she also didn't lob crystal teddy bears into picture windows.

When Tessa returned, she found her friends in the living room. Vee sat on one end of the couch and Kate in a chair nearby. They were speaking in low tones, and broke off as she entered.

Tessa halted in the face of some uncomfortable vibes. "This isn't an intervention, is it? Been there, done that, got the Painkillers Are Not My Friend bumper sticker to show for it."

Vee and Kate glanced at each other, then back at her. She'd been joking, but it seemed that she'd hit close to the target.

Tessa sat hard on the couch. "Jesus, I go upstairs to get rid of some damn panty hose and you two start conspiring."

"We weren't conspiring," Vee replied. "We're worried about you."

"All right, then," she said. "Let's hear it. And you can skip all of the 'we're only doing this because we're your friends and we love you' blah-blah-blah, too." She gave Kate an extra glare for the countless times she'd covered for her in a meeting or bailed her out at work. Some gratitude.

"Then here it is, friend," Vee said. "I don't like what life's done to you. Tessa, where's the woman who painted those glorious murals in our apartment, who wanted to learn how to tango and to speak Russian?"

"Dumped and unemployed?" she suggested.

Vee shook her head. "Not relevant. This goes deeper than current events, no matter how godawful they've been."

Even in her heart-of-stone state, Tessa couldn't stay flip

in the face of her friends' concern. "I'm touched that you're worried, but—"

Vee shook her head. "Nope. Just listen, okay? You're a pro at taking care of other people, you know? I've watched the way you coddle Jack, and the way you head home to Evanston if your mom has so much as a hangnail, but you're doing a really horrible job of taking care of yourself. You need to change your focus…change your life."

"I'm okay with where I'm going." She was growing fairly comfy with Hell, actually.

"Now's the time," Kate said, apparently picking up her part of this tag-team approach. "You've got severance money, no house payments and nothing to keep you in this rut. You're moving straight from justifiably pissed into scary-land, Tessa."

Last night Tessa had dreamed that she'd become Virgina Woolf, stones in pockets, taking a long walk into icy, deep and embracing water. And that had been the cheeriest of her dreams. "Okay, maybe I have a few issues to work through."

"What is it you want? What's your bliss?" Kate demanded.

"My bliss?" She laughed, and even to her ears it was a sound straight from scary-land. "I want my old life back. I want my job. I want my marriage before the doctors, the Clomid hormone hell days, the IVF and the insane race to pregnancy. I want to pretend that none of this has happened. I want Jack back and I want… I want the goddamn impossible!"

Yes, she definitely knew how to scream.

"Great, then," Vee said after an uneasy silence. "What's your backup bliss?"

Hollow and beyond sad, Tessa shrugged. "No clue, but I think it might include a cabana boy and a whole lot of rum."

Vee leaned forward, her expression earnest. "I'm glad you said that. Irv and I have a house in Costa Rica overlooking the Pacific that we love, but we just don't seem to make it there anymore. Clients want to stop in at the condo in Belize or our house on Lake Como, but Costa Rica? Never." She smiled. "They don't know what they're missing. The place is paradise. It's in a village so small that it's not even on the map. Why don't you go spend some time down there? Stay as long as you like and think about your backup bliss. You'd be doing us a favor."

"A favor, as in 'keep the crazy screaming lady south with the other nuts wandering the beach'?"

Vee laughed. "Not quite. We have Don, Irv's third cousin twice removed or something, as a caretaker, but he lives in his own house on the property. The main house just sits empty. Houses need occupants to keep everything working. And besides, the more people on the property, the less likely squatters will target it. That's the one problem with this particular paradise."

"So I'd be alone in the house?" Tessa asked. Alone sounded distinctly unappealing.

"If you'd be more comfortable, bring Kate," Vee offered. "You've got an open schedule, right?" she asked Kate, who nodded in return.

"I don't know. It's not as though changing my location changes my problems. Part of me wants to tough it out."

"Then part of you probably wants to end up in jail, too," Vee said. "I always wondered about those stories—you know, the ex-wives who vandalized houses…rotting shrimp in the shower curtain rods, and all that. I wondered what it would take to push a woman so far. And I'm beginning to understand."

It took Tessa a moment to catch Vee's meaning. "Unbelievable. You think that I'd…"

Now that Tessa considered it, rotting shrimp seemed like a damn fine idea. It would just be a matter of getting in the house while Jack-and-Uterus were at work. She was sure they hadn't changed the locks yet. Jack was too arrogant to think of it, and—

Tessa's heart plummeted. Vee was right. She was in danger of taking her dance with the dark side one step too far. "Come on, Tessa, ditch all this garbage for a while. Seize your goddamn bliss," Kate urged.

Bliss… How very sick she was hearing of bliss. But she was also sick of being afraid to do anything for fear of somehow making her life worse. And the truth was, save a freak lightning bolt or a case of hemorrhagic fever, it could get no worse.

"Fine," Tessa said. "I want to fall off the map."

CHAPTER 4

San José International Airport, Costa Rica

Tessa couldn't fault an airport that offered beer and fried chicken at breakfast time. In fact, after a sleepless overnight layover in Houston, Costa Rican carbs and fat grams had seemed wonderfully festive. She could, however, fault Kate as a travel companion. Or more accurately—and more kindly—perhaps not so much Kate as her dogged insistence that her new bike make the trip, too.

Whether it was their hasty breakfast, the knowledge of the relentless heat and sun just outside this air-conditioned enclosure, or the stress of two overtired women hauling six enormous bags and a bicycle, Tessa was sweating. Her shirt clung to her back, and her hair had begun its humid weather snake-dance into dreadlocks.

Vee had told them that Don, the house's caretaker, would be waiting for them once they cleared customs. However, after twenty minutes spent scouring the crowd, it had grown obvious to both Tessa and Kate that Don wasn't among its numbers. Tessa had seen tour guides gathering their pasty white charges, who looked like so many chicks scattered in a barnyard. She'd witnessed tired families rushing for the comforts of home, and in a swift and evil kick to her battered self-esteem, she'd watched lovers reuniting. Not just one couple, but seemingly everywhere she looked. She wanted to warn them that love was a lie, that they should guard their hearts against this fraud, except she knew that just *hers* had been false. And so her gaze had jumped from point to point, unable to hold fast to any one thing, any more than Tessa could.

But that was why she was to spend three months in this unfamiliar place, where the Spanish in which she'd believed herself fluent flowed by her like water rushing down a mountainside. She had twelve weeks to learn to hold fast to herself...not to Jack or a job no longer hers, or even to Kate, her cranky human security blanket.

"I'd kill for a cigarette," Kate said, bike braced in one hand and stacked luggage by her other side. "This was the wrong time to try to quit."

"There is no right time," Tessa replied, in no finer a mood. "And forget the cigarette. I'd kill for a phone."

She had seen a full bank of pay phones while they'd been waiting in line at Immigration, but on this side of the great divide? Two phones, one of which was broken, and the other well occupied. As her antiquated cell phone was useless in

Costa Rica, Tessa held her spot six back in line. Tucked in the pocket of her allegedly wrinkle-proof travel pants was a crumpled bit of paper with the house phone number on it.

"You should call Vee if no one answers at the house," Kate said.

"And Vee can do *what* from L.A.?" At Kate's surprised expression, Tessa schooled herself to patience. "Kate, I'll get this fixed, I promise."

Tessa looked through the thick plate-glass window to her left. A younger man who'd been there fifteen minutes ago still remained, leaning against the side of a dented and dirty green Volkswagen van. He wasn't Don, she was quite sure, as he was too tight of skin and short of hair to match Vee's description of a grizzled Haight-Ashbury veteran. Still, it was time for a bold move, since Tessa had already been told that Kate's bike eliminated both the bus system and the currently available rental car stock as means of reaching Vee's promised land.

While gathering the last of her brainpower, Tessa rubbed her thumb against the rough skin at the back of her left ring finger—all that was left of the engagement ring and wedding band she'd tucked into a safe-deposit box back in Michigan. She'd toyed with the idea of selling them, but when it came down to it, she hadn't been ready.

Most everything else she'd gladly ditched in a garage sale two weeks earlier: the furniture that Jack-and-Uterus had deemed substandard and thus not negotiated for, the fussy

Wedgwood china from Jack's mom, the golf clubs Tessa had owned purely to humor her spouse. Other than her clothing and pre-Jack keepsakes, she'd held on to only her dozens of movies (on VHS tape and therefore nearly as obsolete as she was feeling) and her art supplies. Both collections were being shipped to the house in Playa Blanca, where they'd likely gather dust. And at this rate, arrive before she did. She again glanced at the van.

"I've got an idea. Hold my spot in line," she said to Kate.

Her friend grumbled, but nevertheless wrangled bike and luggage to the proper location. Tessa headed out the door, where the heat sank through her clothes and into her skin, a jolt of energy that she knew from tropical experience would soon turn to lassitude. She took advantage of the brief surge, striding over to the rusty van.

A hand-lettered sign reading *Tourista* sat behind the windshield. The sight of it was a stronger lure than a chilled Dr. Pepper. Tessa worked up an outgoing smile for the clipboard-wielding male, who had to be about the same age as Kate's bartender-plaything.

He smiled in return, and Tessa absently noted something like a sensual thrill chasing down her spine. Maybe the past month hadn't rendered her completely dead inside? Interesting trivia, but about as relevant to her current situation as Hollywood gossip.

Tessa focused on her more immediate need of language

skills. It had been a million years since she'd used Spanish for more than *hello* or *thank you*. Four years of high school classes, a summer program in Spain after her freshman year of college, all amounting to… In sum, not nearly what she'd thought she'd known last week as she'd glibly chattered along with the Berlitz CDs she'd borrowed from the library.

"*Hola*," she said to the van's possible owner. "*De—deseamos ir a Playa Blanca.*"

"Playa Blanca?" She nodded, then tried to explain where it was located. "*Está cerca…al lado…de Quepos?*"

"Across the mountains and south from Quepos," he replied with a nod. "It's hours from here, you know?"

His English was far less halting than her Spanish, thank God.

"So, are you for hire?" she asked.

He hesitated, and Tessa's palms began to sweat. She would tolerate no more failure.

"I don't go that far, too often," he said.

Hope rose. "But you do sometimes?"

He smiled. "When the money is good."

She'd make it good—highly tempting, indeed—if it meant they could leave this purgatory of an airport. "I have a friend with me," she said, then glanced toward the window, where Kate was giving her a broad smile. "Come inside. Let me show you what we've got."

"I don't know," the driver said, edging closer to his van.

Tessa dug deep and found the smile of charm and confidence that had once stood her so well in business. "Give it a shot," she said. "I promise the price will be right."

A two-lane freeway skirted San José's hardscrabble edges and led to narrower and rougher roads threading through a rise of mountains to the Pacific coast. Their driver Alonso's van, also rather hardscrabble, bounced and shook like the amusement park rides Tessa recalled from childhood. From her perch on the front passenger seat, she tried to fix this moment in her memory—the lush green landscape deep enough to drown in, the humid air, the grayish-whitewashed houses in scatterings too small to be called villages, and even the fine dust and dizzying exhaust drawn into the open window next to her.

Kate sat on the bench the next row back, loosely fastened into her seat belt, with her perpetually suntanned legs swung onto the seat and her arm clinging to the seat back. Eyes closed, she'd cut herself off from chat, which was fine by Tessa, who had no desire to converse over the half-tuned blare of the radio and Alonso's incessant, rapid-fire talk on his cell phone.

Tessa was usually a relaxed traveler, but the knowledge that she had no sense of certainty about where she was going, how long she'd wish to be there, or if even this exotic place would be enough to lift the drab gray folds of her depression, had left her nervous and empty.

As they jounced along and drowsiness began to overtake her, Tessa drifted back to long-ago car trips. She'd sit in the rear of her father's Eldorado (his sole bit of male overcompensation), and in that seat-belts-optional era, she would slide across the slippery white leather interior as they rounded each bend in the road. She'd hummed pop tunes to herself, trying to block the sound of her parents' bickering. They had loved each other, but they'd never quite bought into an attitude of quiet contentment. Her mother had been the mapper of the couple, each mile of a trip marked, measured and timed. Her father had been the detour man.

"It's all about the trip, Brenda," he'd say when her mother would squawk as he pulled from the freeway to take a back route.

Tessa had always thought herself more a detour girl than a mapper. Back when time had permitted, she'd been the one proposing surprise weekends away with Jack, the one to persuade him to stop at the neon glow of a roadside diner in the middle of nowhere.

Now that she'd been stripped of the guideposts she'd taken for granted, she was beginning to think that she was comfortable only because she'd been planning the detours. Maybe she'd always been a milquetoast mapper cloaked in a detour girl's bohemian clothing. To consider that she knew herself this poorly was sitting no better than her beer and chicken breakfast.

When not on his cell phone, Alonso acted as a casual tour guide. As they traveled past a palm oil plantation, he explained that the stunted trees had been chosen for the ease of reaching the palm kernels. Tessa found the endless vista of fat, dwarf trunks with their soldier-straight rows foreign on some Hansel-and-Gretel, evil-forest, vestigial child's level. Following Kate's cue, she let her eyes slip closed until the van made a rough turn onto what Alonso said was the coast road.

The blue slice of Pacific she'd briefly seen from the mountains was closer now, but no longer visible. Still, Tessa fancied she could smell the delicious tang of the sea mixed with the van's leaky exhaust. After fifteen or so minutes traveling south, Alonso flipped shut his cell phone, slowed, then pulled up to a set of battered gas pumps in front of an equally worn market of some sort.

"We stop here," he announced.

Kate roused herself from her doze.

"How much longer do you think?" she asked Tessa.

"I'm not sure," Tessa replied, paging through the maps in the three Costa Rican travel guides she'd jammed into her oversize pack. No one map gave sufficient detail, which was the reason she'd had to buy so many guides. Two of the books slid to the floor, and she clutched the last while grabbing for the escapees. Once she had the jumble safely back in her lap, she ruefully acknowledged the depth of her map dependence. She could nearly hear her father's deep laughter.

You're a mapper through and through, Tessa mia, he would have said.

Tessa's throat tightened and her eyes began to sting. God, she was tired of being weepy, but how she longed to hear her dad's voice. And how she'd needed him these past weeks... his wisdom, his dry sense of humor, his unfailing support. She was now a month away from forty, and it seemed that she still hadn't moved beyond being a daddy's girl. And one with no daddy, at that. Her brief smile was involuntary as she considered her dad's response to this "poor me" aria. *Laugh away, Dad, but you have to admit that right now, it's not all that easy being me.*

Kate was worried, one of her least favorite states, pulling second place only behind humiliated. Heartbroken rounded out her personal bottom three, except she handled that by simply pretending she had no heart. Hearts were inconvenient things, anyway—making one live when living was no longer fun, and making one feel to the painful degree that Tessa seemed to.

And that was the foundation—not heart...hell, no—of Kate's worries. She wasn't a psychiatrist, but it was already clear to her that Tessa needed more than a little R & R and a fifth of good rum. Kate had been restless with excitement last night. But Tessa? All night long, she'd been that eerie, staring-into-the-darkness variety of quiet. Each time Kate had wakened, it was as though she could see Tessa's thoughts tangling in dark contorted knots that Kate knew she was too emotionally shallow to even begin to unravel.

Coming to Playa Blanca had seemed a lark, the ideal antidote to a two-faced lover and the loss of a job. Besides, she knew she owed Tessa for the time or two at work that she might have claimed one of Tessa's ideas as her own. Never anything big, of course. In any case, a bit of tropical hand-holding while Tessa regained at least a measure of her former fight had suited Kate quite nicely.

But, hey, shallow is as shallow does, Kate reminded herself. And except for her suspicion that Tessa might commit some stupid and/or dire act in the near future, and that she'd be powerless to respond, it wasn't a bad trip. Kate loved what she'd seen of the country so far, even getting a kick out of the small, washed-out bridges that meant one had to drive through the streams they'd once spanned. She adored the ugly stray dogs on the side of the road, the sight of packs of kids tossing a baseball to one another, even the smell of eau de jungle-rot that had begun to permeate the van.

As they passed through the town that Alonso assured her was Quepos, Kate made mental note of the white-water rafting tour shack and a couple of sea kayak rental spots. If she didn't get moving soon, old age was going to catch her sorry ass, and she had no desire to let that happen.

She also saw a small hotel-casino, and a store with cigarettes—ah, sweet, sweet, cigarettes—advertised in the front window. She asked Alonso to stop, both because she'd soon go insane without a smoke and because she wanted to get a rise out of Tessa. "Hey, Tessa, I'm going in for some cigarettes," she announced after the van had been lopsidedly perched with its left tires on the sidewalk, facing oncoming traffic. "Want anything?"

"No," Tessa replied, eyes still closed and voice so distant that it sounded as though it had traveled over a bad phone connection.

"Nothing?" Kate racked her mind for prime Tessa-tempting lure. "Not some chocolate or cookies or—"

"Just get your cigarettes, Kate."

How could a woman enjoy a good smoke with Tessa the Ghost to worry about?

"Cruise on," she said to their driver, who did just that.

It took much mental wrestling for Kate to shove the lovely initial hiss of the word *cigarette* from the front of her brain. She'd just succeeded, when Alonso again slowed the van.

"Playa Blanca," he said, pointing at a broad crescent of beach to their right.

Kate looked at the dark sand beach and saw nothing *blanca* about it. She was about to comment to Alonso, when he asked, "So where do you go?"

Damn good question.

"Tessa," she said, nudging at the base of her friend's seat with her foot. "Tessa...reengage."

Brown eyes were briefly visible, then Tessa shielded them with the sunglasses she had propped on the top of her head. "What?"

"We're in Playa Blanca," Kate said. "Do you have the house number?"

Silence hung as thickly as Tessa's withdrawn mood.

"I'm not sure," she finally said.

Seeking higher guidance, Kate looked to the putty-colored and dirt-streaked fabric lining the van's roof. She found nothing but a hitchhiking spider.

"Do you have any bright ideas?" she asked the striped creature.

It kept its silence, knowing less—or possibly more—than the van's human occupants. And either way, they were officially screwed.

Tessa scowled, thankful for the shade of her sunglasses. She didn't want to leave her dark and quiet place. She'd been happy there.

"But you have the house's phone number, right?" Kate prodded again.

Tessa reached into her pocket and, after a short scuffle with the seat belt holding her down, extracted the scant information she had.

Damn, she thought as she read. It was a bleak testimonial to her muzzy-headedness that after shipping off her boxes to Playa Blanca, she'd pitched the address and kept only another slip with the phone number. Vee had assured them that Don would get them to the house, and that had seemed enough. But this, too, could be fixed. And doing so was far simpler than facing all the matters she couldn't repair.

"Alonso, could I borrow your phone?" she asked.

He pulled to the side of the road, this time lodging the van in a patch of scrubby weeds. Tessa now understood how the vehicle had taken on its battle scars…one lost tourist at a time.

Tessa dialed. The phone rang several times, then the answering machine message kicked in. A gravelly male voice informed her that she'd reached the Silverman residence. She could leave a message and someone would get back to her soon.

This was not an option that she embraced. Tessa hung up and returned the phone to their driver.

"Playa Blanca isn't very large, is it?" she asked.

"It has more than one house," he replied, nodding his head toward the road, which just ahead rose and moved inland from the dark sand beach.

"You're not proposing a door-to-door search, are you?" Kate asked.

Her friend's skepticism was well-founded. Tessa dug

through her memory for anything that Vee might have said about the house's surroundings, but came up empty.

"Not a house-to-house, but we might as well keep moving until we find the village."

Alonso pulled back onto the road. They made the top of the rise in less than three beats of Tessa's weary heart.

"That's it," Alonso said, pointing at a few one-story buildings sitting at the very edge of the road. "Beyond are some hotels."

Tessa decided to go with her instincts. "Let's move on a little," she suggested.

Around the next sweeping bend, a few large buildings cropped up higher on the mountainside to their left. At the mountain's foot sat some smaller structures.

"Stop up there," she said, pointing at a small cinderblock sundries-and-souvenirs shop that had been brightly painted with a mural of butterflies, monkeys and birds. The art was primitive, with the size and perspective oddly skewed—likely the work of children, and wholly charming.

Alonso parked.

"Let me see if I can cut down on the door-to-door. I'll be right back," she said to Kate.

Tessa slipped from the van, her sandals skidding in the sand that coated the parking lot. She stilled an instant to take a daunting self-inventory. Her hair had escaped its ponytail holder and knotted around itself. A fine coating of road grit covered even her teeth. Her deodorant had begun to fail hours before, and she'd gladly shower under a garden hose.

All the more reason to get to Vee's house.

Tessa stepped into the shop. Its cluttered interior was an oasis of air-conditioning. She would have lurked in a corner and cooled off, except a toucan she'd assumed was yet another wildly colored souvenir, on shelves thick with the same, proved to be real. Tessa's startled screech as it took flight competed with the toucan's greeting.

A man and woman at the sales desk, the only other people in the store, stopped their conversation and looked her way.

"Sorry," she said, then bared her gritty teeth in an apologetic smile. The woman behind the counter, young—annoyingly so—golden-skinned and beautiful, smiled in return, but said nothing. The man, older but no less attractive than the woman, watched her with equal curiosity. The toucan, now standing in the middle of the counter, angled its oversize head her way and peered at Tessa, too.

The man nodded to her. His skin was a deep burnished bronze, and he wore a golf shirt with a pair of khaki shorts. Like Jack, he looked the sort to think it fine to call a woman "babe" or whatever the Spanish equivalent might be. Jack also favored golf shirts when out of the office. She hated them, along with overconfident smiles and Maui Jim sunglasses, just like the pair resting on the counter near the man's hand. The toucan stealthily approached the glasses. Tessa briefly hoped the bird might be strong enough to do them harm.

"I'm looking for the Silverman residence," she said to the couple.

Her words were met by silence, except for the scrabbling noises the toucan made as it tried to work the man's sunglasses into its fat bill.

"*Estoy buscando la residencia de Silverman,*" she repeated. "Playa Blanca? Silverman?" She awkwardly hitched a thumb in the direction of the road. "House?"

The woman gave the man an intimate half smile that Tessa wished she hadn't seen. Jealousy—appropriate or not—nipped at her.

"Silverman?" he repeated to Tessa, his expression impassive.

She nodded.

"Go to the black gate on the ocean side, the second drive south from here, but you'll find they're not in residence."

Alonso's bilingual ease had been tough enough on her linguistic pride; this man, with his smooth English nearly better than hers, decimated her self-confidence.

"Thank you," she said, backing away and nearly knocking over a rack of sarongs in the process.

Fringe knotted in a vivid tangle of orange, red, turquoise

and yellow. The toucan squawked its disapproval of the commotion, and from behind her sunglasses, Tessa sent it the same evil eye with which her late Nona DiPaulo had been so adept. Though Tessa's heart was racing and she wished herself anyplace but knotted in cotton, she managed a gloss of manners for the humans.

"Sorry," she said to the duo watching her from the register as she straightened the garments.

The man's dark brows rose marginally, but there was no other outer indicator that he found her nearly as clumsy and ridiculous as she was finding herself. She hurried from the shop before she could do more damage to her ego.

"Well?" Kate asked once Tessa was back in her seat. "Victory?"

"In a Pyrrhic sort of way."

Kate laughed. "That's better than nothing."

Tucking this recent embarrassment in with the other bits of baggage she'd been carrying lately, Tessa gave Alonso his marching orders. She couldn't reach Vee's quickly enough. Once there, she would bar the gates and kick back in solitude. At least, as much solitude as she could wrest from Kate and the mysterious Don, should he appear.

"There!" Tessa pointed to the second oceanside entry.

Alonso wheeled hard into the drive, and Kate hung over the back seat, holding her beloved bicycle steady.

The black security gate that the man in the souvenir shop had described was partway open.

"We might as well go in," she said to Alonso.

The narrow road was paved, which he seemed to interpret as an invitation to speed. Just around one curve, a drive broke to the left, and a small stucco house with a clay-tiled roof sat on a wedge cut into the steep incline to the ocean. This, she knew, had to be the caretaker's house.

"Keep going," Tessa instructed.

Alonso gunned it. Kate, still draped over the back seat and gripping her bike, muttered her standard word of choice, and Tessa held tighter to the armrest.

The drive curved into a circle, the center of which held a tall and sinuous modern bronze fountain set in a reflecting pool. Beyond the artwork sat the house, with its two low-slung wings stretching out to form, appropriately enough, a broad V.

Alonso's low whistle made for faint praise. Vee reigned as the darling of the *Architectural Digest* set for good reason. The confluence of exquisite taste and a bottomless bankroll could result in fine things, indeed.

Tessa felt a small ripple of optimism as Alonso pulled under the shelter of a glass and rich tropical wood portico that extended over the drive at the house's entry. Only good could come of a place like this.

Kate, finally assured of her bicycle's safety, turned around in her seat and gazed silently at the splendor in front of them. "You're sure this isn't a spa?"

Tessa smiled at the small stone sculpture of a frog perched at the base of one of the portico's rough-hewn columns.

"Positive."

The frog was whimsical, incongruous and always had been one of Vee's signature items. Even their college slum of a house on Mary Street had been graced with a frog sculpture. That particular amphibian had also become a shrine of sorts, surrounded with beer cans left by horny serenading fraternity boys. Tessa was struck by how far they had risen in the world. Or at least Vee had.

"Do you think Vee has any white wine in there?" Kate asked.

"Probably a cellar full."

"In that case…" Kate opened the van's side door, then busied herself extracting her bicycle.

Tessa met Alonso at the van's cargo area and helped him retrieve their luggage. She pulled the cash she owed him from her wallet, then, because she was now feeling nearly content and soon-to-be cosseted, she added a tip for good measure. Alonso departed with the same haste he'd used in getting down the drive.

Tessa approached the house's massive front door and pressed the doorbell to its left. While she waited for an answer, she let the sound of the water cascading down the fountain behind her repair her spirit. A breeze curling down the hillside rustled through the vegetation and ruffled her hair. Peace settled into her bones.

Then Kate stepped beside her and pounded on the front door. "Enough of this waiting around," she said to Tessa. "There's no car, no caretaker...and I'm willing to bet my backup stash of cigarettes, no one home."

Peace had always been a rare and delicate commodity.

Kate reached for the door's bronze handle that echoed the lines of the fountain. She pushed on it, then looked at Tessa with obvious surprise when it gave under her hand and the door swung inward a fraction.

Tessa hesitated. It was like violating a taboo, walking un-invited into a house not hers. However, the choice of stay-ing curbside until someone arrived lacked appeal, as well.

She stepped into the haven of cool—in more than one sense. Even with her knowledge of Vee's flair for perfect homes, she marveled at the broad, sweeping stairway that curved to floors below. The house was even larger than she'd first thought, and had clearly been designed to meld into the hillside, with the entry at the peak.

"Five-star, all the way," Kate murmured from next to Tessa.

And just below the soft sound of her friend's comment, Tessa fancied that she'd picked up another noise.

"Did you hear that?" she asked Kate.

"Hear what? The sound of bliss?"

"Not exactly," Tessa replied, her pulse speeding. "Hang on. Hello?" she called to the floors below. "Don?"

After a moment during which the loudest sound she heard was the drumming of her own heart, she decided that she'd imagined the noise. Anyone with a measure of manners would have made themselves known by now. She shook off her jitters and again cozied up to the promise of a respite in paradise.

"It must have been my im—"

Just then the faint yet unmistakable sound of a smoker's hack echoed upward.

A chill rippled across Tessa's skin. She hadn't been mistaken. They were not alone.

CHAPTER 5

"Okay, *that* I heard," Kate said quietly. "Three packs a day, minimum." As a recently former smoker, she knew of whence she spoke. "Go on down. I'll cover your back."

"My back. Right," Tessa said. "As usual."

Her friend's tone held a little barb that Kate hadn't heard in a very long time. She found herself amused by it, and relieved that Tessa seemed to be coming out of her odd daylong near-silence. Maybe soon she'd be back in fighting form, and they could tackle bliss as a team.

Kate knew that bliss was a state achieved by whatever route was required, so long as a woman won. And counter to that "it's imperative to get there the fastest" mentality, she also believed that coasting off another's efforts was both smart and economical. Hence, her symbiotic relationship with Tessa—they helped each other, and they both won. Okay, maybe she usually scored a little better than Tessa, but that was a technicality.

Further pondering ended when the individual below floors worked up another bottom-of-the-lungs cough.

Kate trailed behind Tessa down broad treads made of some dark and glossy exotic wood she couldn't identify.

"Don?" Tessa called after taking no more than three steps at a snail's pace. "Is that you?" The hacker probably couldn't suck in enough wind to answer.

Kate stayed on Tessa's heels as she picked up pace, pausing only briefly to scope out the vacant formal living room on the first floor down. She finally came to a halt on the ground-floor landing. Kate pulled up two steps above, captured by the sight of what awaited them. It was as though someone had created a "find it" drawing—the sort she'd stare at in tattered kids' magazines while fighting nerves in the dentist's waiting room.

"Circle two things that don't belong," she said to herself.

Tessa looked over her shoulder long enough to give Kate a "what the hell?" look.

Kate shrugged, and, as she joined Tessa, let her focus slip past the seamless beauty of million-dollar furnishings and settle on the room's unusual occupants.

"Well, you're definitely not Don," Tessa said to the two women seated opposite each other in low armchairs. Kate knew from having listened to Tessa yammer on when she'd furnished her now-gone dream house, that the chairs were placed in a "conversation cluster." Ironic, since neither female seemed inclined to speak.

Kate observed as Tessa pulled on the diplomatic yet somehow subtly dominant persona Kate had seen her use in difficult meetings. It was a skill that Kate envied, and one that she knew would never be hers. Hank had once told her that she had the subtlety and nuances of a pit bull. At the time, she'd taken it as a compliment.

Tessa moved closer to the women. "I'm Tessa DiPaulo. And you'd be…?"

The older woman, who had hair the color of faded apricots pulled back into a bun and walnut-colored skin so leathery from the sun that Kate couldn't begin to pin an age on her, stubbed her cigarette on a china dinner plate holding more of the same. Some of those butts still looked long enough to smoke, too, dammit.

Both females kept their silence. The younger, dark haired and golden-skinned one—maybe sixteen, maybe even less, but definitely with a big, fat bun of her own, except this one was in the oven—stared intently at the stone floor. The elder woman at least met Tessa's gaze.

"This *is* the Silverman residence, isn't it?" Tessa asked in a masterpiece of a tone that made it clear she knew she was in the right place, yet would never be pushy about it.

No answer. Tessa tried the same question in her remarkably poor Spanish. The pregnant girl fought back a smile, as did Kate, who traveled to Mexico each spring and could at least survive when compelled.

"You are not Tessa Wright?" the older woman finally asked

in a heavy accent. Not Spanish, either. German, Kate guessed.

Tessa's smile carried with it some major relief. "Good, then. So you do know who we are. My last name was Wright, but now it's DiPaulo...again. Tessa DiPaulo," she repeated as if reminding herself. She gestured to the terrace, complete with a swimming pool that seemed to flow out into the silver-blue line of the ocean far on the horizon. "And you are?"

"Guests of the Silvermans," the older woman replied.

"Vee had told me that only Don was here," Tessa said after an instant.

"We're very recent," she answered in a flat voice, all but daring Tessa to argue.

Tessa, like any skilled negotiator, declined the bait. "And where's Don?"

"In San José, looking for two women he was told to bring here. You, I would think," she added, while inserting a fresh cigarette into an ebony-colored holder that Kate would have considered overkill, except that it fit this woman.

"I am Mila. And this is Isabel," the woman added, gesturing at the young girl opposite her. "She speaks no English."

"Ah." Tessa lapsed into silence after that, leaving Kate to step into the breach.

"So...Mila," Kate said. "Does Don have rooms prepared for us?"

"You will have that area, the next floor up," she announced, pointing to the hall extending in a northerly direction off this central room.

Kate could almost hear *"and you veeel enjoy it"* appended to the statement with a dominatrix's iron command.

"Hey, so long as I have wine and a tub to soak in, I'm a happy camper," Kate replied.

Decades of noisy Murkowski conflicts had taught her to pick her own battles…and battlefields. At the moment, Mila knew the lay of the land, and she and Tessa did not.

"Does Don have a cell phone?" Tessa asked. "I'd like to be certain that he's on his way back, and not still looking for us…as we're here."

"Yes, I see," Mila replied after lighting her cigarette.

"Are you sure you should be smoking in the house?" Tessa asked. "Especially with Isabel being, uh—"

"Pregnant," Kate supplied, wanting Tessa to call retreat *now*, for God's sake.

Tessa shot to the glass sliding door closest to Mila and opened it a crack. "About calling Don?"

"Do not worry. I will call him," Mila said. She waved her cigarette in the same direction she'd pointed moments earlier. "Your rooms…"

Kate knew when she'd been dismissed, and at least this dismissal was more entertaining than what Midwest National had dished up.

"Come on, Tessa," she said. "Let's go find the wine."

But Tessa was exhibiting pit-bull tendencies. She'd opened the sliding door wider. "Really, Mila, I have to be firm on the cigarette issue. If you knew Vee at all, you'd know she'd never permit smoking in here. Even Irv has to go outside to smoke."

Mila rose and made an exit sufficiently dramatic for someone fond of ebony cigarette holders. She slid the terrace door shut behind her hard enough that it bounced back open a few inches, then turned her back on her audience, presenting a view of a posture stiff with anger, that apricot bun and skinny, varicose-knotted calves beneath a faded floral dress.

Kate squelched her impulse to applaud.

As Tessa focused her attention on the pregnant teenager, her smile grew several teeth too broad to be anything short of deranged. The teenager, apparently one sharp cookie despite her early plunge into reproduction, rose and scurried upstairs.

Kate decided to try again. "Come on, Tessa, let's find some wine, have some food and let the mystery guests take care of themselves, okay?"

Tessa closed the sliding door the rest of the way, then picked up the dinner plate with its crop of butts. "I'm going to go find the kitchen."

"Perfect," Kate said. "I'll just come along and—"

"*Alone*."

Damn, but she'd made Mila the dominatrix sound like a sweet milkmaid.

"Sure," Kate replied. Some alone time was suddenly sounding very appetizing. And one hell of a lot safer than being around these sharp-toothed women.

It had been years since Tessa had permitted herself something as immature as a full-blown snit, but she intended to pitch one now. Once she confirmed that one *pitched* a snit, as one did a fit. And the pitching, or whatever, would be done in private, naturally. She paced the room she'd selected as hers, angrily stuffing handfuls of clothing into dresser drawers.

Those females certainly didn't seem to know Vee. That they even knew each other stretched Tessa's concepts of friendship and connection. The pubescent-and-pregnant set, even Costa Rican style, would have little reason to hang around cranky, chain-smoking German retirees.

"Too bizarre," Tessa decreed as she tossed her swimsuit onto the king-size bed. She absently noted its ivory silk duvet embroidered with small palm fronds. If she were in a better mood, she'd stop to admire the craftsmanship of the furnishings designed for this space. As it was, she'd be equally comfortable in a Holiday Inn...circa 1968.

Solitude, semisolitude, or even a corner to hide in. She didn't care which providence sent her way, so long as it sent something. And if she stood a chance of exorcising her anger, she would need to stretch her admittedly short legs.

Tessa scrutinized the bathing suit she had laid out on the bed. It had fit four years ago, before the rituals attached to inconstant fertility had played havoc with her shape. Certainly, she could have bought a new suit before leaving Detroit, but would it have been esteem-building to look at herself in a three-way mirror under color-sucking fluorescent light? She thought not.

She stripped out of her travel-weary clothes. Toiletries in hand, she padded to the bathroom attached to her quarters, pointedly ignoring the mirrors both above the sink and on the opposite wall. She briefly debated between the comforts of the deep tub for two, with its window into the verdant tropical forest beyond, and the shower with a shower head that was suspended from the ceiling like a mammoth sunflower.

The shower won today. Tessa switched on the taps and stood there, stewing. She attempted to reel out her snit to its fullest extent, but the warm rain pouring down began to soothe her stress-tightened muscles. She tried some of the vanilla-scented shower gel waiting on the marble corner shelf and hummed a snippet of an Alanis Morissette song. And like the former queen of bitter, in time Tessa's temper calmed.

Those women probably didn't know Vee, but she could accord them the courtesy of waiting for Vee's caretaker to verify this. A few hours of patience would buy much goodwill, and heaven knew she'd been short on that since walking in the door. She would feign solitude, even if deprived of its balm.

After washing her hair, she dried off the best she could and wriggled her way into the too-small suit.

"Lycra, the miracle fiber," she said to her potbelly, now somewhat flattened but not fully conquered.

After pulling a beach towel from the bedroom armoire, Tessa dredged out her sunblock and found her way to the telephone, where she called her mom, gave her contact information and let her know that she'd made the voyage to Playa Blanca mostly intact. Mom sounded a lot more certain of that outcome than Tessa still felt, but she was nonetheless pleased when Tessa promised to call every couple days.

Home fires tended, Tessa found the wine cooler in the kitchen's pantry. The cooler was a moderate affair, a climate-controlled unit that would hold only one hundred bottles or so. She smiled as she recalled Irv's three-thousand-bottle cellar in Holmby Hills. This must be his idea of roughing it.

A quick look unearthed a bottle of Napa chardonnay that Tessa recognized as not being obscenely expensive. One corkscrew and a glass later, she was in business. Tessa exited the kitchen and was making a beeline for the terrace when Kate came downstairs.

"Hey!" Kate said.

Her calm smile grated on Tessa, a sure sign her snit wasn't in full remission.

"Two hours," Tessa said. "Give me two hours of peace, please?"

She didn't wait for a response, relying instead on seventeen years of friendship. Tessa escaped to the terrace. She set her wine on a teak table shaded by a large canvas umbrella, then dropped her towel poolside. One foot dipped in the water was enough to let her nerve endings know that cooler times awaited. First, though, she wanted to check out this property that Vee loved enough to keep and yet never see.

The center portion of the terrace was consumed by the infinity pool, which flowed over its seaside edge and then circulated back to a waterfall at the far end. The broad strip of patio to the left of the pool held the obligatory outside kitchen with sink, refrigerator and grill. If life inside grew crowded enough, Tessa would happily relinquish the air-conditioning for this pampered edge of the jungle. To the right, stone steps disappeared down the hillside.

Tessa followed them, truly curious for the first time in ages. Halfway down the hill, she paused to get her bearings. It was then she noticed another house surprisingly close by. It sat to the left of and at least twenty yards higher than Vee's. Tessa was sure that it was luxurious enough, but in size it wasn't much larger than Vee's caretaker's residence. Though Tessa knew she was no better than a snoop, she cupped her hand above her eyes, trying to cut the glare of the sun and absorb some details of the house.

She liked it, that much she knew. It was real, not the fantasy stuff of Vee's existence. Still, she wouldn't turn her nose up at fantasy freely offered to her out of love and concern. Even she, in her current arid emotional state, couldn't be that callous.

As the stairs wound to the base of the steep hill, she paused to note the tangle of greens...vines leading to plants mating with taller plants clinging to sturdy trees.

Tessa took the last bend to the shore below. It was a small, sheltered spot with sand the same dark hue she'd seen in Playa Blanca. She considered taking a swim, but pulled up short when she saw young and round Isabel sitting beneath a palm at the beach's fringe.

Isabel nodded to her, the measured greeting of one party sizing up another.

"*Hola*," Tessa offered, and received the same in return. Then the girl stuck her nose in whatever book she was reading.

Tessa debated expanding the conversation beyond one word, but in truth, had no interest in doing so. It wasn't as though she hated the overtly fertile, but avoidance remained a painless route.

Tessa turned back to the stairway and began to climb. When she took a break to ease the stitch gripping her right side, she noticed a man standing on the deck attached to the other house on the hillside. He was tall and dark, with a thick mustache. And he wore sunglasses...Maui Jims, she assumed, based on the way the hairs at the back of her neck had risen in alarmed recognition. He appeared to be the man from the souvenir shop, and she didn't want to be seen.

Head down, she took the rest of the stairs at an uncomfortably quick pace. One word sounded in her mind as her sandaled feet hit the steps: *Recluse...recluse...recluse.*

In some mysterious place, a pantheon of recluses must be enshrined. Emily Dickinson...Howard Hughes...Greta Garbo...and...and...

Tessa paused to drag in a labored breath. This walk had been deceptively simple while going downhill.

Did she know of any other recluses?

Hell, of course not. A well-known recluse was an oxymoron of the highest order.

Tessa gained the terrace, and the stone was warm under her feet. She dove into the pool, surfaced and began a leisurely swim, practicing the breathing that had been second nature in her days as high school swimmer. When she'd relaxed enough, she flipped onto her back and floated.

Garbo. She would be Garbo. Alone. Blissfully alone.

Isabel always woke early. Even before the baby had begun growing inside her, making her feel as clumsy and unhappy in her skin as her fat and evil cousin Luz, she had risen with the sun. Nothing could change that, not the wonderful bed she now slept in alone, and not the first feeling of safety she'd had since age eleven. And so this morning, as with all others, she read the simple children's stories Mila had bought her, until the birds had stopped their hungry songs and the monkeys had swung through the trees from their sleeping places up the mountain to look for food by the shore.

Isabel set aside her book, yawned and stretched, then worked her way to the edge of the bed. Past Mila's room she walked, smiling at the snores that sounded louder than storm waves hitting the shore. In the bathroom, she showered and brushed her teeth. As she wove her wet hair into a fat braid to hang down the middle of her back, again she gave thanks to Don—who she was sure must be one of God's very best friends—for the miracle of her own toothbrush and tube of toothpaste, a toilet that flushed and soap that smelled of flowers.

The kitchen was empty, and the house sleepy. This made Isabel happy, but not surprised. All the Americans she had ever met had been lazy and selfish, thinking only of their own needs...their own pleasures. She couldn't believe these two newcomers were any different.

Isabel opened the refrigerator and pulled out the bowl of red beans and rice she'd made the day before. Now that she had mastered this kitchen, breakfast was her daily feast. Banana and papaya and mango...rice and beans and warm tortillas. The tortillas were never as good as Mama could make, but since Mama had other, bigger faults, Isabel had learned to live without those tortillas.

She was tossing the banana skin into the trash when the shorter American—Tessa? What kind of name was that?—came into the kitchen. The American said hello, and Isabel was willing to nod, but nothing more. There was too much to be lost by being friendly. She finished preparing her meal in silence and was about to slip from the kitchen, when this Tessa-woman stopped her.

"Where is Don?" she asked in Spanish so slow that Isabel wondered if she might be as stupid as Luz. Surely these simple words could be spoken with more speed. And surely Isabel could think and speak quickly enough to outwit this woman. Especially in Isabel's native Spanish.

"He has gone to Quepos to bring back supplies," she said as fast as her tongue would move. "The fishermen are back early and he wanted to be first to the boats for fish, and the market will be open today for fresh fruit."

The American nodded in such a way that Isabel knew she'd understood nothing.

Good, then, Isabel thought. Mila had given her a strong weapon when she'd not let these strangers know that Isabel spoke English enough to bargain...and to listen. And the American had handed her more protection in not understanding Spanish.

Isabel smiled at the woman. "I will go eat in peace, now," she said in her Spanish. "I hope your day is filled with burn from the sun, heat that will empty your brain, and insects large enough to send you screaming home."

The silly woman nodded her thanks, and Isabel took her meal outside.

After a breakfast of toast, banana and some of the best coffee she'd ever drunk, Tessa ventured out to see if Don had returned. She wasn't clear on where that might be, except that it seemed to involve the town of Quepos and fish…or fishing.

She was crystal clear, however, regarding the tinge of malice in the teenager's smile. She'd chosen not to take it personally, though. She had seen enough adolescents hanging about shopping malls to be familiar with the fact that snottiness was a rite of passage. Add to that the hormone surge of pregnancy and the kid was bound to be a little sour, and perhaps a lot manipulative.

No matter. Tessa had feet and eyes of her own, and knew how to use them. The morning sun was already merciless as she walked up the drive, taking the turnoff to Don's house. No car was nearby. In fact there was an emptiness to the place that Tessa more sensed than saw.

Curiosity pushed her on. She stepped onto the covered front porch, noting the rich sprinkling of leaves and other bits of tropical detritus that had settled on the clay tile beneath her feet. This level of neglect didn't strike her as natural for a man who was a caretaker. The double windows to the left of the front door were useless for snooping, as the fat wooden venetian blinds inside had been rotated closed. The windows to the right of the door afforded a marginally better opportunity. Tessa cupped her hands and put her nose to the glass, peering between the blind slats, which angled just a little off fully open. Scant light shone inside, though, leaving her to fill in more blanks than what the slats obscured.

The far wall of what had to be a sitting room was covered with a mad jumble of objects. One was obviously a red plastic cup. The rest weren't as easily discerned. She glimpsed slips of paper about the size of airplane boarding passes, rectangular bits smaller than that and countless photos, none of them framed and many of them overlapping. Tessa wished for a flashlight or the nerve to try the front door, but she had neither. Instead, she blinked a few times and willed her middle-aged eyes to focus. The harder she concentrated, the more details popped out at her. She spotted a grinning skull emblazoned with a ziggy lightning bolt, then something about the size of a bumper sticker with happy dancing bears in a rainbow of colors....

"The Dead!"

No doubt about it, given the icons being revered, she was spying on a shrine to the Grateful Dead. Tessa was no Dead fan, as she lacked the patience required to appreciate jam bands. The closest she'd ever come to that scene was attending the Lilith Fair with Kate when it stopped in Detroit, back in '99. She'd had a great time, coming home sunburned and more than a little giddy, but had felt no need to incorporate the event into her decor. But Dead Heads, she knew, were a cult unto their own.

Dissatisfied with the information she'd managed to glean, Tessa left the porch and followed a trail through the lush ground cover toward the back of the house. She'd just rounded the corner when some creature came crashing toward her from the wilder land that lay beyond.

"Oh God!" Panicked, she made a dash for the front porch while her mind riffled through the animal possibilities she'd read about in her tour guides. Jaguar? That nasty little pig thing with big tusks? What the hell was its name? Tessa reached the front door and began to shake its locked handle as the predator closed in. It cleared the trees just as she was drawing breath for the scream of her life.

And all this for a...*dog*.

"Well, shit," she said, feeling relieved and at the same time vaguely disgusted that she'd let this beast rattle her.

The dog, part beagle and part something bigger, stopped in its tracks and gave her a look that carried about the same measure of disgust. Tessa had time to note its collar made of hemp and seashells and tag it as likely Don's dog before it turned about and retreated to the shade.

"Hey, Jerry," she called on a whim.

The dog didn't return.

"Garcia?"

Still nothing.

"Fine, then."

The disused state of Don's house—and the loneliness of his potential dog—had raised enough alarm bells that it was time to put in a call to Vee. Tessa returned to the big house and the phone she'd earlier spotted in the kitchen.

Isabel sat at the small table in the dining nook, doodling with the yellow stump of a pencil on a piece of paper. Because she couldn't help herself, Tessa tried to steal a glimpse of the girl's drawing, but Isabel quickly covered the sheet with her left hand.

Be that way, Tessa thought, accepting that she had managed to piss off both dogs and children this morning. Well, at least the singular of each. Which led to the question…

"A dog. Does Don own a dog?" she asked, too cranky to even try to break out her Spanish.

The girl raised her hands and shrugged, international sign language for "You might as well be speaking Lithuanian."

"El perro," Tessa repeated, ceding at least that much.

The girl shrugged again.

"Thanks loads," Tessa said, then turned her back on at least one of her troubles.

She dialed Vee's cell phone number, the surest way to find

her friend. The phone rang just once, then switched to her voice-mail greeting.

"Vee here. Well, actually not here. Irv has surprised me with a photo safari to Borneo, which is a tad short on cell towers. Leave a message, and I'll get back to you when I can."

While she waited for the message tone, Tessa rubbed her forehead with her palm, trying to sort through her thoughts. Much as she wanted some answers, she didn't want to telegraph her stress across the deep blue sea.

"Hi, it's Tessa here. When you can, give me a call. I have a few questions about some of the—" she glanced at pregnant Isabel, doodling away, and suffered a flashback to Jack's new Uterus "—equipment here at the house. Hope you're having fun. So…'bye."

As she hung up, she felt more than actually caught Isabel giving her an odd look.

"Problems?" she asked the girl.

And for the third time she received that "I've got no clue" shrug.

In that, at least, she and Isabel were in the same boat, for Tessa had no idea what to do next.

CHAPTER 6

The Americans, proving their craziness, left the house without water or hat at just past two, one on a bicycle and the other on foot. They'd be as wise to drink a stomachful of seawater and then roll in the hot sand of the cove. Upon their return, Isabel might suggest that as an evening activity. But while they were gone, she at least would use her brain and speak with Mila.

She knocked on the old woman's bedroom door, then, upon Mila's grunted acknowledgment, opened it to a cloud of smoke.

"The cigarettes will kill you one day," she said to the German.

"Something had better."

Isabel, who was well used to Mila's bite, smiled. "A large dose of poison, I think, would do the job."

Mila pushed back the chair from the fancy little mirrored table where she'd been sitting. "I'll trust you to bring it when it's time."

"Only another seventy years," Isabel replied, then brought

Mila around to today's problems. "The smaller American—Tessa—she senses that something is wrong."

"Bah. Let her drink a few Imperials and sit by the pool. So long as we make sure there is food and liquor, she will have no reason to think."

Isabel shook her head. "She's not that way. She has already called Don's boss and is now walking to the village since the van is not here. She was far too curious about where Don might be with the van, too."

"You worry too much," Mila said. "The van is well hidden. We have a roof over our heads and food to eat. Let tomorrow take care of itself."

Isabel supposed that was easier for the old to believe than for her. Mila had seen many more tomorrows. And one tomorrow…one coming far too soon…Isabel would have not only herself but this baby elbowing her insides to take care of. She knew she was smart enough, but still, she was just fifteen, and most in the village saw her as only another piece of street trash blown across the mountains from San José. Without this house and Don's protection, all she could do was go back home.

Home? Ha! As if she had one. She lived in terror of Hector, Luz's boyfriend, finding out where Luz had dumped her and bringing her back. Hector had always found Isabel a more valuable object than Luz ever had, which was, Isabel knew, the greatest reason Luz had wanted her gone.

"Is there nothing from Don today?" Isabel asked, trying to find a whisper of hope.

Mila ground her cigarette into a teacup on her bedside table. "If there were, I would tell you. I look at the computer every morning, do I not?"

"Yes, but it's been three weeks now since he should have been back. I worry that he's hurt, or—" She didn't say what else she thought because to give it voice might make the horrible thought more real, and she did not sleep well as it was.

"You worry far too much. Don will be back," Mila said. "He forgot about time, just as he does when here. If there were a problem, he would have called."

"But three weeks? We should tell this Tessa what has happened. I don't know her well, but this much I can already see—if we don't and she learns what's going on in this house, she'll be angry. She *is* angry."

"I'm angry, too," Mila said in a voice as bitter as unripe mango. "Why did they have to come here? And why now, damn them? But in confessing, we'd be as foolish as those tourists gambling away their money at the casino in Quepos. The shorter one might be kind, but she also might not. You want to guess wrong and lose our home?"

"But you told me that the first computer message from Mrs. Silverman to Don said they will be here for months. *Months!* We cannot lie so well or for so long. Tessa has this way of looking at me as though she knows already, and I—"

"You're talking nonsense. These women know nothing, and Don will be back before they can find their wits. I promise you this, Isabel." Isabel had heard many promises in her life. She had seen few kept. Yet Mila had helped her since the night she'd found her beaten and wishing to die by the trash bins behind the Hotel Paraiso. For Mila, and Mila alone, she would bear the strain of deception at least a few days longer.

"Then if we are to do this, you must go buy fresh fish and fruit," she said. "I told Tessa this was where Don was today. I don't think she understood, but if she did…"

Mila gave a resigned sigh and then tucked her cigarettes into her pocketbook. "I'll go get the van from its hiding place."

"May I come along to town?" Isabel asked. She longed to see Quepos and perhaps buy some sweets and page through the magazines in the market.

"I suppose you should," Mila said. "It will stop you from having a weak moment and spilling your heart out to this Tessa."

Isabel agreed, even though she had no heart left to spill. It had been ripped from her long ago.

Playa Blanca: three hotels, all in need of refreshing, the souvenir shop where Tessa had tangled with the sarongs, a one-room real estate agency with an ATM machine appended to its side, and a building bearing the word *Supermercado* in faded blue paint.

Tessa found the store's label wildly ambitious considering the scant groceries sold inside. Still, she had managed to pick up a few odds and ends that she'd neglected to pack. Never again, though, did she wish to try to ask an elderly male shopkeeper for tampons. The language and dignity barriers had proven insurmountable. After far too long spent standing in front of the fat boxes of sanitary napkins with Kate doing her best not to laugh aloud, Tessa had decided that the wisest course of action would be an Internet order for next month's needs.

If not for the beach, Tessa would hold out no hope for the village. But the beach…it was enough to excuse the actual lack of a town. Children cavorted in the foamy surf, and flirtatious teenagers clustered at picnic tables by the walk bordering the sand. Except for a few vendors at folding tables, selling cheap jewelry and offering henna tattoos, most adults had taken shelter from the relentless sun. Some lounged beneath gaily colored umbrellas planted in the sand, and others had chosen to relax beneath the corrugated metal roof of an open-air cantina. Tessa, earlier abandoned by Kate, who'd spotted a tempting dirt road up the mountainside, had stopped in the cantina for a break before beginning her return trek.

A solo at her table for two on the seaside border of the cantina, she pretended to read a travel guide while she eaves-dropped on adjacent conversations. She heard German in happier tones than Mila's, a smattering of English, and Spanish everywhere. She was pleased to know that she could now understand rudimentary menu orders such as beer, ham sandwich and salad—no matter how quickly spoken. From time to time she glanced up from her book and used her fingertip to trace rivulets of moisture creeping down the label of her Imperial, a local beer that was proving as tasty as it was inexpensive.

While the walk to the village in new sandals had given her blisters, it had also provided a sense of accomplishment. Who cared that a stroll of about a mile was hardly the stuff of which new lives were made? It had been one sore foot in front of the other…something accomplished completely on her own. And she hadn't thought of Jack for nearly half the day.

Damn. Until now.

Tessa took another sip of her beer and reminded herself to be a realist. It was normal to think of Jack. It was normal to feel angry, betrayed and diminished in her soul because she'd been blindsided. And it was normal that these feelings were swamping her less and less each day. Soon she'd again be able to focus on the good days in their shared past, not just the sound of Swedish lead crystal shattering plate glass.

"To me," she said, raising her bottle in a toast before finishing off the last few swallows. Tessa leaned back in her white plastic chair and smiled at the brightly colored party flags tied to the rafters of her shelter. A breeze eddied in from the ocean, and the triangles of red, yellow and orange danced in the current. She closed her eyes and tucked away the image.

"You're smiling," said a smooth male voice she'd heard before. "Shall I take that to mean you are enjoying your visit?"

Tessa opened her eyes. Yes, it was the man from the souvenir shop. He was as tall as she recalled, though virtually any man seemed tall to her, so he was probably a respectable six feet. She still wasn't wild about his mustache, but he'd tucked his Maui Jim sunglasses into the breast pocket of his tropical-patterned shirt, giving her at least one less reason for a gut response of dislike. That still left a twinge of embarrassment over her sarong-tangle, plus a very healthy hesitance to talk too much to anyone. Neither, though, was she capable of ignoring him. She weighed his question.

Despite the unexpected twists in the road, was she enjoying herself? The answer surprised even her.

"Yes," she finally said. "I think I am."

"I like that you took a moment to consider your answer," he said. "It lets me know you speak the truth."

"Or I'm horribly slow," Tessa replied, one beer tarter of tongue.

He laughed. "That, I doubt very much." It was his moment

to hesitate. "We have not been formally introduced. My name is Javier Ruiz."

He extended his hand, and Tessa shook it. His grip was firm, warm and dry, sign enough that she should invite him to sit.

"Hello, Javier. I'm Tessa DiPaulo. Would you like to join me?"

"I would." He pulled out the chair opposite her and settled in. "Tessa...that's an unusual name," he said after summoning the waitress with a subtle wave.

"It's a nickname that saves me an arrogant full name."

"Which is?"

"Contessa," she said. "I think my mother might have had delusions of grandeur for me when she talked my father into it."

He smiled. "But that name suits you, as well."

It had once, when she had been able to walk into a room and know that she'd capture attention simply by doing so. The light that had shone from deep within had hit a scorching flashpoint, though, leaving her little desire to rekindle it. At this moment she was well aware that she was pudgy, perspiring, and that her hair had to be in a witch's tangle.

"Thank you," she replied all the same.

The waitress arrived, and Tessa declined Javier's offer of another beer, asking for a soda instead. It was a straight road back to Vee's, but two beers would make her lazy and without ambition to follow it. Javier and the waitress conversed for a moment, and Tessa had no clue what the upshot of all that talk might be.

"So," he said to Tessa once the waitress had gone, "why simply Tessa, now?"

"I'm more comfortable with it. I've tried to outgrow my Contessa phase. You reach a certain age and it's just unbecoming to be spoiled, you know?"

"And all Contessas are spoiled?"

She peeled the wet beer label off her bottle and stuck it to the cover of her travel guide. It suited her mood better than the stern-faced monkey that had been staring up at her. "This Contessa was. Still maybe is…a little."

"Then we are two of a kind."

"Really?"

He gestured to the beach and the azure sky. "Any man lucky enough to spend time in paradise is spoiled, no?"

The waitress arrived, bringing tea and a plate of what appeared to be tuna sashimi. Tessa wondered for this man's sanity, ordering raw fish in a place that looked to have little more than a rusted refrigerator in the way of cooling equipment.

"Do you like sashimi?" he asked.

"On the rare occasion."

The corner of his mouth turned up at her hedging reply. "Then try some," he said, nudging the plate marginally in her direction.

"Thanks, but…"

He laughed. "You think if one of the two of us is to have food poisoning, it might as well be me?"

"Oh, no, that's not what—"

"Ah, but where's that honesty of yours?"

Tessa smiled. "Yes, the thought did cross my mind."

He pointed toward the counter from which a dark-haired and very pretty woman served beers and soda. "See that lady?"

"Yes."

"That's Margarita. She owns this place."

"Not a bad job," Tessa said.

"A fine one, except in the rainy season," he replied. "Margarita's husband is a fisherman. You'll have no fresher fish anyplace on earth. It's off the boat, and to here. Now try some…just one bite."

Raw tuna was not her customary lunch, but Tessa felt ready to branch out. She selected the smallest piece possible and slipped it into her mouth. Far more facile at perceiving colors than flavors, after she'd eaten it, all she could think to say was, "It tastes clean."

He laughed. "Like soap flakes?"

"No, like the color of the sky after a thunderstorm has passed."

"Ah," he said. "You think like an artist. Are you one? We have many who visit here."

"Not me," she replied flatly.

Her luncheon-mate's dark brows drew briefly together. "Have I tread where I should not?"

Tessa shook off her past the best she could. "Sorry, old regrets and all that."

"If it is a regret, fix it now," he said with an easy shrug of his broad shoulders.

Shoulders that Tessa had no good reason to be noticing. Except she was.

"Easier said than done," she replied to his suggestion.

He smiled. "But most things are."

True enough, she supposed, though she refused to admit so aloud.

"But enough of regrets," he said. "At the least you can enjoy more of this fish that tastes like clean sky."

She thanked him, and then they ate in a silence that Tessa couldn't quite call comfortable. She knew he was only being hospitable, but unfamiliarity held relaxation at bay.

"So what do you do when not in paradise, Tessa DiPaulo?" he eventually asked.

She liked the way her name rolled off his tongue, an exotic mix of ethnicities.

"I'm between things right now," she replied in a quiet bit of understatement. "And you?" He didn't have the well-used hands of a fisherman or farmer, and his wardrobe was too polished, as well.

"I'm a lawyer in San José, because that's where I must be to have enough clients to pay my bills. And I keep office hours here in Playa Blanca when I can, as this has been my home since birth."

"It's a lovely place," she said, though her mind had already moved on. If he had been in the community this long, he should know about Don, and perhaps the two women living in Vee's house.

"But the sun is strong," he said. "And I think you might have burned yourself already."

The touch of his fingertip to the skin of her forearm where it rested on the table jolted Tessa, reminding her that she didn't really know this man. Certainly not enough to ask him questions about matters Vee might not want addressed outside her usual circle. It also reminded her how long it had been since a man had touched her at all.

Disturbed by her thoughts, she edged back and folded her hands in her lap, leaving him no further opportunity for casual contact.

"This time, I have offended you," he said calmly.

She wished she hadn't been so transparent.

"No, I'm sorry," she said while searching for the words to explain to a virtual stranger how vulnerable she was, and yet not lose what little armor she still possessed. "I'm just...I don't know...jittery, I guess." She rubbed her hands over her arms, thinking how odd it was to have gooseflesh while in tropical heat. "I'll definitely put on more sunblock before I walk back."

She glanced up at him, but his attention had been redirected elsewhere.

"Ah, I see the person I was to meet," he said, pushing back his chair. "Claire operates on our more relaxed local standard of Tico time. You know that someone had been born and bred in Costa Rica if they don't rush." He rose and nodded to the waitress, who began setting another table for two. "I've enjoyed talking with you, Tessa, and hope you don't mind that I've bought your drinks for you. I also hope you find our country more fully to your liking."

With that, he turned and greeted the willowy woman Tessa had also first seen in the souvenir shop. They kissed one another on each cheek, and Tessa recalled a tour guide she'd once had in Paris, who'd struggled to explain the social intricacies of *faire la bise.*

That Parisian sojourn was in her past. Now Tessa sat with Javier Ruiz's empty plate, lukewarm soda and a nearly painful yearning to be the sort of woman who would *faire la bise* and not pull away from an innocent touch. Perhaps it was time to find long-lost Contessa. Just a spark of her, though, for Tessa didn't want to burn again.

Kate felt like the middle-aged version of a sport drink commercial. She had pedaled ass up a narrow dirt road leading to a smaller and more rutted version of the same. Sweat dripping and water bottle quickly emptied, she had treated the ride as a race. Never mind that she had no competition or even a good idea of the direction in which she was headed. And forget taking in the countryside, as she'd first intended. Those were all inconsequential matters. By the time she'd reached the top of the final incline, she'd convinced herself that she was fast and as sleek as a large-boned, barely in shape, cigarette-craving Pole could be.

But then something amazing had happened. A bird had cried out. Kate didn't know a whole lot about birds in this part of the world, but she knew that the creature who'd gained her attention was damn big. No teeny canary could make that sound.

Curious, Kate had slowed and started to look around. And the more she'd looked, the more she'd wanted to see. She'd risen enough in altitude that the trees weren't so thick, and while the air was less humid, it still carried the full heat of the day.

Now Kate pulled to the side of the road—such as it was—next to a small, gated farm with a handful of chestnut-colored horses grazing on already short-cropped grass. A hand-painted sign in bright green hung from the front gate, reading Finca O'Rourke. Sitting on the farmhouse porch was a silver-haired woman reading a book. She looked up, as though sensing Kate's attention.

Kate waved, and the woman returned the greeting. Kate knew she should move on, head back downhill to Tessa, the squatters and the general muddle that this "vacation" had become, but she wasn't ready to face reality.

Kate lingered, looking at the woman on the hillside and her idyllic life. As she watched, a large and brilliant red bird flew over the farmhouse, chattering as though talking to the woman below. Identifying the bird was simple; even non-birder Kate had tripped across a few photos of scarlet macaws in her Costa Rican research.

"Incredible," she murmured.

The bird screeched and changed course. Kate followed it low across the blue sky, until it disappeared into the treetops.

"Beyond incredible."

She looked back to the house and the woman. As she did, reality changed up on her. She could see herself on that porch. *Really* see herself…her face for the lady's, her shorter blond hair in place of the longer silver. She made a grab for her water bottle, thinking that dehydration had set in, but the bottle was empty.

"Jesus," she muttered, and for the first time since she had drifted into the nonbeliever camp, she meant it more as a prayer than a curse.

She wanted to be this lady. Literally. She wanted the farm, the porch, the book. Okay, maybe not so much the horses, since she'd always been frightened by them. But in their place she could see a few random llamas and maybe a cow or two. And she could see acres and acres of land all hers...and bicycles, and people sitting around a pool at the end of a hard day's ride. Sure. Finca Murkowski, where the bicycles ran wild and free.

She laughed, a manic sound loud enough to carry to the reading woman. Kate remounted her bike and pedaled off, thinking that sunstroke had to be imminent.

Finca Murkowski?

It was absurd. Her big move had been from Warren, the city where her sisters and brothers still lived in walking distance from her parents, to Birmingham. A handful of miles, not thousands.

And still the silly words played in her head: *Finca Murkowski.* And finally two more words, daring her to grab that bastard bliss by the balls: *Why not?*

As she headed downhill to the main road, Kate let numbers roll through her head: the number of times she'd come up with ideas like this and not followed through (six), the number of drinks she'd need to chase this one from her head (five, minimum) and the number of times she'd have to kick herself in her semifit butt if she didn't at least come up with a business plan before rejecting the concept out of hand (infinite).

Optimism settled over her. She would grow this idea, nurture it like the children she would never have, and in leaving no mark on this land, she would leave her paradox of a mark on the world. Now to rope in the dollars and believers sufficient to make her dream come true....

Kate reached the main road, waiting for a break in the passing vehicles so that she could cross to the waterside of the road. And as she rode toward the village proper, not that it had much proper about it, she tried to keep her feet from matching her racing mind. Her attention was too divided for any show-off, "watch the old chick pedal" maneuvers.

Just when she'd given herself an atta-girl for being so good, a dark blue van blasted by. "Holy shit!"

Kate, who'd been on the very edge of the pavement, was forced to go cross-country, her bike's tires skittering across gravel, weeds and pieces of roadside trash. She held it together for as long as she could, but in her panic, braked unevenly. She was over the handlebars and flat on the ground before she could even work up another outburst.

The world fell quiet as even her thoughts were knocked from her, along with her wind. Cars continued by, either not noticing her among the weeds, or not quite sure what to do.

Kate wasn't too sure, either.

As she lay in the dirt, running her tongue across her teeth to be sure all were where she'd left them, and trying to remember critical facts like her ATM card's password to be sure her brain hadn't turned to mush, the downside of a life riding wild in the mountains above Playa Blanca occurred to Kate.

Had she even seen a hospital?

Okay, so a hospital was overreaching, but how about a clinic of some sort?

She recalled nothing.

Kate brushed a clump of grass from her forehead and laughed. So if she screwed up, she'd be roadkill, plain and simple. What the hell, at least she'd be going with a smile on her face.

Wishing for fewer years on her bones, Kate sat upright and swiped at the blood dripping from a wide, dirt-filled scrape on her left elbow. All in all, she'd gotten off lucky, and it was the last damn time she'd ride anywhere without her helmet.

Feeling closer to four hundred years old than forty-one, Kate slowly stood, then righted her bicycle. Everything appeared to be in working order on the bike, at least. She took the road through the village carefully, not giving a rat's behind about the people doing double takes at the mess she'd become.

Just past the clump of hotels, she rode up behind Tessa, who had a grocery bag in one hand and a definite limp going. Figuring they might as well suffer together, Kate dismounted the bike and walked next to her friend.

"Ever find those tampons?" she asked.

Tessa's brown eyes grew wide. "What the hell happened to you?"

"A blue van," Kate said.

"Jerks. You could have really been hurt."

Kate laughed, her near-bliss experience still outweighing the near-death one. "Trust me, I *really* hurt."

Tessa stopped, and as she dug through the daypack she'd had slung over one shoulder, she asked, "Was this the van traveling at the speed of light? It kicked up enough road dust that I thought a sandstorm had started."

"That would be the one."

Tessa handed Kate a couple of pieces of tissue. "You might want to clean up that elbow a little."

"Thanks," Kate said. "Just out of curiosity, is there a hospital around here?"

Tessa frowned, then got that sure look that always arrived before she was about to spout chapter and verse. "According to the tour guide, there's one in Quepos, though if it's anything major, a MedEvac flight to San José's better. Why? Do you want to go get checked out?"

"No, just thinking ahead."

"To what?"

"The next time those jerks blast by," she fibbed. "It's a small town. We'll see them again."

And if Kate Murkowski had her way, she'd be seeing them the rest of her life.

CHAPTER 7

Isabel sat behind the wheel of Don's blue van. She and Mila had again hidden it at a long-vacant house across the road and up the hillside from its real home. Frightened and angry, she tried to calm herself as tears leaked from her eyes.

"You should not have let me drive," she said to Mila. "You should have said no."

"But why, when you wanted to so very much?" Mila asked.

"Because I'm a child, and you should have said no!" It was easier to deliver guilt to Mila's lap than to let it sit with her any longer.

"You're no longer a child, whether you want to be one or not," Mila pointed out. "And as for the driving, it was for less than a handful of minutes. No one was hurt, even if you did frighten the bigger American off her bicycle."

Isabel looked through her tears and caught Mila's wide grin.

"This is nothing to smile at," she said. "Someone could have died."

"But no one did," Mila replied. "And now you'll have to

distract the Americans long enough for me to get our fish and fruit into the kitchen."

It seemed there was a price for every pleasure—even one as fleeting and questionable as trying to drive—and Isabel was so very tired of paying.

She walked the road to the large house, first stopping at Don's place. Her heart rose like a bird on the breeze, with the hope that he would be there. And then it plummeted. His house remained as it had been that morning when she'd last checked. She watched as Jerry, the dog who would come for no one but Don, slunk back into the green of the trees. She offered a few words of comfort, since that, food and water were all she had to give the poor thing, with its heart breaking.

From her time spent with pencil and paper, drawing what her slow and stupid hand would let her, Isabel knew the narrow and hidden paths through the rich gardens surrounding the big house as well as she did the stone walkways. This time, she stayed in the shadowed landscape, carefully making her way down the hillside until she rejoined the walk that led to the blue and chilly swimming pool.

So she was to distract the Americans? She should have given Mila this job and carried in the fish, with its cold, unseeing eyes. Dead fish were far easier to handle.

Making herself as small and quiet as a mouse—a skill that had saved her much grief until she turned eleven and grief had become her jailer—Isabel tiptoed to the pretty glass doors leading to the house from the terrace.

The Americans were inside, and she saw in their hands the household file that Mila had been keeping since Don had failed to come home. Isabel muttered a low curse—one of her elder brother Estefan's colorful favorites. She needed them to stop nosing about, and she must think quickly!

Seizing a plan, Isabel went to the edge of the terrace, where the gardens met the stone, then drew in a breath until it hurt.

"*Aiiii!*" she cried shrilly, the sound echoing off the terrace and down to the water. "Snake!" she screamed in Spanish, then repeated it, pointing into the bushes that Don always kept trimmed so neatly.

Isabel didn't allow herself even a glance toward the house to see if her plan was working. "The snake will kill the dog! Run! *Aiiii!* Snake!"

She relaxed when she heard the house's door slam.

The Americans were at her side soon after she managed to work up a few tears still left over from the guilt of nearly having killed Kate.

"What is it? What have you seen?" asked the larger woman in Spanish so good that Isabel began to worry.

"It was a snake. The biggest I have ever seen…with green shiny skin and evil, beady eyes the color of night. It was big enough to swallow a chicken and then want three more. It was after Don's dog, and… and…" Mother of heaven, she hadn't thought about where in this tale of hers Don might be.

"And?" Kate asked, looking at her much the way her own mother had after catching her in a lie about where the six thousand colones under Mama's mattress had gone. Isabel had learned her lesson with a belt sharp against the skin of her back. If you would lie, do it well.

Good thing the Americans had no belt.

"And?" Kate asked again.

Isabel fluttered her hands to distract from the panic in her eyes. "And Don has gone to help a neighbor with a—a—house problem. And now his dog will be eaten," she finished in a rush.

"A house problem?" Kate echoed.

"Yes. A house problem." Isabel began to wade into the green of the garden, as though she meant to hunt and strangle the snake.

"And where is Don's dog? I don't see him."

"Maybe your eyes are bad."

"Not as bad as your story." Kate reached out a hand and hauled Isabel from the garden.

Isabel wrenched away, but it was too late. She was swamped by the sick feeling that came with being touched by strangers. Oh, how much simpler life had been when she'd felt nothing at all.

"Don't touch me," she said, wishing for a knife to protect herself, or better yet, her lie of a snake to come swallow this woman. "Don't ever touch me." She shook with fear, and hated that she'd shown the Americans her weakness.

"Do you want to tell me what's going on?" Tessa asked Kate, who was looking at Isabel as though she was crazy.

And maybe she was, Isabel thought. Crazy to do what Mila had asked of her. Crazy to think that she deserved a place as fine as this.

"Isabel, here, saw a snake right out of *Jurassic Park* chasing Don's dog," Kate said.

Isabel didn't know what this "Jurassic Park" might be, but she knew she was being mocked. She was ready to give the same back to the blond one when Mila came from the house onto the terrace.

"What are you doing?" she asked Isabel in Spanish, using a scolding voice.

Ah well, at least the groceries were now stocked.

"Nothing," Isabel replied. "It is nothing."

"She saw a snake," Kate said in English, staring at them both curiously. "Or so she says."

"Kate, we don't have any reason not to believe Isabel," Tessa said.

Isabel stared at the ground, thankful she was not supposed to be able to understand Tessa, who was doing that thing again, where her words held one meaning and her face another.

"And maybe we should do something, if it's *Jurassic Park* big," Tessa added.

Mila stepped in front of Isabel. "This is the tropics, and snakes come in all sizes. But if it will comfort you, I will notify Don when he returns from the village."

"I thought you said he was at a neighbor's, Isabel?" Kate asked in Spanish.

"Javier Ruiz's," Isabel supplied.

"Interesting," Kate said, switching to English.

"Not very," Mila replied in the same tongue. "He went first to the village and then to Ruiz's."

"Good, then," Tessa said. "He'll be back soon. I'm looking forward to meeting him."

Isabel kept silent, awash in languages. English…Spanish… It did not matter. All she knew was that she was doomed.

Cali, Colombia

The broken leg and ribs were real bitches, but it was the fever that had nearly killed Don.

"Dirty wounds," he remembered one doctor saying as he was brought into the hospital.

What did the guy expect? It wasn't as though having your motorcycle taken out by a truckload of stinking cattle would give a guy *clean* wounds.

But Don hadn't been in any position to argue the point, since a faltering heartbeat later, he'd begun hanging out around the ceiling of the little emergency room, watching his Don-body, already pretty messed up after sixtysomething years of hard living, get messed with some more.

Amazingly enough, he'd lived. He knew he was getting stronger, too, because today the nurses had upgraded him from no food at all to some really puke-worthy juice. And he was happily drugged, which was the only way he could manage to put up with this life of tubes jammed into places that tubes sure as shit should never be.

And earlier, just before the nurse had given him something to knock him out again, he'd also learned that he'd been in this bed for three goddamn weeks. He supposed it was better than the alternative, which had flashed through his mind as the truck crossed to the wrong side of the road and come straight at him.

Don shifted a little on the narrow bed, wishing he were home in Playa Blanca with "Hell in a Bucket" playing on the stereo and an ice-cold Imperial in his hand. In his three-week-long nap, he'd had some wild dreams. In one, he'd wanted to give it up, but Jerry had told him it wasn't his time. He had things to do, lives to fix. Like maybe even his own, first, Jerry had pointed out with a fool's grin.

Don wouldn't have put up with this kind of garbage from the dude, except Jerry had been looking pretty damn good for a guy whose big heart had finally blown to hell over ten years before, leaving him dead and Don severely pissed off.

But, hell, he was alive and Jerry wasn't. He was even thinking that some more of the citrus mystery juice wouldn't be a bad thing. Based on the pain when he breathed, though, he knew he was more likely to get a nurse with a long needle and a bad attitude. Don settled in for the wait.

Just as he was having a fine flashback to the early days when the Dead weren't…well, dead, and he'd followed each concert tour, hitching rides or scraping up pennies to take the Hound from city to city, a young nurse he'd never seen before came into the room.

Pretty nurse.

Reminded him of what Isabel would look like in a few years, which got him to worrying, and he hated worrying.

"You're awake again. This is a good thing," she said.

"But it hurts less to sleep," he pointed out.

She gave him a half smile and then began flipping through his chart. "We have no name for next of kin, your house phone was not listed and you had no emergency number in your passport."

"I meant to get around to that," he said. Of course, he'd also figured that he'd taken on Jerry's mantle of immortality when Jerry had done the unthinkable and croaked.

"Too many of you men say that. What will your family say, with you gone this long?"

A few months ago, he'd have been able to say that he had no family, but now that would be a lie. "They'll tell me I've been an ass."

She laughed. "Would you like to make a call? We can get you into a wheelchair and to a phone."

Don tried to concentrate on what he'd had with him before his motorcycle had been reduced to a bunch of pieces small enough to fit in a baggie. "I don't have a calling card...I don't think."

"Don't worry. We'll handle that for you."

At a price, he knew, but whatever they charged, he'd find a way to pay. "Yeah. A call would be great."

Anxious to let the ladies back home know he still breathed, he worked his way up in the bed, ignoring the young nurse's warnings to go slower. The hell with slow. He'd been at *stop* for too long, and Mila and Isabel had to be sick with worry. Isabel, at least. Mila was made of cast iron.

He struggled some more, but it was getting harder to find the edge of the bed, with all the white dots shooting through his field of vision. Darkness began closing in, and Don realized that he'd been stupid, hurrying this phone thing along.

Damn. Jerry's really gonna chew my ass this time.

And with that, it was naptime.

Playa Blanca, two days later

Tessa's patience had waned sliver thin, along with the moon in tonight's sky. All four women in the house knew that Don was nowhere about, but according to Mila and Isabel, over the past two days Don had been everywhere but brokering peace in the Middle East.

Tessa floated on her back in the swimming pool, her hair drifting around her like dark seaweed. Countless stars shone in the sky, a sight far different from night in suburban Detroit. She thought about the usual things that captured a woman's mind at moments such as this: what lay beyond the stars, where her father's spirit might be and if she could possibly sneak one more bit of ice cream from the freezer before sleep.

Sleep...

She'd had little of it. Vee's talk weeks ago of squatters and the need to have a house occupied had been keeping Tessa up at night, wondering exactly with whom she'd been sharing a house. For her peace of mind, tonight she would have to end this runaround. It no longer mattered that Vee remained in Borneo. The question had grown beyond whether Mila and Isabel were welcome guests to whether the caretaker still existed.

Tessa's fingertips, extended above her head, brushed the edge of the pool. She rolled onto her stomach and moved closer, resting her forearms on the rough stone of the pool's deck. Off in the underbrush, away from the glow of the terrace's lighting, the dog with no name howled to the barely there moon. Tessa knew how he felt.

She would talk to these women and rely on the instinct that had flitted off to God-knows-where when it came to the issue of Jack's fidelity. But she was far more together now than she'd been then, far less wrapped in her own net of small daily miseries. In some strange way, she was nearly thankful for her job loss. Now to cage instinct and put it to work.

Tessa smiled into the darkness. Good luck, there.

The dog howled again, the sound closer now.

"I hear you, friend," she said to the beast.

Tessa watched as Kate stepped onto the terrace, then came and sat cross-legged at the edge of the pool by her.

"You've been out here since before sundown. You have to be waterlogged," Kate said.

"Probably. I was doing some thinking. What have you been up to?"

"Just toying with an idea...sitting in my room and crunching some numbers."

"And how did it go?"

"The numbers crunched back."

"Sorry." Tessa stretched out, fluttering her feet behind her while resting her fingertips on the pool's edge. She felt weightless and wonderful. This was far more her sort of exercise than the endless rides Kate had taken the past two days. Kate had even been lobbying for Tessa to get her hands on a bike and join her. Not damn likely.

"Are Mila and Isabel still awake?" she asked.

"Awake and in front of the television. I don't think *Friends* will ever go off the air."

"Imagine being one of them and seeing your young self on television thirty years from now."

"Depressing," said Kate.

"Without a doubt," Tessa affirmed, then worked her way over to the pool's broad steps. "I've been thinking it's time we have a good old-fashioned 'Come to Jesus' meeting with our friends inside," she said as she climbed out.

"Time to pitch 'em?" Kate asked.

"Time to figure out what's going on, at least," she said while toweling herself off. "I can't take another of Mila's tall tales."

Kate chuckled. "And I'm not sure she has another one left in that staid Teutonic body. So, do you want me to back you up?"

"Naturally," Tessa said, wrapping the beach towel around her hips and tucking the top under to create some terry-cloth camouflage. "You do it so well."

"Just currying favor," Kate replied in a casual tone.

Tessa walked into the house, knowing full well that Kate would follow. The women were just where Kate had said they'd be, watching television. Still damp, Tessa stepped in front of the screen and switched it off.

"You were wanting something?" Mila asked. The words carried a strong "screw you" subtext.

"Yes. I want the lies to end."

"Lies?" Mila echoed.

"Where's Don?" Tessa asked. "And don't bother telling me that he's fixing a roof, buying a donkey or whatever the lie of the night might be. Just tell me where he really is."

The older woman remained silent, and the teenager began rocking back and forth in her chair.

"One last chance. Where's Don?" She gave a mental count to twenty, readjusted the towel at her hips and then said, "You're leaving me with no option." She reached for the phone where it sat on an end table next to Isabel. "I'm calling the police."

Mila made a scoffing sound. "You're being ridiculous. How will it look when they arrive and Don is sleeping safely in his bed?"

"Sorry, but we both know he's not," Tessa said, then began to punch 911 into the handset, which was a complete bluff. She didn't know whether Costa Rica even had a 911 system and she hadn't hit the on button, in any case.

"Stop!" Isabel cried.

And in English, too, Tessa noted. She'd at least sniffed out this scam.

Isabel unleashed a torrent of Spanish at Mila, who an-

swered in angered tones. Then the young pregnant girl focused on Tessa.

"Don is missing," she said in heavily accented English.
Her shoulders began to shake and fat tears rolled from her
eyes. "I am afraid he is very hurt." One sob became many,
and Isabel folded in on herself.

"She loves drama, that one," Mila said. "And she should
not have concerned you with a matter as trivial as this.
Don went off on a motorcycle vacation. Walkabouts, he
calls them. I have known him since he came to Playa
Blanca, and in all those years he hasn't followed a schedule," she added. "He leaves for weeks on end, but he always
comes back."

Hands over her face, Isabel said something. Tessa sorted
the words *three weeks* from the jumble.

"He's been gone for three weeks?" she asked Mila.

"Less, I'm sure," Mila replied. "Isabel sees him as a grand-
father and misses him very much."

The girl pulled her hands away from her face and swiped
her palm across her eyes. "Five weeks he has been gone. He
should have been home almost three weeks ago."

"And you lived here five weeks ago?" Tessa asked the girl.
She nodded.

Five weeks. Tessa mentally counted back to early November. That was about a week before Vee had offered her the
house, and Tessa was sure that Vee would have mentioned

the two females already in residence. She said as much to Mila.

"Maybe Vee is forgetful," the woman offered.

Actually, Vee was the only woman her age Tessa knew wasn't lying to herself or puffing for others when she said that she didn't need a date book to keep track of matters. Middle-aged fog hadn't yet set in, and Vee forgot nothing. Damn her. And damn Mila for making this harder than it had to be.

"Why not just tell me the whole truth, or do you lie for sport?" she asked the German.

"I lie for survival," the woman replied.

Tessa didn't know what to say in return. She looked at Isabel, with her pregnant belly popping out on that incongruously childish body, and then at Mila, who suddenly seemed diminished from her usual dragon self.

"Tell me how you ended up in this house," she finally asked.

Mila shifted in her chair, settling her knotted hands in her lap. "Isabel and I were living in another place, a small house on the mountainside south of the village. I had been there since I came from Germany in 1990, and the rent was modest. But then the owner put the house up for sale and told us that we would have to move if I could not afford to buy it. And with my small pension, I couldn't, of course. Playa

Blanca might be just a speck now, but it's becoming very popular with land speculators."

Kate, who stood on the outside of the inquisition's circle, muttered something beneath her breath that sounded like *no shit*.

Mila continued. "We had moved our belongings to a shed behind an empty vacation villa near here. Don, who was watching the property for the owner, found us." She sat a little taller. "I have my pride, and would not have gone to him with our troubles. But he offered on his own to put us here until we can find someplace else, and I accepted."

"Great. Missing-in-action Don, patron saint of the poor," Kate said.

"Be fair," Tessa warned her friend.

"No need. We've got you in line as his protégée. You didn't ask, but here's what I'd suggest. Tell them to pack their things, Tessa. They lied. They don't know Vee, and it's not our problem that her caretaker is gathering lost sheep."

"They're not our sheep to boot," Tessa pointed out. "They're Vee's, and she's not reachable." But that problem, the best Tessa could figure, currently ranked second behind the missing caretaker.

She turned her attention to Vee's uninvited guests. "Where did Don say he was going?"

"South," Isabel said. "Maybe all the way to Colombia."

"Has he called since he left?"

This time Mila answered. "No, we had some e-mails and one postcard from Panama, but nothing recently. This is not unusual, though. I've watched this house for him while he traveled, before."

Kate snorted. "So he's in Costa Rica, Colombia, Panama or dead. After three weeks I'd be betting on the last."

Isabel stood, fists clenched and face drawn tight. "Shut up. Just shut *up!*"

"We'll find him," Tessa promised in an effort to calm the girl. "All we have to do is track his possible routes."

"Do you have any idea of the number of possible routes around here?" Kate asked. "No, of course you don't. You haven't even left the property in two days."

"Kate," Tessa said in her best diplomat's voice, "why don't you let me finish this off?"

"You're going to get suckered," her friend warned.

"Too late," she replied, and Kate stalked off.

"So what now?" Tessa asked, though she expected no answer from the women in front of her.

Despite what she'd said to Kate, Tessa knew that if she were to be a good friend to Vee, she should show these two the street. Vee was generous enough to friends, but Tessa doubted she'd take kindly to people who'd been abusing her hospitality for weeks. Still, Tessa could think of nothing worse for her karma—and her sleepless nights—than putting a pregnant teen and an old woman, no matter how toxic, curbside. In any case, it wasn't as though Vee had suffered actual harm, thus far.

"This can't go on forever, you know," she said. "This isn't your house, or even Don's."

"So you will call your friend?" Mila asked.

"That depends on you."

The older woman bristled. "If you are thinking that we'll be your slaves…"

"No, not at all."

Actually, Tessa was only half-sure about what she was thinking. Instinct seemed to be reeling her back to her mother's alarmed words about self-sufficiency. Maybe her mother had had a point, no matter how poorly Tessa had taken it over twenty years ago. She decided to let instinct roll.

"Mila, I want you to come up with a plan," she said. "One you show me and we work on together."

"What sort of plan?" Mila asked, her curiosity clearly piqued.

"You need a home, and you obviously need income other than your pension. And, Isabel, have you thought about what you'll do after this baby is born?"

Isabel hesitated. "Not what I did before."

Tessa didn't want to think too deeply about what that might have been. "Then you have to start planning, too. Have you even seen a doctor?"

The girl laughed. "To be told that I am having a baby? I know that."

"No, for prenatal care," Tessa said, feeling her fix-it urge kick into overdrive. "You need to be sure the baby's growing as it should, and that you are, as well."

Mila held out one hand. "Money for food…" And then she held out her other. "Money for doctors…" She pretended to weigh the two. "Guess which we choose."

"That's my point. There has to be a way to choose both. Today's the fourth of December, right?"

They nodded.

"Kate and I are scheduled to be here through the third week of February. If we can all get along…which means no lies, no smoking in the house and no manipulation…I won't tell Vee about you, and I won't ask you to leave. And in that time, I want Don found and you two to get your futures sorted out."

Tessa didn't miss the irony of telling them this, but hell, they might as well all be sorting together. She quickly tapped into her thoughts about the missing caretaker. "And I'll be telling Vee about Don. I have to," she added at the alarm plain on their faces. "If she decides that she needs to fly down here, then we change our course a little, okay?"

"Change our course to what?" Mila asked, her expression having shifted from scared to cynical.

"I don't know," Tessa replied. "We'll wing it."

She'd never spoken more freeing words. They were loose and free Contessa words, actually. And even though she'd just taken on the woes of an MIA Dead Head, a pregnant teen and a cranky impoverished pensioner, Tessa could have danced with joy.

And, she promised herself, some night soon when the moon was growing full and the dog with no name had ceased his howling, Contessa DiPaulo would.

CHAPTER 8

Kate paced her bedroom until she couldn't stand its four posh walls and had to move on to her suite's small balcony. Even the fresh air and the sounds of the night creatures venturing out weren't enough to settle her.

She braced her hands on the wooden railing and stared into the darkness, wishing for both a cigarette and two fewer household occupants. It wasn't as though she had anything against the squatters. It was more that she had problems of her own and didn't need them clogging up the airspace with theirs. She wasn't the woo-woo type, didn't much care about her spiritual path, but was damn well determined to have both Tessa and herself simplify, simplify, *simplify* until the path to Finca Murkowski was clear.

She had never wanted anything with such passion. Growing up in a three-bedroom house with six brothers and sisters had made sole possession pretty much the Holy Grail for Kate. When she'd bought her house years before, it had been the first place that was hers alone. Still, though, even then it had felt like a place-filler—a nice one, sure—but not the home of her dreams. But this land was different. This *country* was different.

She knew it was insane that a Polish-American might find her true roots on a Costa Rican mountaintop, but life was too damn short to worry about whether she was losing it. New Kate, Costa Rican under the skin, would make her mark here…live each day for the pleasure of it and give pleasure to others. Banking and pleasure had almost never bumped up against each other.

But now she knew what she wanted, and by God, she would feed that want! Even logical Tessa would see what a solid quality-of-life plan she'd put together. Granted, the financial end of the plan was riddled with more holes than a termite-infested log, but once Tessa signed on, some would be plugged. Kate wasn't certain how to broach the subject with her friend, but knew it would have to be soon.

Old Mila had been dead-on about land speculators. Even the property Kate had spotted yesterday, so far beyond Finca O'Rourke that it was actually on the other side of the mountain, had other buyers snapping at it. And Kate didn't even want to think about the improvements that would have to be made. How did one get heavy equipment to the backside of a mountain? She hoped like hell it didn't involve resorting to helicopters.

Restless, Kate moved back inside. She checked out the

magazines in the basket next to her bed, but she wasn't the
Vogue type.

A knock sounded at her door.

"Yes?" she called.

"It's me...Tessa."

Kate opened the door and admitted her friend, who'd
changed into shorts-and-T-shirt pajamas. With her hair
pulled into a ponytail, she appeared closer to twenty than
forty. This seemed inherently unfair to Kate, as Tessa's favorite form of exercise was turning the pages of a novel.

"What's up?" Kate asked.

"I wanted to talk to you before I go to sleep," Tessa said
as she closed the bedroom door.

"Okay." She checked out the frown lines between her
friend's brows. So maybe Tessa looked closer to a very cranky
thirty.

"Did the crone-and-wench show wear you out?" Kate
asked.

Tessa's expression grew darker yet. "Kate, what's going on
with you?"

Kate debated engaging in a little denial, though Tessa
didn't appear to be in the mood to allow that luxury. But because there was no rule against trying, she put on a bewil-
dered expression.

"I'm not sure what you're talking about," she said.

"I mean your attitude in the other room, and here, with

that crone-and-wench crack." Tessa pulled out the chair from the dressing table and sat. "Don't you think those women have enough going on? I'm serious about this. What's up with you?"

What's up with you?

From a purely technical point of view, this was the perfect opening to bring up the request she had in mind for Tessa. But emotions came into play here, as well as Tessa's equally foreign compulsion to bond with and nurture all and sundry, including the squatter duo. Kate somehow managed to clamp down on her need to move along her agenda.

"I think I have jet lag," she said, knowing the excuse was puny at best. "I guess it's all the travel catching up with me."

"We're a two-hour time difference from Detroit and you've been feeling good enough for day-long bike trips," Tessa pointed out.

Damn. Did she have to mention bike trips? So much for self-control.

Kate wanted to think that she glowed with joy, but she felt more like a victim in one of the *Alien* movies. Her excitement was going to burst from her one way or another, and she'd rather not rip a gut trying to hold it in.

"Tessa, this is going to sound insane, but I've found my bliss."

Tessa's brows briefly arched. "Already?"

"I know it was a little fast, but now that I know what I want…" Kate's words trailed off as she tried to pin down the words to describe the thrill that made her blood rush in a way that no job—and for that matter, no man—ever had. "It's like my life has finally started."

"And what is this life?" her friend asked, sounding not exactly bored, but certainly lacking the level of enthusiasm Kate had hoped for.

"Come on, be happy, Tessa."

"First, why don't you tell me what I'm being happy about?"

Good point. Kate stood in front of Tessa, more nervous than she'd ever been when presenting a new client to the bank's senior loan committee. This time, it was her future on the line, and that mattered to her a helluva lot more than some auto parts manufacturer's. She moved closer to her friend, not in her space, but also not easily avoided.

"I want a bicycle ranch," she announced, figuring shock value had its merits.

"A *what?*"

"Some people have dude ranches, and I want a bicycle ranch. Tessa, I'm sure this will be a money-maker. I want a big piece of property and a guest house with a wonderful pool, and maybe even spa treatments. I want to take people out on multiple-day bike trips, and have them catered to and pampered while camping out at night. I want—"

"Hang on. *Where* do you want this?"

"In Costa Rica. Above Playa Blanca, to be specific."

Tessa quickly shook her head, as though she was trying to

dislodge Kate's words. "So in three days, one of which was spent just getting to Playa Blanca, you've decided that you're going to pick up your entire life and resettle in Costa Rica?"

"I saw you fall for Jack in less time than that," Kate shot back, then couldn't believe she'd said that.

Over a decade had passed since, at a chance meeting, Kate had been forced to introduce Jack, her secret and newly minted lover, to Tessa. Kate had had such consistent miserable luck with guys—two dates and they were gone forever— that she'd kept silent about Jack. They'd passed the five-date milestone and were working their way toward ten. She'd been almost ready to admit to herself and others that this might be the real thing. Except it hadn't been real to Jack. He'd quickly dropped her and married Tessa.

"Jack's a poor example, don't you think?" Tessa replied after their mutual silence.

Poorer than Tessa would ever know, so Kate conceded the point with a nod. "About the bike ranch… I have the concept worked out. Between the land, marketing, equipment and the improvements, plus a stash of working capital to keep me going until the money comes in, I figure I need about four hundred thousand in outside investment."

"Dollars," Tessa said flatly.

Since there was no turning back, Kate barreled on. "Yes, dollars. Tomorrow I'll take you up the mountainside and let you see the property I've been looking at. The house is a wreck, and there are no outbuildings to speak of, but it's gorgeous, Tessa. Really! I met the nearest neighbor, too, and she says that anything is possible here, so long as you have money and patience."

Tessa briefly smiled. "I don't suppose that now would be an appropriate time to point out that you're usually short on both?"

"Not appropriate at all. And listen, I know how much I can get out of my house in Birmingham and some investments I have outside my 401K. Plus there's always my severance package... Which leads to...you."

"You want me to invest in a bike ranch?"

"Look, I know I've been a pain to deal with over the past couple of days, but I want this so badly, Tessa, and I don't know how to pull it off. We've always been a team, haven't we? I'm only asking for a small investment to start with...fifty or sixty thousand, tops."

"*Small?* You think that's *small?*"

She should have known better than to float numbers before she had Tessa hooked. Kate went into damage-control mode. "Come to the property with me tomorrow. It's gorgeous. I promise you'll love it."

Tessa stood. "Kate, I don't even like bicycles."

"They're a hot trend in tourism."

"Hot and highly uncomfortable in this climate, I'd bet."

"Just come with me tomorrow," Kate pleaded.

"No," she said. "I need time to think."

And that was the problem. Kate didn't want Tessa to think; she wanted her first to hunger for this…to *feel*. And given Tessa's current attitude, Kate might as well wish for higher breasts and a man who wouldn't screw her over.

"Never mind," she said, feeling more hurt than she should. "I couldn't have expected you to want this as much as I do. Why don't we just both get some sleep?"

"I'm sorry, Kate, but—"

"Really, it's okay," Kate said. "I'll figure something out—cash in that 401K, maybe."

"You can't do that. It would be fiscal suicide." Tessa's voice carried a note of alarm.

It was then that Kate recalled the best way of all to gain Tessa's attention. She gave a casual shrug of her shoulders. "Sometimes you've got to take risks. And in any case, if I bomb out I have Social Security to fall back on, right?" She opened the bedroom door. "But as I said, I'll handle this. Don't sweat it, Tessa," she said as she shooed her out.

Tessa hesitated in the doorway. "Do you have a written plan you can show me?"

"Nothing finalized." Kate went to the sheaf of papers on her nightstand. She riffled though the information, pulling out the most positive calculations and ignoring the gaping holes that she hadn't quite wanted to face. "This is rough, so don't take it as gospel."

Tessa took the information, nodded absently, then left. After Kate had closed her bedroom door, she got one step into a victory dance before guilt cut in. Maybe it had been a smidge underhanded to toy with Tessa, but it had been necessary, too. She considered the adages supporting her position: To the victor go the spoils.... No guts, no glory.... And her personal (albeit modified) favorite: Just freakin' do it and deal with the consequences later. Finca Murkowski would be hers, and Tessa would come to love the place, too. After all, who could hate a place where the women lived large and the bicycles roamed free?

The next morning as Tessa tiptoed by Kate's bedroom door, she had a two-part prayer: that Kate was out riding already, and that her friend would happen upon a great deal of money before she returned. And while the money would be highly convenient, Tessa would settle for having only the first part of the prayer granted.

When she reached the house's front door without crossing either Kate or the other two residents, Tessa was feeling blessed indeed. She paused on the drive in front of the fountain to be sure the new sneakers that Kate had harangued her into buying before departing the United States were snug. She didn't need new blisters to go with the set from her last sandal-clad hike to the village. As she knelt, the books and supposed necessities she'd stuffed into her daypack shifted her weight forward. When she awkwardly stood again, she saw the dog with no name lurking just down the way.

"Hey, Pooch...uh..." she called, belatedly realizing that she couldn't name a single Grateful Dead member other than Jerry Garcia. The dog slunk away, apparently sniffing out her philistine status.

Tessa walked on, pretending she didn't see the beast shadowing her. She'd just passed the turnoff to Don's place when a dark blue van, engine roaring, chased her from the road. She hardly had time to inventory every nick and ding before it turned into Don's, but blindfolded she would have recognized the vehicle. The sound of its failing exhaust system was unmistakable. This was the same van that had taken out Kate three days earlier.

Ready to rip the skin off the driver, Tessa sprinted to the vehicle, which had pulled into the spot next to Don's house. The driver turned off the engine. The driver's door slowly opened, but no one appeared.

Tessa came closer, but was cut off at the pass by Kate, who'd come hauling uphill from the main road on her bicycle. She flung herself off her bike. Sweat dripped from the tip of her nose, and her eyes carried a fury that flirted with demonic possession.

"Get out of the van!" Kate bellowed.

Tessa supposed that was a convincing approach, even if it did smack of Kate's having watched a few too many cop shows on television.

"Don't make me come in after you!"

Slowly, two bare brown female legs—rather swollen at the ankles—appeared. Tessa watched as Isabel awkwardly slid from the seat to stand on the ground below. Her expression was as defiant as Tessa was sure her own had been at the same age, when caught up to no good.

Kate stalked closer. "You! You're a menace!"

"I am just learning," the girl said, holding up one hand in a nervous gesture of self-defense.

"Right. Sure you are," Kate scoffed. "I know how it is down in these parts. You start driving as soon as you can see over the steering wheel. You damn well know how to drive, and you intentionally ran me off the road the other day."

Isabel's chin rose. "These parts? What do you mean by *these parts*? That we are so backward that we have no laws? That we sleep with chickens in the house?" She would have been nose-to-nose with Kate, except her belly got in the way.

Tessa, as always, refocused her gaze upward. She could deal with Isabel much more easily if she disregarded the physical evidence of her pregnancy.

"I mean that you tried to kill me."

"I did not, but now I wish I had," Isabel spat.

Tessa had never raised a child, but it seemed she had two in front of her. Their war of words continued as she circled them and peered into the van. Mila sat in the front passenger seat with her belt still fastened.

"This is Don's van, then?" Tessa asked.

"It belongs to the house. He left me the keys when he began his walkabout."

Tessa slipped off her daypack, put it on the bench seat, then slid in next to it. "Perfect," she said to the dour German. "I now have a ride to the village."

Mila, no one's fool, didn't object. Instead she wished Tessa a fine trip before exiting the van.

Tessa closed her door and started the engine, smiling at the gaseous rumble of the leaky muffler. She had backed from the parking spot, carefully avoiding both the combatants and Kate's bike, before Kate noticed her escape.

Tessa lodged the van in Drive and waggled her fingers at Kate.

Can't hear you, she mouthed at her friend, who was waving her arms and shouting something about "the property."

Definitely can't hear you, she repeated, then took off.

Now that she had wheels, Tessa headed north out of Playa Blanca and took the winding road to Quepos. She supposed the drive was lovely enough, but she didn't dare be certain. She had work enough becoming accustomed to the narrower roads and the way cars thought nothing of pulling out of side drives without a glance for oncoming traffic. Relatively speaking, this was no worse than Detroit traffic, except that it was so…foreign.

She smiled at her obvious thought, then, feeling brave enough for some distraction, switched on what at a glance appeared to be the radio's knob. Instead, an old cassette lodged in the van's tape player squealed and whirred. Tessa winced. She was ready to eject it when it caught.

"Truckin'," sang the Dead, and Tessa joined in, substituting "blah-blahs" for the lyrics that escaped her. The next song she didn't know at all, so instead she thought about Kate's mad proposal.

And it *was* mad. She didn't have the sort of cash sitting about that Kate had asked for. True, she had some inheritance money she'd carefully stashed to pay for an adoption once she'd warmed Jack to the idea. It was closer to thirty thousand dollars than sixty, and she didn't find trading off the baby she'd now never have for a bike camp, or ranch, or whatever Kate had called it, a fitting substitution.

Still, she and Kate *had* been a team for seventeen years. They'd lasted longer than many marriages. Hers, for example. But a life centered around bicycles and catering to an endless stream of guests? Tessa shivered at the thought. She was gregarious enough, but without her downtime, she also grew snappish. And Kate already had that job covered, along with finding her bliss in a Kate-like style, too—sudden, wild, and with a passion that Tessa yearned for. In moderation.

As she pulled into Quepos, Tessa promised herself that she'd at least consider Kate's proposal. Somebody had to protect Kate from her passion, and Tessa was the woman for the job.

After finding a parking spot near the harbor, Tessa strolled the small pier, past the fishing boats tied at their moorings. The scents of fish and sea—a sort of tidal stew—lingered in the air. Scavenger gulls still sat on pilings, hoping against hope, and a marmalade-colored cat nosed around a large garbage can. But for the heat, this could be a smaller version of Dingle Harbor, in Ireland, which had been a favorite travel spot of her parents. Dad would have loved this place, too.

Tessa enjoyed the small luxury of being a tourist, walking slowly, taking in the every day. The fishermen had carted off their catch sometime before and were now cleaning, repairing and stowing gear for tomorrow's work. Some smiled and waved as Tessa walked by. She returned their greetings, feeling feminine and deserving of notice for the first time in months.

From the harbor, she walked the streets of the town, stopping in shops that caught her eye. It was nearly noon when her arms were too full to let her gaze wander further. She'd bought a long white cotton skirt embellished with bright embroidery simply because she'd liked the way it twirled around her like a bell when she spun in front of the mirror. On a total whim, she'd purchased lovely dangly earrings on fine wires, though her ears were unpierced. And she had indulged in a flowery, tropical yellow-and-orange two-piece suit. She wouldn't go so far as to call it a bikini, but it was less than she'd worn since putting on her baby-stakes weight. It didn't matter that she curved out where maybe she shouldn't. There was no one she cared to impress. Reinforcing that attitude, her stomach growled.

Tessa deposited her purchases in the van, locked it and went off in search of food. Half a block from where she'd parked, she came across a restaurant with a wide, covered veranda and a pretty tiled fountain. She glanced at the menu posted by the entrance, found fresh fish on it and ventured in. The hostess was leading her to her table when she spotted a familiar man seated alone by the fountain. And this was a man owed an apology.

"If you don't mind…one second," she said to the hostess, then headed in Javier Ruiz's direction. He was reading a newspaper, what looked to be the financial section.

"Jav— Mr. Ruiz," she quickly substituted, uncomfortable with the idea of using his given name.

He looked up, and a smile stretched across his face as recognition dawned. And what a smile it was. Almost adolescent-giddy, she found herself smiling back.

"Tessa," he said as he stood. "It's good to see you again. Please…have a seat. Join me for lunch."

She didn't even think of saying no.

In a gesture she could only call courtly, he came around the table and pulled out the chair opposite his. Once settled in, she looked up and thanked him. Their gazes met, and one very underused feeling came to Tessa: *passion*.

Somewhere deep inside, Contessa stirred and made herself known. And this she told Tessa: Javier Ruiz might not be her bliss, but he held distinct possibilities.

Tessa smiled at the man one more time, earning herself a quizzical yet distinctly interested expression in return.

Welcome home, Contessa, she thought. *It's been too damn long.*

Cali, Colombia, three days later

Don wasn't crazy about Neil Sedaka. Nothing personal, mind you. Sedaka's music just wasn't his thing, any more than sloe gin fizzes or sardines were. So when he wandered out of unconsciousness to a mental soundtrack of the S-man singing a bastardized version of "Breaking Up is Hard to Do," Don was damn glad to have both drugs and a fever to blame. Especially because he wanted to sing along. Words weren't an option, though. Instead, a gagging *weugggh*-sound seemed to be coming from his parched lips.

Don opened his eyes and wondered if, like a vampire, he'd fry at the light. He didn't, but holy Jerry, he smelled like death. He wanted a shower, more real food and the hell out of this bed. And unlike his last extended dance with consciousness, this time he *really* felt better. He wasn't surfing that zippy sort of high that comes with knowing you haven't yet managed to splatter your brains on the highway. He hurt, but now it was the kind that came with healing.

He waited patiently for a nurse to arrive, and his patience was rewarded. Pretty Nurse came in. Ava—he recalled her name as being. She must have told him during one of his earlier short wake-ups.

"So, this time you mean to stay awake," she commented before jamming a thermometer under his tongue.

"How'd you know?" he asked around the intrusion.

"No more talking," she said, then added, "This time you look determined." She extracted the thermometer after it beeped, read it, then gave a pleased nod. "Normal. The antibiotics have done their job."

Speaking of which, he needed to get back to his.

"After I eat, shower and shave my tongue, do you think we could get me to a phone?"

Smiling, Ava nodded, and Don knew he was back in business.

Playa Blanca, Costa Rica

Tessa sat at the swimming pool's edge with Isabel, their feet dangling in the cool water. Kate was off chasing real estate agents, and Mila sat in the shade, thumbing through pages of an importer's catalogue. Javier was in San José for the next two days. Three days ago, when she'd run across him in Quepos, he'd stopped for lunch on his way there. He had also invited her to his house for dinner when he returned. Tessa had accepted, her blood running warmer at the prospect.

And as for Don, Mila had plied some surprising computer skills combined with phone hours to confirm that he was in no Costa Rican or Panamanian hospital along his most likely route. They still awaited responses from a few hospitals in Colombia. It was small progress, but Tessa, who had begun to time herself to the slower Tico beat, was content. Isabel, too, had calmed a bit.

"So you don't know how to swim?" Tessa asked, repeating Isabel's surprising admission of a few moments earlier. "You've lived by the water all your life."

"No," Isabel corrected her. "I lived in San José…in the city. It was only four months ago that I came here."

"And had you lived there all your life?"

"Yes," she said in a flat tone.

Tessa gave the girl a sidelong glance. Isabel's mouth had turned down at the corners. She appeared distinctly uninterested in continuing this line of chat, and Tessa saw no reason to push her.

"Well, you're by the water now," she said, kicking her feet at the pool's surface and splashing both of them.

Isabel laughed, and the sound was genuinely youthful. Tessa had one last question.

"Isabel, how old are you?"

"Fifteen," she replied. "I will be sixteen in April."

Tessa, who'd thought her older, was shocked. Fifteen and a mother seemed too much a burden for any girl to face.

While she reached about in her mind for something to say, the house phone began to ring. Tessa scrambled upright and hurried across the terrace, her feet making sloppy water stains on the stone. She grabbed the handset she'd brought outside and placed on one of the patio's small teak tables.

"Silverman residence," she said, a little breathless.

Her announcement was met by silence, so she tried again. After a three-count of silence, she was about to give up. Then a gravelly voice spoke.

"This is the *Irv* Silverman residence?"

"Yes," Tessa replied. After another instant of silence, Tessa made the logical leap. "Is this, by any chance, Don?"

Nearby, Mila dropped her catalogue and stood. *"Don?"*

Tessa tried to focus on the call.

"Yeah," the man said. "And if you don't mind my asking, who are *you?*"

Mila and Isabel were hurrying her way. She gave them a quick nod.

"My name is Tessa DiPaulo," she said to Don. "I'm a friend of Vee's. I've been staying at the house, along with a couple of people who have been pretty worried about you."

"Mila and Isabel? Are they okay?"

"Yes, they're fine. The bigger question is how are you?"

"A little busted up, actually. And stuck in Cali."

"Colombia?" she asked.

"Yeah. It was Harley versus a cattle truck, and the cows won. I'm lookin' better than the bike, though. Can you tell the ladies that I'm gonna make my way home as soon as I'm sprung from this place?"

"The hospital?"

"Could be…might also be Hell. It depends which nurse is looking after me. So you'll talk to the ladies for me?"

"Better yet, you can talk to them yourselves," Tessa replied. "That is, if you're up to it."

Don was, so Tessa handed off the phone. Mila and Isabel took turns assuring themselves that he was fine, and each showed their love in their own particular style—Mila by scolding, and Isabel by having her torrent of Spanish turn to one of tears. Tessa eventually retrieved the phone from the girl.

"I guess we have some things to talk about when I get home, don't we?" Don asked.

"We do," Tessa said. "But it can wait until then. Do you have your return trip planned, or do you need help?"

"I've got it."

"Then would you mind hanging on while I get paper and a pen?"

When she was ready, he listed a convoluted chain of buses that would finally land him in Quepos.

Tessa was awed. "How are you going to survive that?"

He laughed, then drew in a raspy breath that she imagined signaled increased pain. "Good drugs," he said. "Very, very good drugs."

Good drugs. Tessa flashed back to the lost and empty days after her father's death. "That's a start," she said as lightly as she could, knowing he'd meant the words jokingly.

Good drugs and bad days. She was pleased to have both behind her.

CHAPTER 9

Isabel had once been a patient girl. Slow, her mother had called her, and stupid, too. But Isabel knew she was neither of those things. She had simply always been willing to wait. As the second-youngest of six, there had been much waiting to do. Waiting for what food her brothers didn't gobble, waiting in line to use the toilet, which never worked as it should, and waiting until she went the way of her evil cousin Luz.

Waiting now made Isabel feel as though ants were crawling across her skin. She had been waiting the two days since Don's call. She wanted him to call again, or at least send word that he was on his way home. And she had been waiting forever, it seemed, for this baby to be ready to be born. She had weeks yet until it was time, but she was so tired of feeling clumsy and huge, of wanting to move slower than the sloths in the trees that surrounded this house. She knew it was all of these things nibbling at her, not just the two mysterious boxes that had arrived for Tessa.

They sat in the middle of the entryway, where the delivery man had left them: two fat boxes, each big enough for a child to sleep in, addressed in neat print to Tessa DiPaulo. Isabel walked yet another circle around them, then nudged each with her bare toes. One rattled, almost calling her to give it another push.

Tessa should be here to open these boxes. Now! Why did she feel that a simple meal this evening with their neighbor required a trip miles away to the salon at the fancy hotel in Quepos? All that fuss for a man. Hah! Isabel knew them for the rutting creatures they were. Mama should have called all men stupid. Then she would not have been wasting her breath.

Mama had never given her so much as a surprise piece of candy on her birthday, let alone two mysterious boxes begging to be opened. Though it was no easy drop, Isabel settled on the floor next to them. She wished someone was in the house to distract her. Even Kate, with her blade of a tongue, would do. But, no. It was Isabel, two boxes and no patience.

"Enough," she said, then began picking at the shiny tan tape sealing the closest box shut. And because she knew she was wrong to do so, she began to gather her excuses...*the packaging was already loose...she was worried that a small animal might be suffocating in one....*

A rat, maybe—which she was no better than for tearing into what wasn't hers. But as with so many other events in her life, the deed was done and there was no undoing it. She tore the tape the rest of the way off, folded back the box flaps and peered inside.

More boxes, each with printed covers. She pulled one out, and then made a sound of complete disgust. She'd just sacrificed her honor over *movies?* She could already watch those in English or Spanish on the house's many televisions.

"Dirty Dancing," she said with a look at the couple on the cover. They seemed clean enough to her. Isabel shrugged, then resettled the movie with all of its friends. But as long as she was doomed…

Isabel ripped the tape off the next box, wondering if this is what she would have felt like if they'd had the money to celebrate birthdays…to celebrate anything. Her heart pounded even harder when she saw what awaited her.

Paints! Countless wonderful little bottles of paint, a wooden box filled with brushes, and beneath that, flat white canvases to cover. It was almost too much to absorb. Then Isabel uncovered a box with sharp pencils in all the colors that she had ever seen or dreamed.

A sob ripped from her throat, surprising her as much as if a frog had jumped from her lips. She threw her hand over her mouth, but still the cries continued, shaking her frame until the baby inside her turned and pushed against her belly, showing its displeasure.

The baby could just be still and wait, for what held Isabel

was so huge that she could not begin to stop it. She ached with hurt that no one had ever given her even one pencil, with awe at the riches and, most of all, with hunger. More hunger than she had ever felt. This was not her gift, but she would die—*yes, die!*—if she could not squeeze just the smallest amount of crimson out of its bottle and see if it smelled of blood and anger, or perhaps thick and flowery, like the perfume of the rich lady tourist who'd once given her twenty American dollars for no reason at all.

Isabel's hands shook as she opened the large plastic bag containing at least a dozen small bottles of paint. To think that three more bags like this waited in the box! She pulled out the crimson, then set it down and dug through the box for something less serious than the fine canvas to try it on. At the very bottom was a pad of paper.

She flipped open the paint's white plastic top, then let a daub fall onto a sheet of paper. She would have bent to sniff it, but her belly was in the way. Instead, she brought the bottle to her nose, then quickly set it down.

"Eugh!" She sneezed once, then again. The color was far prettier than the scent, which was not blood, nor anger, nor money, but like the polish remover that Mila used on her sharp pink fingernails. Ah, but for this, Isabel would hold her nose. The pictures she saw in color but could only draw in black-and-white, they were hers, now…down to the bright orange of Mama's favorite Sunday skirt.

This was theft, but it was also in some strange way her right, Isabel thought. She would draw and paint as her hand and mind demanded. Tessa would either understand or toss her to the street. And in that moment of passion, Isabel didn't care which.

Hair tamed and nails polished, Tessa drove the final bends of road from Quepos to Playa Blanca, trying to recall her last first date...not including Jack. That it had been over a decade prior didn't help. Neither did the fact that just before Jack had come her great flame-out, that dance with self-destruction spurred by her dad's death.

And Tessa wouldn't call what she'd done in those months "dating," exactly. *Dating* was such a pleasant term...benign, positive, none of the things she'd been. There had been a man she'd drunk and partied with, then sometimes had sex with because she'd been too empty and numb to care, but those had not been dates.

And before that? She supposed that being memorable was too much to ask of that nameless, faceless male, over eleven years in her past. She also supposed she was pushing matters to call this dinner tonight with Javier Ruiz a "date." She had no idea what to call it, though, other than unsettling. She wanted a pleasant evening—no hassles, no false expectations. Her greatest goal was to survive unscathed.

And she knew that was asking a lot.

Tessa stopped at the gate to Vee's house, pushed the button on the remote control that opened the gate and drove in. She wondered what Javier was doing, one gate over. Did he feel even a fraction of the ambivalence that she did over this dinner that was *not* a date? God, she hoped not. One of them was going to need to carry the conversation, and she suspected it wouldn't be her.

Tessa parked the gassy van in front of the house, instead of in its far more natural Don-environment. After she climbed out, she gave a wave to the antisocial dog, who'd been stalking her from the underbrush since she came onto the property.

"Sorry, it's just me," she said as the beast turned its back on her and slunk off. "Good thing you're nice to Isabel," she called to it. "Or you wouldn't get fed." An empty threat, but she felt she'd regained the upper hand...or paw.

Tessa stepped into the house and almost immediately froze. Her boxes had arrived. And it appeared they had also been savaged. She closed the door behind her and moved in for a closer inspection. Her VHS movie collection was relatively unscathed, but her art supplies—dammit, they were *everywhere*.

Her nearly new box of Prismacolors had been opened and the pencils were scattered across the floor like one-hundred-twenty brightly colored pieces to a child's game of pick-up sticks. Her hard board canvases teetered in a random stack, and farther into the room waited one of Tessa's vellum pads, its cover flipped open and a blotch of red acrylic paint on the exposed page. Tessa's anger rose. Just because she hadn't been interested in her supplies for a while—okay, a *long* while—didn't mean she welcomed others to play in them.

"Kate?" she called, following a loose trail of abandoned, half-finished sketches, scooping them up as she went. "Mila? Isabel?"

No one answered, but someone had been busy, for while the common space on the next floor down was clear, chaos awaited Tessa on the ground floor. Vivid paintings, in various stages of drying, sat on nearly every flat surface.

Tessa marched into the kitchen, where she found Isabel at the table, surrounded by dozens of little bottles of paint, paper and all of Tessa's brushes—including her favorite sable ones.

Tessa's hands closed into tight fists as she tried to hold in her anger and silence the possessive little voice inside her crying, *mine, mine, mine!*

"Isabel, what have you been *doing*?" The question escaped on a wave of emotion, as it was damn self-evident what the girl had been doing. She had been painting. Wildly.

The girl looked up from her work, no remorse, no contrition on her paint-streaked face, just a sort of concentrated passion that Tessa would have sold her soul to feel.

"Painting," Isabel simply said.

"Apparently," Tessa replied, her voice sharp. She pulled out a chair opposite the girl and sat. "You do know these paints are mine, right?"

Isabel swished her brush in a tall crystal tumbler she'd filled with water, then wiped the bristles with a hopelessly stained dish towel before nodding. After dipping the brush in a bit of black from a palette improvised from a dinner plate, she focused on the painting in front of her—a rough and savage fuchsia-colored flower that somehow came close to making O'Keeffe's work look sexless.

Tessa's fury waned in the face of Isabel's utter absorption. In its place came curiosity…and another tug of envy.

"You should consider apologizing, and quickly," she suggested.

"Apologize…sorry," Isabel absently replied.

"It might work better if you sound like you mean it."

The girl looked up, a fierce frown drawing her dark brows together. "When I am done, I will do whatever you want to pay for the paints. Until then…go away."

Tessa laughed. "Go *away?* You've got some nerve, kid."

Isabel said nothing in response. She kept painting, and Tessa continued to watch.

"I'm not going to go away, you know," she said after a few minutes had passed. "So you might as well show me what you've been up to…with *my* paints."

Isabel sighed. "If I do, will you let me finish in peace?"

"I might," Tessa replied, unwilling to totally cede control of the situation. She pushed back her chair. "Let's start in the other room," she said, then left without waiting for Isabel to follow.

Tessa was standing over the first work—a street scene done in large, almost abstract, blocks of angry color—when the girl joined her.

"Where I lived," Isabel said with a shrug. "It is not so pretty."

As they progressed down the line, it was apparent to Tessa where Isabel had begun to slow enough to let her hand keep pace with her mind. She stopped in front of a painting that particularly caught her eye. This scene covered the full of the paper. There was no background, just a group of males, their postures those of pride and territoriality.

"My brother, Estefan, and his friends," Isabel said. "Every night they stand on the corner by the gas station. He is handsome, my brother. All the girls love him."

Tessa nodded. "And this is…?" she asked, pointing at the next work.

"My cousin Luz."

Luz had been given medusa-like black hair, lavender skin and pointy red teeth spiking from an open maw.

"I take it you're not very fond of Luz?"

"I would spit on the fat bitch if I saw her again," Isabel replied in a tight voice. "But I never will. *Never*."

Whatever it was that had happened between Isabel and her cousin, Tessa was pleased that the girl had found a safe form of catharsis. She moved on to the last few paintings, all of which were familiar—the beach below, the cantina in the village and the antisocial hound. She complimented Isabel on her work, but the girl didn't seem interested in comments, just in getting back to the kitchen and painting more.

"Okay, here's the deal," Tessa said. "I'll share my supplies with you on two conditions."

"What are they?" Isabel asked, her crossed arms resting just above that round belly.

"First, you ask my permission. And second, you clean up your mess. This won't do, Isabel," she said, gesturing at the papers everywhere.

"I am sorry," she said, and this time the haze of creativity seemed to have cleared enough for Tessa to see sincerity in her eyes. "I could not stop."

"I understand," Tessa said, though she didn't fully grasp what had happened to the girl. She'd never experienced the need to paint to the degree Isabel had today.

"And I accept your rules," Isabel said. "But I have one of my own. You must paint with me…teach me."

"Isabel, I'm an amateur. I haven't taken classes in years."

The girl shook her head. "You tease me. You own all these beautiful things. You must know what to do with them. You teach me, and I will help your Spanish."

There was no denying that Tessa's Spanish was in dire need of help. And while she was nothing more than a rusty though once fairly talented amateur artist, she supposed she had a few pointers on perspective and composition. Truly, the thought of painting again was tempting, if also a little daunting in the face of Isabel's mad, passionate revelry.

"Okay," Tessa said. "We'll start tomorrow."

"Now," Isabel replied in Spanish. "We will start now."

Tessa glanced at her watch. She was due at Javier Ruiz's house in less than two hours. "Tomorrow," she said. "I have—"

Isabel raised her paint-flecked hand. "In Spanish," she warned in that tongue. "Always in Spanish, or you will not learn."

Tessa sighed. "Fine. In Spanish. Tomorrow."

Isabel took Tessa's hand in hers. "Now. Your dinner can't be for hours. Paint with me. *Please*."

Tessa looked at her own pale hand, clasped in that browner (and redder and bluer) hand. Something inside her shifted, and her heart began to ache a little. But it was a very, very good ache.

"I will," she said to the girl. "Now."

Because suddenly, nothing seemed more important.

Kate clocked her downhill speed on the bike's digital speedometer. She was kissing thirty-seven miles an hour. It killed her to think that race cyclists considered this a decent pace with no hill to push their collective skinny butts. All in all, it was a good thing that she wanted to lead only leisure tours, since her forty-one-year-old former smoker's lungs and decidedly not-skinny butt were up to no greater challenge. It was ungodly challenge enough to figure out how to buy her land, then proceed from there.

Bright and early this morning she had called a real estate buddy back in Michigan and asked that he fax a listing contract to her at Vee's house. Since it had been even brighter and earlier back at the place she used to call home, she had received a sleep-garbled "okay" from Todd. Kate was sure once that "big fat commission" concept sunk in, he'd move more quickly. Possibly even faster than she was moving at this moment.

Kate wheeled to Playa Blanca's nearly indefinable outer edge, then slowed to her cool-down pace. She was thankful that for a Friday, the weekenders were surprisingly sparse. The fewer cars parked along the beach, the lower the risk of being suddenly and bone-crushingly cut off by a distracted tourist. She laughed when she realized that in just over a week, she'd somehow decided she was a Tico, as much a part of the landscape as the fierce-looking iguanas.

Maybe she was as crazy as Tessa thought her. Kate considered the possibility but concluded she was only bullheaded Kate, doing what she did best: pushing on. A few more leisurely turns up and over a hill and she was back to where she'd started hours before.

And now she was also prepared to maneuver around Tessa's hesitance. Since Tessa would not come to the mountain, Kate had brought the mountain to her…digitally. After stowing her bike under the house's front overhang, Kate took a moment before going inside to unzip her fanny pack, pull out her camera and review the pictures she'd taken, mentally rehearsing the pitch she'd prepared to accompany them. When she was done, she restowed her camera.

"It's show time," she announced, then went inside. Or maybe it was cleanup time. Kate detoured around random piles of stuff and followed the sound of pop music down the stairs and to the ground floor.

"Scary." The place looked like an art gallery for the criminally insane. She tilted her head and checked out a picture of a woman with red dagger-teeth.

"Tessa, are you here?" she called over the music, even though she knew that being heard was a long shot.

On to the kitchen Kate strolled, placing a mental bet on who she'd find there.

"As expected," she said to herself, then went to the radio on the counter and turned down the volume. "Occupational therapy?" she asked Tessa, who had at least glanced up, if not offered a greeting.

"Just working out a few kinks," Tessa replied.

Kate took in her friend's painting. It was pretty standard fare, looking to be a view from the cantina in the village to the beach. That meant the paintings with the serious kinks had to be the work of the resident child not-quite-bride.

"Nice," Kate said to Tessa, not daring to see what Isabel was painting now. One look and she might well be marked for life. "Thanks," Tessa said. "It feels great to be doing this again."

"Looks like you've been at it for a while, today," Kate commented.

"Not long, I don't think." She glanced up again. "What time is it, by the way?"

Kate checked her watch. "Almost six."

"Shit!" Tessa dropped her brush and pushed away from the table, panic in her eyes.

"What?"

"I'm going to be late!"

"Late?" Kate echoed.

"Dinner with Javier Ruiz…at six. Isabel, could you clean my mess?"

As soon as the girl nodded, Tessa bolted from the room. Because she was enjoying the show, Kate followed.

"A date, huh? So what are you wearing?" she asked as Tessa bounded up the steps to the floor above.

Tessa stopped at the landing. "Wearing?" she repeated. "Shit!"

"Doubt it," Kate replied, then trailed after Tessa to her

room. When her friend opened the closet, Kate did the merciful thing.

"You might want to wash up first," she said, gesturing at Tessa's unintended body art.

She looked down at her hands. "I'm sunk."

"Just slow down," Kate said, aware that she was probably the least qualified person to give that advice.

"No time," Tessa replied, then went into the bathroom and turned on the sink's taps.

Kate flipped through the contents of Tessa's closet, searching for something that looked like what Tessa might choose to wear. For a tropical first date, Kate would have opted for shorts, a golf shirt and flip-flops, but she knew her friend would go the feminine route. After pulling out a couple of sleeveless dresses and laying them on the bed, she glanced through the open bathroom door to where Tessa scrubbed her hands, a Lady Macbeth in little need of training.

"I can't believe I did this!" Tessa heaped on more liquid soap. "It's almost as though I wanted to screw up."

Kate shrugged. "You're out of my league. I'll leave that for a shrink to sort out. But look on the bright side—at least we're getting a little time together. You know, a paranoid woman would have thought you were avoiding me all week."

"I was," Tessa said.

Kate laughed. "Then my faith in paranoia is renewed."

Tessa quickly dried her hands, then began shedding her

shirt and shorts. "Kate, I don't want to be rushed with your bicycle ranch, or whatever you want to call it. Everything in my life has changed. *Everything*. If I learned one lesson after my father's death, it was that during a crisis my judgment stinks."

This was a problem. Time was ticking down on paradise. "What are you talking about?"

"Me…painkillers…Rosehaven," her friend impatiently replied.

Rosehaven. Funny, but unless Tessa brought it up, which she almost never did, it seemed to Kate as if Tessa's visit to the private clinic had never occurred. Tessa had returned pink and serene, snagged Jack and turned into Lady Bountiful, out to aid one and all. And somewhere along the line, Kate had just adjusted. Having Lady Bountiful as a friend came with certain advantages.

"That wasn't such a big deal," Kate fibbed, lacking any other way to brush aside her friend's concern.

"A month of detox and therapy isn't exactly a little deal," Tessa replied, while holding first one dress then another in front of her and scrutinizing her reflection in the mirror. "Help me out here," she said to Kate. "Which dress?"

"The red one," Kate replied. Tessa stood a much better chance of getting laid in red, and God knows she needed it. If she'd just relax, she'd recognize their true calling before someone else bought it out from under them.

Tessa gave a frantic nod. "Red. Okay."

While her friend wriggled her way into the crimson number, Kate tried to distinguish a little bit of investing from Tessa's long-ago and long-fixed crisis. "Making an investment while changing jobs isn't the same as dealing with what you did back then. And I'll make this totally painless—promise! I'll even call a lawyer in the States and have us form a partnership or whatever."

Tessa hurried back to the bathroom, makeup bag in hand. "Except we're talking about an investment in a foreign country."

Kate shrugged. "Can't be that big of a deal. We're in a house owned by Americans, aren't we?"

"Vee and Irv aren't regular folks, Kate. They have their own legal staff."

"You're just throwing up roadblocks for the fun of it. You *are* considering going in on this with me, aren't you?"

"Yes," Tessa said after she'd finished putting on mascara. "I'm considering it, but seriously, if you don't back off and let me get ready for this dinner, you can forget the whole thing."

"Wow. A little touchy there, aren't you?"

Tessa closed her eyes for an instant. When she opened them, Kate liked what she saw a great deal better...except where the mascara had migrated beneath her friend's lower lids. Tessa noticed it at the same time, swore under her breath, and attacked the smudges with a piece of tissue.

"You're going to be okay," Kate offered.

"Sorry," Tessa said. "It's just these nerves. It's been so long since I've had a first date that I can't even remember it. Except Jack, of course," she hastily added.

Sure, except for Jack. Kate pushed back the bitterness that was escaping from some unknown crack in her composure. Hell, if she were land, she'd be toxic right now.

"Just have fun tonight," she said, not sure how else to wrap this up. She wasn't going to get what she wanted, so Tessa might as well.

"Right. Fun," Tessa echoed as she grabbed some lipstick, then set it aside, seeming to realize she had neither pockets nor a purse. She jammed her feet into some gold sandals that looked to be totally impractical outside the house. "I'd better get going."

Kate followed Tessa out of her room, then down a floor to the pool terrace. "Going overland?" she asked.

Tessa nodded. "It's faster, and I'm beyond late."

Yeah, but hopefully not beyond being laid, Kate thought. Because one of them had better end up feeling satisfied, and it definitely wasn't Kate's lucky night.

CHAPTER 10

Tessa should have taken the high road...or carried a machete. One glance had told her that the cross-country route to Javier Ruiz's was impassable by virtually all but the spider monkeys who called the canopy of trees their own. So, in a parallel of her life as of late, she'd had to go down to ascend again.

By the time she'd begun the march from the beach, up the zigzag wooden stairway to Javier's home, nerves and heat had combined to make her a nightmare of a test case for her antiperspirant. She paused in her climb long enough to wriggle her feet from her sandals—far more uncomfortable than they'd looked, the buggers—and clutch them in one hand. She could feel her hair fighting the gel and spray with which the stylist had tried to tame it, and springing into its usual curls. If this was what her prior first dates had been like, small wonder she'd conveniently forgotten them.

One final "zig" before reaching the deck, and then Tessa bent and began to slip her sandals back on.

"Did you take the sea route?" a male voice called from above.

So much for a graceful entrance. Tessa wedged the second sandal into place, straightened, cupped her hand over her eyes and looked up at Javier. He stood at the edge of his deck, hands braced on the rail like a captain well in charge of his ship—so sweat-and-nerve-free that she, too, settled a little.

"I'd call it the scenic route, except everything around here is scenic," she answered, before finishing her climb.

Smiling, he took her hands, then brushed a kiss against her cheek. If she'd been expecting it, she would have responded in kind, but at least she was now halfway to that continental *faire la bise*. A small step when viewed alone, but a large one considering where she'd started out just days before.

"Red suits you," he said, with a nod to her dress. "Welcome. Would you like something to drink? I have iced tea, Imperial, some white wine chilling…"

"A cold beer sounds wonderful," Tessa said. If she could dull the edge on the last of her damn nervousness, this evening had potential.

"Come inside. We'll sit where it's cool."

Tessa glanced around as she walked beside him. This yard had no swimming pool and the house had none of the upscale finishes of Vee's, but it suited its wilder landscaping. The center of the deck held a table and chairs hewn of a thick golden-red wood. Overhead was a large dark green umbrella, shading the spot. A grill sat in one corner, and in the other, two lounge chairs. It was a man's place, no potted plants and no frills about it.

He ushered her into the house. It, too, bore a rugged stamp. The floor was of large squares of reddish-orange tile, and the ceiling of wood much the same color as the outdoor furniture.

"Have a seat," he said, gesturing to a modern-style sofa and two low armchairs. "I'll be right with you."

As Javier left through a doorway that she assumed led to the kitchen, Tessa made a tactical decision in choosing the sofa over the isolation of an armchair. Another small step, true, but she was pleased with herself. Music played from an unseen source, its beat sensuously Latin.

Javier returned and set two beers and pilsner glasses on the coffee table in front of the couch.

"One thing to go," he said, then disappeared again.

Tessa used his absence to let her gaze wander. On a far wall was a large bookcase with two broad shelves devoted to photographs. She leaned forward, as though those few inches would bring her the details from the many framed shots. She was certain she saw Javier in some of the group photos, but lacked the time for a closer inspection.

"Do you like *ceviche?*" he asked as he set two small, shallow bowls on the table, along with tortilla chips, napkins and spoons.

She waited until he'd settled in next to her to answer. "I've never tried it, but it's raw fish again, right?"

He answered with a broad smile.

She laughed. "I'm beginning to worry that you have a fixation."

"I have my fixations, as you say."

By the light in his eyes, she knew he was hinting of her. Her Contessa side liked that very much. Practical Tessa doubted the truth of his words. She took a sip of her beer, breaking the brief spell.

Javier tapped the side of the bowl in front of him. "But, yes, this is raw fish with peppers marinated in lemon and lime juice. Try some… I promise it's much better than I'm making it sound."

Tessa required little prompting, and was soon glad of it. "You made this? It's wonderful!"

He shook his head. "As much as I'd like to be a fraud, it's not in me. Margarita made it."

"I'm glad," she said impulsively.

"That Margarita made the *ceviche?*"

"No. That you don't want to be a fraud." The word *fraud* had brought thoughts of Jack, of course.

Javier briefly hesitated before speaking. "I see."

Tessa didn't want to waste this dinner on husbands best divorced, so she forged on. "So, Margarita is the woman who owns the cantina?"

"Yes, and she is also my sister."

"Really?"

"Really," he responded with a nod. "And as long as I'm disclosing family links, Claire from the souvenir shop is my sister-in-law. And she and Margarita were so pleased I'd invited a woman to dinner, that along with making our meal, I'm surprised they're not peeking in the window to be sure I entertain you properly."

Tessa laughed. "Is there anyone in Playa Blanca you're not related to?"

"Many," he said. "It just so happens that you've seen me with my family first. That's not so strange, is it?"

"No," Tessa replied, even though the thought was truly as foreign to her as the taste of the tangy *ceviche*. She had only her mother, and while they talked on the phone frequently— again likely tomorrow—miles kept them apart. She found the idea of a close family warming.

"I have a son, too," Javier said, pointing toward the framed pictures on the bookshelf. "Mike is in law school in Florida."

"Why not in Costa Rica?"

"First, because I advised him to get dual law degrees, as I have. And second, his mother is in Florida. He lived mostly with Susan after we divorced."

Tessa walked to the bookcase. Now that she was closer, she could easily pick out Mike Ruiz. He was handsome, like his father, and appeared to possess the same outward confidence, too.

"You were married, no?" Javier asked.

"I'm waiting for my divorce decree to clear those last technical hurdles," she replied without looking away from his pictures. She lifted a shot of the duo. Mike wore a graduation cap and gown, and his father looked fittingly proud. "I came here to sort through options."

"Options?"

She returned his son's photo to its spot and settled again on the couch. "You know, what to do next."

"Ah."

She watched as he tried to hide a smile behind a swallow of his beer.

"What?"

He waved off the question. "It's nothing. Presumptuousness on my part. Now let's finish our *ceviche* before Claire's chicken dries to the bone."

Tessa finished the appetizer, but his unspoken words still nibbled at her. "I'd really like to hear what you were thinking a minute ago," she said.

He stood and gathered the dishware. "I would have said that a Contessa should spend more time doing and less planning."

A pang of emotional hunger struck. Planning and pondering were her safety net, her twin rituals that staved off the great darkness she'd been fearing would swallow her whole, once again. But over the past days, that fear had receded, leaving curiosity in its wake. What would happen if she stopped considering and just started living? It was a delicious notion, one she would have to...*ponder*. Tessa's mouth quirked at her ability to plan even freedom.

She rose and raised her beer bottle in a brief toast. "Lucky Contessa, then. Now let's go rescue that dried chicken."

He laughed, and she followed him to the kitchen, where the table had been set. A vase of bright tropical blossoms decorated the table's center, lovely but incongruous in this very male place. Had she seen this first, she'd have been immediately tipped off regarding female assistance.

As they ate, they talked of Playa Blanca and of his earlier life in the area. Javier explained how the previously unnamed stretch of buildings had found an identity separate from Quepos in the 1980s, when its "white beach" name had come from a small, hidden airstrip secretively built by smugglers from points south.

The airstrip and the drug smugglers were long gone, but it had taken decades for the village's reputation to fade and productive redevelopment to begin. Javier mentioned that he and other family members had begun expansion of a small hotel they'd bought just south of the village. Tessa liked his commitment to his roots. In fact, at the moment she'd be hard-pressed to find anything about him she didn't like.

The more they talked, the more she became aware of him on a visceral level—the slow curve of his mouth when he

smiled, his quick sense of humor, and an innate courteous-
ness that somehow made him even more sexually appealing.
She recognized her nascent feelings as natural—even hoped
for—but they again left her as awkward as a first-date teen.
And she knew that he'd noticed. He could hardly have
missed her verbal fumbling.

While she helped him clear the table, Tessa scrounged
about for a means of distracting her mind from her awakening body. Finally, she settled on talk of Kate's proposed en-
terprise. When she'd finished explaining the bike ranch
concept, Javier seemed far more receptive than she'd felt.
Then again, Kate wasn't hammering *him* for investment
money. At least, not yet.

"What concerns you about this idea of your friend's?" he
asked once they'd settled back at their places and were waiting for the coffee he'd started to finish brewing.

"That she's not thinking it through."

"Ah, but she has you for that task."

She ignored his teasing. "True," she conceded. "But her
idea is so far from my interests that I can't grasp its appeal."

"What are your interests, Tessa?"

At the moment, you. They were tempting and truthful
words, but ones she wasn't ready to voice.

"Painting," she said, thinking of the afternoon's celebration of art with Isabel.

"So, you are an artist, as I'd thought?"

"Maybe, but I'm a banker, first." Still, she relished the thought of being an artist at all. "I've only been out of work for a couple of months, but I really miss the flow of deals coming across my desk. I miss meeting new customers, and I miss learning about new businesses. And as boring as this makes me sound, I love the way a good plan fits together, one step leading to the next."

"You think yourself boring? Those who show passion are never boring."

She knew that he didn't mean it in a sexual way, but still her heart skipped a beat. "Passion? I think you're overstating it."

"Not at all. So when you return to—"

"Michigan," she supplied.

"Michigan, then, will you be a banker?"

"I don't think so," Tessa replied, and the answer surprised even her. It seemed that her subconscious had been busy. "I'd rather work for myself, you know? I'm getting too old to want to have some baby MBA grad as my boss. I've already seen too much to put up with a neophyte. I'd guess that Kate's feeling some of that, too."

"So you do see some of her idea's appeal?"

Tessa laughed. "Everything but the bicycles," she said. "But seriously, I understand the desire to do something totally different, or I wouldn't be here. It's her deciding so quickly to stay here that has me concerned. Kate has a heart of gold, but she's also too impulsive. She just goes out and grabs without considering the risks."

"And it's your job, then, to slow her?"

"Not my job, really, but I owe her. She's been there for me every time my life has hit a downswing. Long before this divorce mess, she covered for me at work after my father died, and she's always been there to talk to. She's always made me…" Tessa trailed off, wondering how to put her connection to Kate into words. They shared more than seventeen years of common events. In many ways, Kate was as close to a sister as Tessa would ever have.

"Let's put it this way," she said to Javier. "Kate has a way of making me know that I'm not as alone as I can feel. I'd like to do something for her, even if that's simply helping her reason out this bike ranch idea."

"You're a good friend," he said.

"Sometimes," she answered with the same honesty he'd accorded her all evening. Then she asked a question that had formed in the back of her mind. "Maybe you could help us do this right?"

He took a sip of the wine he'd poured when he'd served the chicken. "In what capacity?"

"A professional one. I'd like you to represent us, and I'm sure Kate will agree."

She bided her time while he deliberated, and as she waited, the idea of having Javier on board grew in importance. She supposed it was the allure of being drawn into his circle—his connectedness to this place—that had captured her.

"I doubt I have any client conflicts," he said. "But I'd have to make sure, and you will need to decide how involved you wish to be in this idea of Kate's—passive investor, active partner, or just friend. Beyond that, I see another stumbling block."

"What's that?"

He reached across the table and settled his hand over hers. "You're not entirely comfortable with me, Tessa, and that's not advisable in the sort of relationship you're suggesting. You'd do better to have other counsel."

"You're the only game in town," she replied, skirting past the more personal issue of *why* she was unsettled around him.

"I can refer you to someone. Most of your business would be handled by fax or phone, in any case."

It was ridiculous to feel as though she were being dumped, but that knowledge didn't dilute the emotional sting. She withdrew her hand.

"But I want you," she said. "I know you, and I know you'll protect our interests and help us navigate the local system."

He leaned back in his chair and simply looked at her for a moment. "Wait a few days, then ask me again if you still wish to."

"What difference will a few days make?"

"Possibly a great deal." There was a silent offer in his expression...a promise of the awakening Tessa wasn't yet certain she wanted.

He looked ready to say something more, but the telephone interrupted the moment. "I'm sorry. If you'll excuse me?" he asked before rising.

Tessa nodded her consent.

Javier went to the counter where the phone sat and answered it.

"It's your friend, Kate," he said, handing it to her.

She was relieved to have the distraction of the call. "Hello?"

"Get lucky yet?" Kate asked.

"Depends on your definition. What's going on?"

"I thought you should know that Don the wandering Dead Head is in the village," she said.

"Right now?"

"This very second. I gave Mila permission to take the van and snag him."

Tessa smiled. "You gave Mila permission?" She was having a difficult time envisioning that exchange.

"Okay, so I didn't tackle her when she announced her plans."

"That sounds closer to the mark," Tessa said, then seized the excuse available. "And I'll be right over there to be part of the welcoming committee."

Her Inner Contessa ruffled her very elegant feathers. *Conflicted to the very end, aren't we.*

"No need to come back," Kate said. "I was just giving an update...and checking in on you."

"Thanks." She let her gaze slip a bit toward Javier. She couldn't dance into physical intimacy without steeling herself for the emotional consequences. All a very fancy way of admitting she was chicken, she knew.

"I'll be there in ten minutes, no more," she said to Kate.

"Tessa! Don't you dare—"

She hit the off button and set the phone on the pretty parrot-green tablecloth.

"I'm sorry, but I need to be going back to Vee's house," she said to Javier.

"Is something wrong?"

"Not wrong, really. Vee's caretaker was in a bit of an accident down in Colombia—"

"Don? On his motorcycle?"

She nodded. "I think the motorcycle was totaled, but Don's recovered enough to make his way home. Mila's bringing him from the village now."

He took the phone and rested it back in its cradle.

Tessa rose. "I should get going."

He led her to the front door, and once they'd arrived, said, "I'll drive you back."

"No, really, I can walk, but I'll be smart and take the high road this time. And thank you for dinner," she added, giving him no opportunity to speak.

Impulsively, she moved closer. *La bise*, she thought. Now was her chance. And she honestly meant it to be a casual brush of the lips against his cheek—a thank-you for companionship she had chosen to abandon. But something happened. Bad aim…Contessa-dominant behavior…no matter what she called it, the result was the same. She had brought her mouth to his.

A new man's kiss. Awkward, imperfect and a little funny as she adjusted to the thought, for the first time ever, of kissing a man with a mustache. And yet this was so compelling that she couldn't bring herself to back gracelessly away. Instead she moved closer, heart pounding, and a small voice—not so much conscience as curiosity—saying, *What is this about?*

It was about pleasure, as he settled one hand at the small of her back. And it was about pleasure, as she allowed herself to touch his hair, threading her fingers into the thick darkness that was so unlike Jack's that the temptation to know its feel was irresistible.

Javier brought the kiss up a notch, his tongue touching hers. A new man's taste. Not Jack. Unfamiliar, a hint of wine and of passion. She'd more or less thrown herself at him, but she had to give him credit for catching her so well.

Tessa had no idea where the moment was going and reveled in being mapless. The feel of his hands at her waist—at least where the dip of her waist had been pre-fertility drugs—made her want to move closer. She wanted to peel off his clothes and hers, and to forget that she was less than a month away from forty, and that she hadn't shown her body to a man other than Jack since she was just shy of thirty.

Javier's mouth moved to her neck. Smart man…one kiss there and she was smooth and clinging as warm honey. She held tighter to him, but he slowed.

"We'll finish this, Contessa," he said low into her ear, and she shivered. "But now, I will drive you home, before I forget that I make you uncomfortable, and that I don't wish in any way to go against your conscience."

His words weren't a cold splash, they were a slow transition back to her reality…the one in which she sought the balance and reason to which he'd alluded.

"You're right," she said. "About both now and later."

He took her hand in his and led her to his car. And as they walked, Tessa smiled. Contessa had danced her way out of the darkness well indeed.

Don had grown even less fond of buses than he was of Neil Sedaka. It wasn't that he didn't think himself part of the proletariat, because he was totally square with the teeming masses. Problem was, the longer he had sat in that tight seat, the more he'd felt as though his left leg—encased in plaster from below his knee all the way to his toes—was teeming, too.

He hadn't wanted to think about whatever had wormed

its way down his cast, but even a healthy handful of his pain-killers hadn't been enough to kill the parasitic images. He'd also felt the irresistible urge to share his experience with his fellow travelers. By the time they'd reached David—a town damn close to Panama—he'd been compelled by the bus driver to give up mass transit.

But, hell, he'd been through worse. With the last of his hard U.S. dollars he'd bought a ride with a trucker heading to La Fortuna, which was the right country but too far from the beach, so they'd parted ways outside San José. One final negotiation with some German tourists had cost him his Levi's jacket, vintage 1972 (a very fine year), but its loss was worth the ability to kiss the dark sand of Playa Blanca. Instead of sand-eating, though, he'd accepted the cold Imperial that Margarita offered him. And he'd barely had time to drink it before Mila had arrived.

Don braced his arm against the passenger door as Mila hauled ass into Casa Silverman. Damn, but he loved his cousin Irv for getting stinking rich…and for recalling the good days they'd had prior to said stinking richness. Life as gatekeeper to Nirvana wasn't a bad payoff for having kept Irv out of jail a time or two.

"Isabel is waiting at the main house," Mila said, breaking into reminiscences of parties long past. "I will take you there."

Don knew a setup when he heard one. "The new guests are there, too, aren't they?"

"At least one, and probably the other," Mila replied.

"Then let me get out at my place."

"They want to see you, and I'd rather please than anger them."

Mila, anxious to please? That was a first....

"Whatever you say, *liebchen*," he answered, then laughed so hard that his mending ribs ached when she growled low in her throat.

"You've missed me. You know you have," he said to her.

"Some," she replied, but he heard the true depth in her raspy voice.

They pulled up in front of the big house, where a welcoming committee waited. Isabel was front and center, even rounder than she'd been weeks earlier. He grinned and waved when she gave that little nod of hers, the one that meant she was happy to see him but far too cautious to let her emotions hang out on the line. Damn, but he'd missed her, and it killed him that this child was going to have a child. He couldn't change what had happened to her, but he'd fight all the way to the gates of hell to make the rest of her life better.

Next Don picked out Javier Ruiz with a curvy little brunette next to him, and then a bigger blonde on the other side of her. In fact the latter was so solid that the word *Amazon* came to mind. Mila shut down the van, but Don took his time opening the door.

First impressions meant a helluva lot in his world. Tequila...good. Sharks...bad. The bitch of it was deciding whether the house's new residents fell into the tequila or shark camp. He was so damn tired—right down to his broken bones—that he didn't want to screw this up. He didn't bother trying to climb out of the van, but he did sit up straighter.

The two women conferred while Ruiz watched with a half smile on his face. Ruiz was no man's fool, and if he wasn't involving himself in the ladies' discussion, Don would watch his mouth around them, too. He had too much to live for, to think that crossing two women would be wise. He'd decided the other night that it was time to write his memoirs, such as they were...and no matter how warped the memories. Someone, someday, would benefit from what he'd seen and done. And even if they didn't benefit, they could always have a good laugh at his expense.

Don looked back out the window. The big-boned blonde watched him skeptically. She had a shark's appearance, but he suspected that there was something more to her. Damn good thing it wasn't his job to figure out what that might be. Her narrow-eyed glare let him know that she'd have his balls in a vise, and scary as it was, he realized he'd probably like it. He'd always been a sucker for women who could beat him two-out-of-three in arm wrestling.

Since he couldn't sit with the door closed forever, Don took the leap. And as he expected, the Amazon spoke first.

"So what hit you?" she asked.

"Cow truck," he answered.

Her smile was about as long as a Morse code blip, but at least it had appeared. "Not good."

"I've had better."

This time her smile stretched out. Whether it was the painkillers or just because he wanted it to be so, Don read that grin as "maybe better, but not as good as me."

Major crapola. This was a complication that his brain flat out didn't want. Now he had to convince the lesser Silverman (okay, not *that* much lesser) down below. He had no use for men who thought with their dicks and he'd be damned if at his age he'd start.

"Maybe I'll come visit you once you're settled in," she said.

"Bring beer," he heard himself say, and knew that if she was a shark, he was destined to bleed out. But until that day came, the fight would be good.

The smaller woman stepped forward. Between the slight frown she wore and the way she was looking him over, he had her pinned as one of those *analyze, analyze, analyze* people who made his brain ache. It wasn't that he was without a philosophical bent. He just figured there was no law against having fun while being smart. And if there were such a law, he'd break it on principle.

"You're Tessa, right?" Might as well get the ball rolling...

She nodded while extending her hand. "And you're obviously Don."

"Yeah," he said, while shaking her hand. He figured the shorter his response, the less she'd have to analyze into subatomic particles.

"I think it would be better if we gave you the night to sleep, but I'd like to drop by tomorrow morning," Tessa said.

Polite words aside, Don knew she wasn't asking permission.

"I'll be there," he said.

As Isabel hurried into the back of the van, no doubt wanting her talk-time with him, Don said his good-nights to the others.

"Get some good rest," Tessa said.

Damn, but he was going to need it.

CHAPTER 11

Darkness had always been both Isabel's enemy and friend. Darkness meant that the men who'd been waiting for the courage to come to her part of the city could wear the night like a mask for their cowardice. When Luz was with her, there was little Isabel could do. But unwatched, she was fast and knew her old streets well enough to walk them blindfolded. In this way, darkness was her protector, too. She would use it to disappear into sweet freedom.

Morning would bring with it an empty, growling stomach, Luz's sharp words, and worse, bruises from Luz's boyfriend, Hector, over their loss of her money. She was growing old, Hector would say, and soon would be of no value. But until then, she would earn her keep.

Now, Isabel was not kept. Tonight she walked the garden paths she had learned as well as the streets of her home. She was as free as the butterflies that flitted from flower to flower during the day. And she had as much money as one, too…a lack she would have to find a way to fill. Until then, she had

Don and Mila watching over her, not parents, and better than them in so many ways. Now that she had Tessa, too, Isabel couldn't describe how she felt about the American, except she was grateful for her arrival, and a little frightened, too, of what Tessa's paints had brought out in her. It was as though a beautiful storm had started inside her head, and now it would never stop.

Isabel sat in her secret spot, one where she could watch and not be watched. Other nights, Jerry the dog had been here with her, but now that Don had returned, Jerry wouldn't stray from his side. She still had her dreams to keep her company, though. Visions of jungles with vines that climbed to consume the sun, of the silly monkeys that swung through the trees, except these were bird-colored in bright blue and red, and of the ocean so thick with life that the water could not be seen. Her heart drummed and her hand involuntarily tightened, as though she held a brush and could capture these mind-pictures *now*.

The noise of a door closing drew Isabel's attention to the house. Music began to play, and the lights around the swimming pool came on. Moments later, Tessa appeared. She was no longer wearing the red dress she had worn to dinner, but her bathing suit. Water splashed as she dove into the pool. She didn't swim long, though. Or it didn't seem that way to Isabel, who had returned to her dreams. When she looked back, Tessa was dancing to the music.

The older woman moved with more grace than Isabel would have imagined. Then again, she might not correctly be recalling how her own body had moved in the months before the baby took charge. She smiled at the thought of standing up and dancing herself. Tessa would be sure some enormous wild creature was lumbering toward her to drag her off.

Feeling like an intruder for watching Tessa, Isabel tipped back her head to count the stars in the sky. When she did, she noticed more lights—these at Javier Ruiz's house up the hillside. Perhaps no one could sleep this hot night.

Isabel sighed, and the baby gave a lazy roll. Slowly she stood and prepared to make her way to the front of the house. The lights from Ruiz's house shone in front of her as she again found the path. Isabel laughed when she saw that he watched Tessa, too. Yes, change hung heavy in the night air, and none were free from its pull.

"And on to the business of the living," Tessa announced as she cracked a fat egg into the butter-slick frying pan waiting on the stove.

She'd awoken absurdly happy this morning. Before showering and then this ravenously hungry venture into the kitchen, she'd briskly traveled the road to the village and back. As she'd walked, one long stride—for her, at least—after another, an odd phrase had taken up residence in her mind.

The other shoe won't drop.

Granted, it wasn't in the All-Time Top Ten of Revelations, but it suited Tessa quite well. She was heartily tired of waiting for that damn shoe, anyway. Kate and Vee had been right. She'd allowed herself to become so engaged in life's bad stuff that she'd forgotten to *live*…to indulge herself with small pleasures. Last night, when she'd danced on the terrace for the joy of feeling her body move, the conscious thought that she was *living* had come to her.

She wasn't so simple as to believe that it was the dancing that had done the trick. And it certainly hadn't been Javier's kiss, though she planned to demand more. He was a wonderful man, but she didn't put stock in Prince Charming fairy tales.

In fact—to borrow Kate's phrase—she had been seizing her goddamn bliss for some time now. Walking the beach, shopping in Quepos, painting with Isabel—all of these were affirmative acts of living. And now that she'd rediscovered the distinction between reacting and living, she would shelter the idea and let it take root in her soul.

As a final farewell to the killer shoe, she'd tried while walking to recall how long this threat had hovered above her head. Had it arrived when her career had begun to unravel? Or earlier, when Jack started his baby campaign, and her body had refused to cooperate? Finally, she'd concluded that she was better off establishing an ending point—*today*—than finding its origin.

Tessa finished putting together her breakfast and had eaten nearly every last bit by the time Kate came into the kitchen.

"You're up early," Kate said as she reached for a mug and poured herself some of the locally roasted coffee Tessa had brewed.

"I've got a lot to get done. Starting with Don and moving on to you."

"I'm not sure I like the sound of this," Kate said. She looked at Tessa more sharply. "What's up?"

"Me," she said, then grinned in spite of herself. "Definitely me."

Kate raised her mug in a toast. "It looks good on you. *Very* good. Are you sure nothing worth sharing happened at dinner last night?"

"Nothing interesting by Murkowski standards."

"Trust me, it doesn't take much," Kate said grumpily.

Tessa nudged the topic along. She was tired of skirting the controversial. She wanted her friendship with Kate back on track; she wanted everything out in the open. "I want you to show me your dream property this morning."

Her friend brightened. "No lie?"

"No lie."

"Why the change of heart?"

Tessa opted for flat-out honesty. "Things haven't been right between us since we got here, Kate. Usually, we stick together, but we've both been just kind of…I don't know… drifting off. I'd like to fix that." At the slightly money-tinged gleam in her friend's eyes, she added, "And before you begin another mad rush at me, I'll tell you now that my checkbook is staying here. This will be an information-gathering trip, only."

"I'll take what I can get," Kate said as she topped off her coffee. "And some time together is a good start. So, we'll go now?"

"You might want to get dressed first," Tessa pointed out, motioning at Kate's ratty Michigan State T-shirt and old flannel boxer shorts.

"Details," Kate replied.

"And I need time to talk to Don."

"Fine, then after that we'll stop at the real estate agent's office in the village and get—"

"Village?" Mila said as she entered the room. "You are going to the village? When?"

Tessa glanced at the clock built into the microwave. "At ten," she said, which gave her twenty minutes to deal with Don.

"I will be ready at ten-fifteen. You will wait for me," the older woman commanded, then left without seeking comment.

Tessa smiled at her retreating form. Tessa might be taking charge of living, but she hadn't quite yet acquired Mila's ability to jam a bit between its clenched jaws and ride it into the ground.

"You're sure about that checkbook thing?" Kate prodded, apparently unable to help herself.

Tessa rinsed her plate and stuck it in the dishwasher. "I said my mood's better...not manic."

"But I need your help, Tessa. 'It takes a village' and all that, you know?"

"The saying pertains to raising a child, not opening a bike ranch."

Kate shrugged. "Hey, if it makes you feel any more inclined to invest, just view me as a child."

Tessa laughed. "Anything to seal the deal," she said, echoing what had been one of Kate's pet sayings during their banking days.

"As always," Kate agreed. "Tell me what else I need to do to get you hooked."

"Slow down, for one. Second, get serious about this. Treat it like a business, because that's what it will be. And both of us need some help navigating the local system." She hesitated, then added, "I've asked Javier if he'd lend a hand."

Kate grinned over the top of her coffee mug. "I'd have thought you'd be asking for more interesting body parts than a hand."

"Funny," Tessa said, trying to be severe, but the problem was, now that her mood had lightened, she was beginning to recall that Kate's tart attitude was one of the reasons they'd suited so well all these years. "And he hasn't agreed to help yet anyway. But tell me what practical things you've done…and don't try to tell me that those half-assed columns of numbers you gave me before are practical. I'm betting that you've just been dancing around your beloved hills like Maria in *The Sound of Music*."

Kate raised her chin to a superior angle. "Setting aside the far-too-virginal aspects, Maria is beneath my dignity."

Tessa snorted.

"Not buying in?"

"Not for a second."

"I'll confess to a certain amount of tree-hugging, but no twirling," Kate said.

"Fair enough," Tessa said, then returned to business. "So, what operations have you benchmarked?"

"Benchmarked! What are you, an undead banker? If I had any garlic, I'd wave it to ward you off."

Tessa laughed in spite of herself, but still tried to deliver her message. "Come on, Kate. It's nothing more than you'd ask from any start-up operation—financial projections, market studies…"

Kate settled her hands over her ears. "Stop! Any more and you'll have flipped me back to a banker."

Tessa spoke louder. "I know you can hear me, and I promise I'm done nagging for the day."

Kate dropped her hands from her ears. "You're too kind. And tell you what, just to reward you, I'll do an Internet search and come up with benchmarks tonight."

Tessa smiled her approval. "Smart move."

"My allotted one per year," Kate replied.

As it was December, Tessa could only hope that the allocation was more accurately one smart move per *calendar* year, but her overall optimism lived strong. She and Kate were talking like friends again, that ghost of another shoe had faded, and she was embracing whatever might come next.

And that, she thought, *is living*.

"So what do you want for your birthday?" Kate asked Tessa as they drove the Dead Head van down the Silvermans' drive.

"Birthday?" Tessa repeated absently while fiddling with the radio dial.

"Yeah. The big four-oh's a week off, remember?" Kate reached over from the passenger seat and tuned in to a station, leaving Tessa free to make the turn onto the main road. She looked up to realize that Tessa had banged a right instead of hung a left.

"Wrong direction," Mila barked from the back seat.

At the same time, Kate asked, "Need a map?"

"I'm mapless," Tessa said, then grinned.

Kate didn't get the comment or the grin, but there were

a number of things she couldn't grasp this morning, such as how Tessa could have been with someone as utterly hot as Javier Ruiz and not jumped his bones. And why the hell, late last night, Kate had had an equally hot dream with that burned-out hippie, Don Silverman, front and center. She'd decided to put the aberration of a Don-fantasy down to the nearly full moon. That, and the fact that her interrupted fling with Mark the bartender had been two long months ago.

Still, she had to admit there *was* something bizarrely attractive about Don's thick silver braid and hawk's beak of a nose. No doubt he appealed to the latent rebel in her. After enough years in corporate America and too many of those spent having bad sex with Hank Kyle, her libido was bound to veer off.

"So where are we going?" Kate asked, trying to pull her mind from sex with a near-stranger.

"We're taking a slight detour."

"That much I'd figured. But to where...South America?"

"I think it's down the road a bit more...." She scanned right and left.

Kate had just resigned herself to a tourist's gawking look-about when Tessa slammed on the brakes, avoiding a concrete truck entering the road. Kate's seat belt locked, and she grabbed the sides of her seat with her hands.

"This has to be it," Tessa said.

Kate looked at the drive just ahead and to their right. "You nearly killed us for a hotel under construction?"

"It's under renovation," Tessa replied.

"Right. That makes me feel a whole lot better." Kate wriggled back in her seat and willed her heart to slow.

The terrain was steeper here than even a few miles north in Playa Blanca, and Kate had to hang on to her cool as the truck's dust settled and Tessa sharply took the turn into the drive. They pulled around a curve and into a parking lot that sat next to a long three-story building. Workers' cars and trucks were clustered near the structure. Tessa exited the other end of the lot and followed a ribbon of road. To their right, fat concrete piers had been poured—probably the base for footings to hold a new building.

"What's this about?" Kate asked.

"Just sightseeing."

"You might want to choose something already finished, if that's the case."

"But something finished would not be owned by Javier Ruiz," Mila said from her perch in the back seat.

"Ah," said Kate.

"*Ah?*" Tessa echoed, shooting her a glance. "What, exactly, does that mean?"

"It means, 'Ah, Tessa's more interested in a man than she pretends.'"

"Curious," Tessa said. "I'm curious."

"Close enough." Kate looked past the buildings and at the property. She doubted there was a spot here without a million-dollar view of the ocean. So Ruiz owned this? She'd give Tessa credit for being interested in someone with some bucks. Kate had never quite pulled that off—except with Jack, who at least had had potential. Wouldn't it be something if someday, some man left Tessa for Kate, drawing level that cosmic balance?

Kate glanced over at Tessa, and took an arrow of guilt that sent the small, evil thought slithering back to its cave. Tessa couldn't have changed what she didn't know. The blame for this hurt lay with Kate, and for the sake of friendship, she needed to keep it there.

"You said we were going to the village," Mila snapped from the middle seat. "Move along, then. I have important business to be done."

"Business?" Tessa asked.

"Yes. At Margarita's. Now, let's go."

Kate's curiosity was piqued, an odd state considering she usually just tried to ignore Mila. The woman smelled of tobacco, and that scent made Kate cranky over all she was missing.

"Important business?" she asked. "Like you need to go pound a couple of cold brews?"

"No beer. Look what it's done to your shape," the German replied. "Awful."

"That's genetics, not beer, but thanks for noticing," Kate said.

Tessa sighed the way Kate's mom had when the Murkow-ski family had bickered…which was always.

"That's enough, guys," Tessa said. She shoved in the cas-sette tape that had been sticking out of its slot, and on came Jerry and the Dead. The truck cruised on north to Playa Blanca.

Kate cranked the volume, propped her elbow on the open window and thought of Finca Mila-free Murkowski. What a fine, *fine* place it would be.

At Mila's command, Tessa parked in front of Margarita's beachside cantina. The older woman was out the van's side door before Tessa had even switched off the rusty beast. It must be pressing business indeed. In the weeks they'd been under the same roof, Tessa hadn't seen Mila move this quickly, except to bolt outside for an overdue cigarette.

"Someone lit a fire under her," Tessa said.

"She's not alone," Kate replied. "I'm going to head over to the real estate shack and get the keys and info for the prop-erty. I'll meet you at Margarita's when I'm done." And then Kate, too, was gone.

Tessa took the keys from the ignition, climbed out of the old clunker, then pocketed the keys. Instead of going into the cantina's small indoor area, she rounded to the beachside, her flip-flops scuffing in the gritty sand.

Mila was standing by a table near the kitchen door, and

Margarita was wrestling a huge box in her direction. Tessa rushed over to help, and as they settled the box onto a table, she introduced herself to Margarita. Javier wasn't the sole Ruiz diplomat. Margarita kindly limited her meddling to asking whether Tessa had enjoyed last night's *ceviche*, and to mentioning in passing that Javier had been called out of town this morning. Tessa felt briefly deflated at the news, but pushed the moment aside.

While they chatted a bit about the kinds of fish that Margarita's husband came across most often, Mila dug through her cracked brown leather purse. She pulled out a pocketknife and flipped it open. The blade was large and evil-looking, and Tessa took an involuntary step back.

"A woman always should be protected," Mila announced, flexing her blade hand.

"No one in their right mind would consider crossing you, knife or no knife," Tessa said.

"This is for the wrong-minded people." Wielding the knife like a scalpel, Mila slit the packing tape across the top of the box.

She folded back the flaps and began searching through the contents, then both she and Margarita nodded with satisfaction.

"Good quality," said Margarita.

"And cheap enough to hold a heavy markup," Mila replied. The cantina owner was about to say something when a squabble erupted between two waitresses. She scurried off, and Tessa moved closer. The box was filled with large folded squares of brightly hued batik fabric.

"Inventory," Mila said, sparing Tessa a glance. "I will be selling sarongs to the tourists, just over there." She pointed to the beach just outside the cantina, where a U-shaped stall that had been made of wooden tables identical to Margarita's now stood.

"That's wonderful, Mila!" Another question niggled at Tessa, though. "So why sarongs?"

The older woman lifted one shoulder in a casually dismissive gesture. "Why not? They're inexpensive enough that I can make a good profit, and my hours and days here on the beach will be my own. Few will hire a bookkeeper my age, and I have no desire to work inside, in front of a computer, when I moved here for the warmth. For this, I will put up with the tourists. It's a small start, in any case."

Tessa was impressed by any start, no matter how small, and told Mila so. Mila was busy ignoring Tessa's praise when Kate returned. Tessa decided to keep up the positive reinforcement.

"Mila's going to be selling sarongs!"

Kate's smile developed a get-even curve. "Think you've got the shape for it?"

"Better than yours."

"Let me see what you've got," Kate said.

Tessa's relief was boundless when instead of witnessing a striptease, she watched Kate reach into the box and unfurl a sarong with a sea turtle in bright blues and greens, and the name *Costa Rica* on one border. A packing slip fluttered down, and Kate picked it up.

"Made in India?" she asked Mila.

"You are not a fan of the global economy?"

"Hell, I didn't even think you knew about the global economy."

"That's because you don't look past your own needs."

Tessa flinched, but Kate only shrugged. "Guilty as charged, but I'm trying to do better."

Mila nodded. "And in time I will use local suppliers and do better, too. Right now I haven't the money. Unless you'd like to lend me some of yours…" she said to Kate.

"You've got the wrong end of that horse," Kate replied.

"I had thought as much," Mila said. "Tessa—"

Kate latched her hand under Tessa's elbow. "Time to hit the road. We've got Finca Murkowski to see," she said, trampling whatever Mila had been about to say. No doubt Kate feared that it might be another hand in Tessa's pocket, not that there was any room, with Kate's crammed into the shallow space.

"Ready to have your socks knocked off?" Kate asked Tessa as they climbed back into the van.

"I'm wearing flip-flops."

"All the better," Kate replied. "All the better…"

Tessa could only hope.

There should be some rule against facing Tessa twice in the same day. Don had already had a chat with her this morning, and he figured that was enough interruption in his meditations. And she'd gotten what she wanted. He'd agreed to let her decide when to tell Cousin Vee that he'd been running a halfway house. Since Vee was one of those organized sorts who made his left eye twitch, Don was more than happy to take a giant step backward in the chain of command. Not that he could friggin' walk well enough to step backward. Hell, between the cast and the painkillers, just standing up was a miserable job.

He'd hobbled out onto the porch a few hours ago, and unless he could think of a compelling reason to get up before nightfall, he planned to stay planted in his chair.

But Tessa DiPaulo was just about reason enough. She came damn close to making his eye twitch, too. True, she was more tequila than shark, but beneath a surface calm, her mind was wound too tightly. If she asked, and she hadn't, he'd tell her to stop doubting her every damn thought and mood.

"So what brings you here?" he asked as Tessa neared.

She hesitated before answering. "Rest and relaxation. Life back home kind of imploded."

He hadn't been quite unambiguous enough for the woman who lived to peel down thoughts like layers of an onion. "No, I meant *here*, as in back on my porch for the second time today, you know?"

She blinked. "Oh. I just wanted to see how you're doing."

"Better," he said, rattling his bottle of painkillers.

"You should watch that stuff," Tessa said. "It can sneak up on you."

Don laughed. "I survived both the sixties and the seventies. My body chemistry is so jacked that these are like hard candies." He motioned toward the chair next to his. "Why don't you sit down?"

She did, then as Jerry slunk off, she said, "I don't think your dog likes me."

"Jerry? He doesn't like anyone. He tolerates me because I keep him in food and out of the rain."

"Jerry? His name's Jerry?"

"Sure. Like the man. You know…Garcia?"

"Figures."

"What?"

"My first guess was right."

"First guesses usually are." He shifted his cast-clad leg. "I guessed that the cattle truck was going too damn fast, and my bike bit the dust because I didn't listen to myself."

"Good point."

"So," he said when she'd sat there with her brain buzzing

on and messing up the quiet afternoon, "do you have any good first-guess stories?"

She sat quiet for a minute more, and Don just kicked back and waited.

"Damn," she said, sounding almost awed. "I've never said this to anyone, but you must have a kind face or something. And it's not as though we're ever going to see each other again, once I leave here…."

"I'll carry your secret to the grave," he vowed, wondering if she knew he was jerking with her a little.

She nodded at the pill bottle he was switching from hand to hand as he waited for drugging time to roll around again. "You'll forget what I said by morning."

"Body chemistry," he reminded her, and she rolled her dark eyes.

"Here's my confession. When I was standing at the altar with my soon-to-be ex, I almost bolted."

"Almost, huh?" That didn't surprise him. She was too anxious to conform to be a successful bolter.

"I didn't want to upset my mother," she said, proving his point. "My dad had died that year, and I'd already gone off the deep end, too. Another embarrassment from me would have been crushing."

"A ditched-wedding crushing? Ha! Now, I ran my parents through the wringer. Car crashes, college dropout, walk-abouts…well, you know about the walkabout habit."

She pointed to the bottle. "I know about a lot of habits—including your little friends, there."

"You?" She looked like a one-chardonnay-to-loosen-up sort.

"What, I should look like you?"

He laughed at that piece of sass.

Tessa grew serious again. "A few months after my dad died, one night when I had no right to be driving in the first place after all I'd had to drink, I was in a car accident. I hurt my back and neck, and while I healed, I found a new best friend. Those painkillers helped me forget all sorts of things—how I was screwing up at work...who my real friends were...how not to blow through my paycheck." She shook her head. "As if coping with my dad's death wasn't enough for my mom."

"Mothers are made of sturdy stock." He used to hate the word *sturdy* for its dullness. But it didn't sound bad to him anymore. It was what he needed to become, and what Tessa DiPaulo hadn't quite figured out she was.

"My mom was stronger than I expected," Tessa agreed.

"And regardless, you wore a hair shirt for one helluva long time afterward, I'll bet."

Her eyes widened. "How did you know?"

He pointed skyward, or at least roofward. "I'm channeling Jerry."

Tessa laughed, then looped some of her wild hair behind her ears. "Bull."

"Okay, how about you're just the right type to do penance? You're here for a little R & R from a tough stretch back home, right?"

"I'm with you."

"And now you say that you're getting divorced."

"Still with you," she affirmed.

"You're not acting like a pissed-off woman who wants to come down and blow the cobwebs from her brain."

"Now you've lost me."

"Instead of running wild, best I can figure, you've spent the past few weeks making a big, messy family of your own, and all the while you've been applauding your sense of freedom. You're one big fraud, Tessa."

For a second she looked as if she might want to haul off and deck him, but then a smile spread across her face. In that instant, Don knew why Ruiz had been drooling over her last night. Tessa wasn't his type, but she sure as hell was most guys'.

"It sounds to me like we've got a serious case of the pot calling the kettle black, wouldn't you say?" she asked.

"Could be. The difference is, now I'm real."

"You are, huh?"

"I'm willing to admit that this is my life. No more running. No more hiding from my screwups, and I've got a ton of those. I've also got a home, a book to write and a family…. The one you've latched onto, as a matter of fact."

"Okay, just for the sake of argument, since I'm not officially buying into this family-seeking theory, if I were expanding my family, you wouldn't share?"

Her question told him that he'd scored a bull's-eye. Despite her sidestepping, Tessa craved family connections the way he did one last Dead concert. He envied her, too. She could grab her desire—though not necessarily at his expense—while he was just pissing into the wind with his wish.

"I'd share if you were worthy," he told her.

"Worthy?"

"Yeah, and there's only one simple rule regarding worthiness. That's spread no bullshit. Be true to yourself because if you can do that, there's less chance you'll screw over the rest of us."

"That's a pretty tall order."

"How so?"

"To be true to myself, I'd have to know what I want."

"You do...you just need to get back in touch with it."

"You're sounding pretty spiritual."

He grinned. "Not bad for a Jew who hasn't seen the inside of a synagogue in thirty years. It's kind of like those bracelets from a few years back. 'Just ask yourself, WWJD?'"

She started to speak, paused for a moment, then tried again. "What would *Jesus* do?"

"Nah. Nothing against the Big Guy. He's one of my people, after all...but I'm better versed in Jerry. What would *Jerry* do?"

"I'll humor you. What would Jerry do?"

"See? This is where being square with Jerry isn't all bad. He'd tell you to hand out some of the good stuff you've received. Give back, since you've been given, and all that embracing philosophical crap. And then, of course, he'd tell you to get stoned."

He'd added the last just to mess with her...to get her to lighten up. Still, he'd bet Jerry wouldn't have minded the addendum. Tessa did, though. A wholly ticked-off look settled on her face. "You really had me going until the get-stoned bit. I thought you were being serious," she said.

"I was," he promised. "Serious as a heart attack." Then he remembered that's how Jerry had taken his Last Big Ride, and could nearly see Garcia's grizzled mug glaring at him, along with Tessa's pretty one.

Don began to laugh so hard that he started coughing. Bright white dots began to dance across his field of vision.

"Need some water?" she asked so sweetly he knew he was screwed.

He managed to nod.

"Get it for yourself," she said, then marched off.

Jerry had no friggin' idea how good he had it being dead.

CHAPTER 12

On a Friday morning, one hour past dawn, Isabel examined eight days' worth of paintings, all so personal to her that she might as well have painted them from her own blood. Eleven pictures; eleven children, some more attractive than others, but all equally adored for what they had brought to—and taken from—her life.

While painting, Isabel hadn't even minded that Mila, her peace and protection, had spent most of her time in the village, selling her sarongs. Tessa had been here and she had painted, although not nearly as quickly as Isabel. But she had expressed herself in a new way, too. Over their times together, Tessa's Spanish had so improved that when Isabel named the picture of Luz *Stinking Street Bitch*, Tessa had understood. She'd also nodded in agreement. A smart woman, Tessa.

Isabel bent down and leaned the paintings one by one against the kitchen's lower cabinets. A sharp twinge raced around her side, and she put a hand to the small of her back. She could not keep this sleepless pace much longer. Though her mind cried for her to paint, her body howled louder yet with its demands for rest. *One more picture*, she thought. *Just one more.*

She'd just finished setting up her kitchen workspace when Tessa came in, face pink and damp with sweat. She took a bottle of water from the refrigerator and drank long swallows before speaking.

"I tried running this morning," she said in Spanish.

"And did you like it?" Isabel asked.

"Hated it. But I'll run again tomorrow."

Isabel didn't ask why. She understood the need to work past pain.

"You're painting again today?" Tessa asked.

"Yes, a little. I'll finish just one more, then I'll sleep in the shade."

"Sleep will have to wait. At two o'clock I'm taking you to see a very nice doctor I found yesterday in Quepos."

"A doctor? I told you I have no money for that."

"I do," Tessa said in such a way that Isabel knew arguing would be hopeless.

And in truth, she wanted to see a doctor. Had she not mapped her tummy with slow and careful hands each night, she would have believed that this baby had more feet, elbows and knees than one child should. Even now, she worried about the unknown. To have an authority tell her that all was well might help her sleep. Something must, and soon.

"I had an idea this morning while I ran," Tessa said. "I think we should put some of your pictures at Mila's stall on the beach."

"Put them there for what?"

"A tourist might want to buy them. Maybe not the one of Luz, as she's very scary, but some of the others…"

Isabel was trying to digest all of this when Tessa spoke again. "If you think this is a bad idea—"

"Not bad. Crazy. Tessa, I paint like a child. Some of these look as though I used my fingers, and I did! Who would spend money on this?" She jabbed a finger at a painting of Jerry nose-to-nose with a green-and-purple-striped armadillo.

"They have emotion, and they're the voice of someone who lives here. Tourists love having those sorts of memories on their walls."

"Crazy tourists," Isabel said.

Tessa laughed. "Crazy, but with money. Can we try this? Please? You have nothing to lose except maybe a bit of pride."

And that was what Tessa had overlooked. Isabel had no pride to spare. What little she'd managed to scrape together was fragile and new, certainly not strong enough to survive seeing her babies wilting unwanted under the hot sun.

"No," she said.

Tessa took her by the hands. "You're good. Very good in a way I never was, and never will be. You're an original. Your style is yours alone, and if I didn't care for you so much I'd be very jealous."

Tessa's work was perfect. A flower looked like a flower, and a house, a house. Isabel would never be able to tame her hand to that degree. "Jealous…*you?*"

Tessa nodded. "You're that wonderful."

Isabel looked into her eyes, seeking a lie or a trap, but saw only kindness. "If I do this, you can't make me go there. I won't see them sit unnoticed."

"Trust me," Tessa said, squeezing Isabel's hands more tightly. And strange as it was, Isabel, who was sure she trusted no one but Mila and Don, realized that her heart and world had opened wide enough to admit one more person.

"I do. Sell them. All but these," Isabel said, drawing her hands away to snatch up Luz, Jerry and the scene with her brother in it. Then she ran to her bedroom where she would hide until her courage returned.

Five days later…

Tessa sat at the computer, ordering acrylic paints and canvases to refresh her supply. Sometime between last Friday and today, a dozen blank canvas boards had dwindled down to three. Tessa had urged Isabel toward the sketch pads last night. With luck, she'd taken the hint.

The situation wasn't dire, though. One could ship virtually anything to Playa Blanca. The question was how deeply the supplier would latch into one's jugular vein for doing so. Today she would be down at least a pint, but that was nothing compared to the full-scale bleed she'd conducted on herself yesterday when writing Kate a seed-money check for ten thousand dollars. It was not much compared to what Kate needed, and Tessa had made it clear that this money was no promise she'd invest more. Tessa saw the act as affirmation that she wanted to rebuild their friendship. How Kate saw it, she wasn't sure. She'd seemed grateful and happy, but also distracted. That, though, was Kate's issue and not Tessa's. She had enough of her own.

"Small potatoes," she decreed the sum now on her monitor, then finished typing in her credit card information.

In another few weeks, she would adjust to all the small accommodations that life, Tico style, required. And in not so many weeks after that, she would be leaving. That thought alone made her throat go tight and her chest ache. Leaving to what—and ultimately where—were matters she chose not to consider, even if considering her options had been her reason for coming to Vee's house in the first place. Being true to herself was something she best handled in small blocks of time. Managing today was good enough.

Not that she had any particular plans. She'd had her morning exercise. Kate was off talking to a couple of bankers in Quepos. Mila was at work, planning a comfortable future one rosy-hued sarong at a time, and while Javier had called to say hello yesterday, he was stuck in San José on business for two more days.

Just to occupy time, she supposed she could take a run and check out the progress at his family's hotel. But she'd already run/walked/staggered there on Tuesday. While winded, weak and sweaty, she'd crossed paths with Margarita. Javier's sister had again been unfailingly kind in the face of this embarrassing (for Tessa, at least) almost-trespass. She'd shown Tessa the plans for the property. When renovations were complete, the hotel would be intimately resort-class, with a small spa, a restaurant and even some shops. Tessa wanted to come back later in the year and see it when she returned to Costa Rica to visit Kate.

Canvases ordered, she'd just shut down the computer when the phone next to it rang. She waited for Don to answer, not really expecting that he would. The man had a way of abandoning his handset like a changeling child in the woods.

Tessa picked up after the third ring. "Silverman residence."

"Tessa, is that you?"

Shit.

"Hello, Jack. What do you want?"

"Just to wish you a happy birthday," he said with the same sort of joviality she'd heard him use when kissing up to car rental clerks for an upgrade.

Birthday? She checked the date bubble on her watch.

Twenty-one, it read. Yes, birthday. Denial might run a deep and winding course, but she had traveled it long enough. She was forty today.

"Thank you," she said, trying for a tone that was polite yet final.

"You're welcome. Have you heard from your mom?"

She definitely had to work on that terminal finality. "I'm sure she'll call tonight, when rates are lower."

"Tell her that I said hello, okay?"

Tessa knew her mother wouldn't give a damn what Jack said, and she had lied when she agreed to relay the message. When that didn't wrap up this most unwelcome call, she added, "Is there something else you wanted?"

"Well...the lock on the door from the kitchen to the garage has been sticking again."

The smart-ass in her wanted to suggest that he just crawl through the window she'd broken, but she knew from the November days she'd spent packing that the window had been replaced. And in any case, Jack was far too literal to grasp the "pound sand" message she'd be delivering.

"You might want to hire a locksmith," she suggested as she stood and moved away from the desk.

"Right," he said.

As she walked to the daylight streaming in from the terrace doors, she swore she could hear his mind clicking through other possible pretexts for this call.

"Okay…" He drew the word out long and slow.

Tessa didn't bother hiding her impatient sigh. "Whatever it is, just say it."

"I, uh… I was wondering how you're doing."

"Tan, fit and relaxed." As though she'd admit otherwise, she thought, and then was surprised by the notion that the words actually applied.

"And you, Jack?" she asked, briefly fantasizing that he'd announce a case of some hideously disfiguring disease. Elephantiasis of the scrotum would be a start.

"I'm fine. Great… You know I think about you, don't you, Tessa?"

"After over a decade together, your thinking of me is no shock," she told her ex.

"Do you think of me?"

"Only when required," she answered, rolling her eyes.

"I want us to be friends, Tessa."

She had lost interest in this particular Jack-Wright-patented brand of manipulation. She glanced outside to where Don sat scribbling away on a notepad in the shade of an umbrella.

"Buddy," she said in her best imitation of the man, "that's one long-dead vulture."

"Do I want to know where the hell that phrase came from?" Jack asked after a momentary silence.

Tessa smiled. "An homage to my shaman."

"Your—"

"My life consultant...friend...big brother." Since Don's return nearly two weeks ago, her talks with him had grown into a twisted daily highlight. He was far wiser than he'd first cared to let on...or maybe the painkillers had finally worn off. Either way, at the moment she had another man to consider.

"Tell you what, Jack, finish wishing me a happy birthday and stop trying to reel me back in. You're only doing it for sport, anyway."

"Sport? Tessa, that's ridiculous."

"Is it? This call is just another challenge to win, though I'd bet its outcome is less important to you than your weekend squash match."

"But—"

Anger wasn't fueling her words, clarity was. "Cheating on me was just another sport, too. Sophie and I were separate pieces of required equipment. Golf clubs...wife...mistress. I'm sure that in your mind, she had nothing to do with me."

"She didn't. Really, she didn't, babe."

"Not babe. Contessa," she corrected. "And you know what? If we'd really, deeply loved each other, this never would have happened."

"Tessa—"

"No, let me finish this. I'm relieved that we're done with each other, because if I met you today on the street, I doubt

I'd take a second look at you, and I'm sure you feel that way about me. Otherwise, one of us would have tried to save our marriage—agreed?"

"That's not fair. Sophie was pregnant. What did you want me to do?"

"Maybe not get her pregnant in the first place?" He didn't answer, and she hadn't expected him to. "And to save us any future calls, have a merry Christmas, a happy New Year and in February, when the divorce is final, I want you to have a wonderful life...far away from me."

With that, Tessa hung up, returned the phone to its base and waited for the inevitable tears to start. Instead, a warm feeling settled over her, almost as fine a sensation as the buzz she got after eating a chocolate bar. It took her a few minutes to peg this new emotion. When she did, she realized it was the joy of freedom.

Divorcing Jack had been more emotionally draining than she'd expected. She hadn't doubted the necessity of divorce so much as her strength to carry on, but she'd proved herself better than a survivor. She'd proved herself a winner.

"So much for marrying Mr. Wright," she said, then went outside and settled on the lounge chair next to Don's. He didn't even look up from his writing.

"I'm forty today," she said.

"A mere child."

It was a tough point to argue, considering all the personal growth she had yet to achieve. "The age has potential."

"Mathematically, more than when you hit seventy," he replied, still without glancing her way.

She scooted up in her lounge and peeked over at his wild scrawl. Words were splattered across the page in outright defiance of the lines. She could pick up only the odd bits here and there—*Bill Walton...Ken Kesey...Egypt...1978.*

"So you're seventy?" she asked, just to rattle him.

"Hell, no! Do I look seventy?"

Tessa smiled. "Tough question, my friend. Some days you don't look fifty, but others..." She finished with a regretful shrug.

He laughed. "That's good genes battling hard living. And I'll let you know for sure about seventy when I land there." With that, he turned back to his writing.

Tessa looked at his craggy features a bit longer. He probably hadn't been any more classically attractive in his youth than he was now, but she doubted that Don Silverman had ever had difficulty capturing a woman's attention.

"Gonna keep staring at me?" he asked as he folded back a filled page and prepared to attack the virgin white of the next sheet.

"Sorry," she said, but didn't look away.

Don grumbled something, then set aside his notepad. "So, birthday girl, what are you going to give yourself?"

She shrugged. "I don't need much. Besides, it's not as though I can go to Nordstrom and buy myself some shoes."

He waved off the thought with one broad hand. "That's just stuff. You need to give yourself a meaningful gift."

Tessa pondered the concept. "Well, I just told my ex to get stuffed."

He shook his head. "Not even close."

A lot he knew. "It felt like a gift."

"Hey, it might have felt like transcendence itself, but it's not something you chose. Now, what good thing are you going to give yourself?"

She tried to think of something wonderful, but couldn't quite get there. Maybe a swim in the ocean, except she lacked the initiative to change into her suit. Or she could always spend the balance of the day counting the spider monkeys as they followed their tree-trail. Both ideas were self-indulgent, but neither fell within the category of a grand gift. She took out her frustration on Mr. Inscrutable.

"Dammit, Don, do you ever ask an easy question?"

He shrugged. "They're easy enough to me."

She stood. "Stomping Jack was the best high I've had in ages, and now you've killed it."

"Find a better one. Think positively. And now go someplace else. I gotta get all of this down before I forget."

"Forget what?" she asked, hoping for just a hint of what he was writing.

"Everything," he replied, then closed her out of his world.

Tessa was growing weary of living in the House of Seized Bliss. Kate plotted, Isabel painted, Mila planned and Don penned.

And she?

She couldn't even think of a P-word other than *procrastinate* that suited her behavior. She was tired of having her nose pressed to the glass as everyone on the inside partied on. She stood and walked beachward.

Isabel was halfway down the hillside, sketchpad and Jerry as company. Tessa waved, but as expected, she remained invisible to the girl, who was riveted on her work. When Tessa gained the shore, she walked to the water's edge. The tide was out, and the boulders that rested at Javier's side of the crescent of a bay were exposed. She headed in that direction for no reason other than it gave her a false sense of purpose.

As she neared the rock closest to tide line, she noticed a crab colony, each dark creature no bigger than a half dollar, teeming over the jagged and pockmarked boulder. Tessa watched, a little repelled by the horror-movie aspects of the scene but unable to look away. Even their random, seemingly aimless hurry held purpose. They reminded her of her actions over the past few years. Point A to Point B, with no idea why.

Maybe she didn't want to be a minutiae-driven mapper, but it would do her good to at least figure out a general direction. North. South. Hell, she just needed to pick one.

Tessa came closer to the crabs' universe and watched as they skittered to their hidey-holes in the rock.

"I get the hint," she said, then moved a nonthreatening distance away.

Heedless of the fact that she was wearing shorts and not a bathing suit, she sat on the wet sand, legs stretched out in front of her, at the point where the incoming surf could flirt with her feet and ankles. She let her eyes slip lazily shut and tried for some of the blissful concentration that those around her reveled in. Instead, restlessness lingered.

Her first impulse was to dig down and think about the dreaded "what now?" but common sense told her that one's fortieth birthday was hardly an objective platform from which to consider life. Instead, in honor of Don, she tried to recall the lyrics to the Dead's "Truckin'." That, unfortunately, led to consideration of what a "doo-dah man" might be. Tessa feared that she had led a sheltered life.

"So, what are you doing down here with the surf?"

Her heart skipped a beat, and she smiled at the surprising sound of Javier's voice. "I'm meditating. What are you doing back in town days early?"

"I had much I missed. You're not pleased to see me?"

She couldn't seem to lose her smile. "Don't know. I haven't opened my eyes yet."

"When you do, you'll see that I'm not dressed to sit with you on the sand."

Curious, she looked to her right and saw feet clad in what she knew were a very expensive pair of leather dress shoes. Using her hand to shield her eyes from the sun, she checked out the rest of his attire. He was better suited for a boardroom than a humid afternoon on the beach, though if he'd ever been wearing a tie, it had escaped.

He extended his hand to her, and Tessa took it. Once she'd gained her feet, she asked, "In a hurry to get down here?"

"Yes, once I saw you," he said. "Will you come up to my house with me while I get changed?"

"Of course." Together they climbed the zigzag stairs.

"What would you like to do today?" he asked, then quickly spoke again. "I'm getting ahead of myself. I had hoped to spend the rest of the day with you."

"It's my birthday." Her words were on their face a non sequitur, but Tessa knew where she was going. For once.

"Happy birthday," he replied, and they finished the climb in silence.

As he ushered her into the house, Tessa took stock of his impassive expression. She supposed he'd be adept at a poker face, with his legal training. Yet in the instant before he was aware that he was being watched, she saw something that gave her hope.

"Would you like a cold drink or something before I…" He gestured in what she figured was the direction of his bedroom.

Awkwardness—mostly his—surrounded them. Yet she

hadn't imagined the warmth in his voice when he'd called yesterday night, or the sexual hunger, imperfectly masked, that he was revealing now.

"It's my birthday," Tessa repeated as she reached out and settled her hands over the dark lapels of his suit. "And I've decided on my gift."

Warmth returned to his face. "You have?"

She smiled, but it was shaky with anticipation. "I want you."

He hesitated, though not for long. "You're sure about this?"

Tessa nodded. "I couldn't be more sure."

His smile started slowly, but grew as she slipped her hands under his jacket and helped him take it off. She neatly draped it over the back of a chair. When he would have unbuttoned his shirt, she stopped him.

"My gift...mine to unwrap," she reminded him.

And she did so, leaving a scattering of clothing—both his and hers—in a path to his bedroom.

A small part of her mind kept waiting for shyness to overtake her, or uncertainty, but neither arrived. Instead there was a newness that ran electrically through her veins. The wet heat of his mouth at her breasts, the solid weight of him above her and finally, when she was close to begging him to join with her, Javier inside her.

He liked to kiss more than Jack had, making her drunk

with pleasure. He talked more, too. Some words were in English, and some in Spanish. She even earned a laugh from him when she told him in his own tongue to keep talking just a little bit dirty to her.

It had been so long since lovemaking had been anything but clinical…anything but a setup for another failure. Javier didn't know her failures, her regrets. She was new again, too, and her heart slammed with excitement. Their lovemaking wasn't perfect, and was far from smoothly choreographed. It was hungry, genuine and without doubt the finest gift she could have asked for.

And later, when they both lay relaxed and replete, that doubting part of Tessa's mind waited for regret to set in. But she had no regrets. She had only the sure knowledge that she'd desired a man and he had returned the favor. Thoroughly, too.

Javier stirred and drew her closer. Tessa snuggled in, and after his chest began to rise and fall in the regular pattern of sleep, she didn't even punish herself when her thoughts strayed to Jack. She knew it was only natural.

Once upon a time, she had loved Jack. He'd also suited the orderly Tessa she'd been rebuilding from the wreckage left after her father's death and her downward spiral. Being married to a goal-driven man had given her structure. For a while, everything had worked. They had focused on growing their careers and their circle of friends. They were the perfect machine.

It had taken her a few years to grasp just how much they were geared toward Jack's competitive bent. As the first of his friends began to have children, Jack decided he needed some, too. His most compelling argument in favor of parenthood had been "it's time." Because he'd pushed—and she'd been trying so hard to be Good Tessa—she'd agreed. She couldn't recall ever fully considering whether *she'd* actually wanted a baby. It had been enough that Jack had.

When things hadn't worked out, she'd agreed to the fertility specialists, too. To distance herself from what she was doing to her body—the twenty-plus-pound weight gain, the stress, the feeling that their entire marriage rested on her ability to conceive (turns out her paranoia had been well-founded)—she'd distanced herself from Jack, as well.

She would bear responsibility for that part of their failure, but it was perhaps the best mistake she could have made. How else would she have realized that a man briefly right for her was also permanently wrong?

She didn't know if she would ever choose to marry again. The idea held no great appeal, especially since she knew now that even if she could conceive, she wasn't sure that she was ready to deal with children.

Still, considering these topics before the court managed to complete the technicality of stamping and signing her divorce papers seemed a bit premature. For now, though, she was happy knowing that she could make a man laugh, and that she could give and accept sexual attention without thinking of basal thermometers and fertility charts.

Life as Contessa DiPaulo was going to be a rich and wonderful experience. Starting now...

Tessa pushed aside the sheet covering Javier. Ready to prowl, she knelt above him, framing his lean hips with her knees. She reached down and ran her hands across the plane of his chest.

His eyes opened, and a lazy smile curved his mouth. "I take it you'd like another gift?"

Tessa laughed with pure joy. Age forty had potential, indeed.

CHAPTER 13

"You'd think with all the other stuff in this closet, there'd at least be a miniature Christmas tree," Kate said as she nosed through the pantry off the kitchen.

"A Christmas tree would have to be *seriously* in the closet around here," Tessa pointed out, then took a quick sip of her morning coffee. She'd had little in the way of consecutive hours of sleep at Javier's last night. Not that she was complaining. Far from it.

"Candles...place mats..." Kate paused in her verbal inventory and looked at Tessa over her shoulder. "What do you mean, *seriously?*"

"Christmas isn't on Vee and Irv's holiday list."

Kate closed the closet door. "Well, that's one *duh* moment for me. I knew Vee was Jewish, and if I had thought about it for even a minute, that lack of tree should have hit me. But after one of my mom's calls I'm lucky if I can remember my name—not that she's ever kept all of our names straight, either."

"Your mom called?"

Kate nodded. "Last night while you were off having fun, I was being told that I couldn't settle in Costa Rica because I'm the only one who will take care of her when she's old. As if seventy-eight doesn't mean she's there already. Seven kids altogether, and suddenly I'm the chosen one."

Tessa felt sympathy pangs of anxiety. Not that her mother ever complained, but she still felt guilty for being a five-hour drive from her. "So what are you going to do?"

Kate looked at her blankly. "Do?"

"About your mother?"

"Oh." She laughed. "I pointed out that I've never cared for an elderly pet, let alone a human. I told her that she'd be a lot better off if we just found her a nice nursing home, and that I'd visit her once every other month. Or she could stop toying with me, since we both knew that she'd badgered Marsha into committing to taking her in, years ago."

Kate walked to the coffeemaker. "She's just ticked off that I'm moving so far away. It was tough enough to micromanage me once I moved from Warren." She poured herself a mug and said, "But she'll get over it. She's got the rest of the family to keep her occupied. And now back to that tree. Christmas is three days off, and we've got nothing."

That Christmas came on the heels of Tessa's birthday had never impressed her as a child. Gifts tended to be consolidated and, selfish as it was, she'd always felt cheated.

"Why the rush for the tree?" she asked, trying to put aside remembered grumpiness.

Kate shrugged. "We've got a kid in the house and this is her last Christmas without a kid of her own to take care of. That hit me last night as Mom talked about what she was doing for the grandkids. A tree isn't much of a gift, but it's something."

Tessa was touched. "This is why I love you. Beneath that take-no-prisoners exterior beats the heart of a marshmallow."

"Marshmallows don't have hearts. And don't be getting all emotional on me. Just help me with the tree before Isabel gets back."

"Where is she?"

"She went with Don to drop Mila in the village," Kate said. "I asked him to keep her busy after that...to take her for a car ride or something. Interesting guy, by the way... Did you know he was a roadie for the Grateful Dead?"

"I figured he was just a fan."

"Nope. He spent fifteen years with them, on and off between other gigs. He and Jerry talked a lot, I think... I know for sure that he misses him."

"It sounds like you and Don have spent some time together," Tessa said, feeling oddly proprietary about the house's resident philosopher-caretaker.

"We've talked some," Kate said. "Mostly about what he did before he came to Playa Blanca."

And Tessa realized that she'd talked mostly about herself.

This Tessa–Don–Kate dynamic bothered her. *She* was supposed to be the unselfish one, not Kate, who was best known for her constant song in the note of *me–me–me*.

"Now, get on task here," Kate ordered. She pulled a chair from the table. "Sit, and let's get this figured out."

Forty minutes later they were back at the kitchen table, making paper ornaments and coloring them with Tessa's pastels. The general plan was to decorate one of the potted palms on the back terrace, as there was nothing pinelike available.

Before starting arts-and-crafts hour, Tessa had conducted another Internet foray. She'd ordered a portable baby crib, gender-neutral baby outfits, a zippered portfolio case and some postpregnancy clothes for Isabel. She'd printed out color photos of the gifts, and they now had red sewing thread loops attached to them so she could hang them from the dwarf palm's fronds.

"Whatever happened to your Christmas ornaments?" Kate asked.

Tessa had a huge collection. Every year since birth, she'd received a Christmas ornament from her mother. Collecting begot collecting, and Tessa had picked up even more at after-Christmas sales.

"I had them shipped back to my mom's house." The idea of putting up a Christmas tree for one this year hadn't appealed.

"We could have used them," Kate said. "This tree's going to be sparse."

Tessa checked out the bird that Kate had drawn and was now coloring. "What's that—a deranged robin?"

"Bite your tongue! This, my friend, is the resplendent quetzal."

"I'll buy in on the resplendent part," Tessa said, noting the fabulously long green twin tail feathers that had to be the subject of many male avian "mine is bigger than yours" competitions. "Does it hang out around here?"

"You'd have to go into the cloud forest around Monteverde to see this guy. I've been thinking about buying a few tourist vans and taking groups up that way. From what I hear, it's wet and cool, but beautiful."

"Shouldn't you be focusing on getting your place together, first?"

Kate gave her a brief smile. "First, I have to get my place. I have to get serious after Christmas. How long is Javier in town?"

"At least until after the new year." They had treaded gingerly around each other before she'd left this morning, each taking care not to cross that unseen line into relationship and commitment.

"I'll snag him on Monday, then," Kate said. "I want my offer on the property presented and a deal done by the new year."

"You have the money lined up already?" They'd both received their settlement checks from Midwest National, but she knew that wasn't enough.

"It's in the bank," Kate said, after a brief pause. "No need to worry about it. Finca Murkowski lives."

Tessa had caught Kate's hesitation, but just nodded absently. She didn't like to think of life proceeding after she left.

"So how does it feel not to have had your big annual bash?" Kate asked, referring to Tessa and Jack's holiday open house.

Tessa shook her head. "It's odd, but I hadn't even thought about it. For ten years those parties grew and grew. The last few years...with the caterers and the throngs of people I hardly knew...those, I don't miss at all. But the earlier ones were special. Remember that first one?"

"Yeah," Kate said, not quite sharing Tessa's smile. She frowned as she colored the brilliant green head and back of her quetzal.

Tessa focused on her slightly more traditional crèche and drew in the details.

That first year, she and Jack had just moved into their Royal Oak starter bungalow. Thirty people had meant a body-to-body press, but they did it. What had started as an open house turned into a late-night house party, with Jack's high school collection of J. Geils albums blasting from the stereo. Tessa had drunk too much cheap champagne, and...

Oh God.

She looked back at Kate and set down her pencil as her hand went clammy. She had wondered the other day exactly when she'd gotten in the habit of waiting for disaster—for that other shoe to drop. And now she grasped what she'd been avoiding—that it had been the night of that holiday party.

She'd drunk too much cheap champagne and had gone to her and Jack's slope-ceilinged bedroom on the second floor. Downstairs, people partied on, and she'd lain face-down on the bed among their coats, wishing the room would stop spinning. She'd slept…maybe for ten minutes or maybe an hour. Time had become all the same to her. Then, the sound of a man had awakened her.

"You're never going to get past this, are you?" It had been Jack, and he'd been furious.

Tessa had stirred, thinking he'd found her among the coats and was angry with her. She'd told him before they married about the weeks following her father's death—how she'd drunk too much, partied too much and driven herself into a tree up in Bloomfield Hills. He'd acted understanding, but whether it was real or imagined, Tessa had sensed a change in him, as though he was waiting for her to fall into that pattern again. And drunk on bad champagne, she knew she'd just given him the ammo he sought.

She had been summoning the energy to push herself up-right when another voice came her way.

"I don't know what the hell you're talking about," Kate said.

Tessa had turned her head in the direction of the ex-change. Kate and Jack were on the upper landing, where the stairs made a sharp right, then climbed three more steps to the bedroom. Even if she'd sat up, she wouldn't have had an unobstructed view of Jack and Kate, and unless they took those last steps, they wouldn't have seen her. If she'd been more lucid, she would have told them that she was there. But words and movement hadn't been at the top of her list.

"Kate, we'd never even been out in public together. We were sex partners...conveniences to each other."

"We were lovers," Kate said in a low voice.

"Bull. Neither of us used the word *love*. Look, I told you I was sorry if my seeing Tessa upset you."

"Of course it upset me. She's my best friend!"

"Jesus, how much have you had to drink? Keep your voice down." After a moment, he'd said, "I married her, Kate. If you want to tell her that you slept with me before we were married, go ahead, but you're just going to hurt her."

"What about *my* hurt, Jack? How the hell do you think I feel?"

"I said I was sorry. What more do you want?"

Kate had cried, and Tessa had tried to keep the contents of her stomach down.

"I don't know... I don't know...."

Jack had huffed an impatient sigh. "Let me find someone to give you a ride home. Stay here until I come for you."

And Tessa had lain very, very still, listening to Kate sob, until Jack had come and taken her away.

For a while after that night, she'd let herself believe that her memory had been alcohol skewed, or better yet, that the overheard conversation hadn't happened at all. Then, when the bad blood between Kate and Jack had become too consistent to deny, she'd done what came naturally to her and ignored it. If Kate had wanted to bring up the matter, she would have. And if she didn't, Tessa could feel no guilt over what she wasn't supposed to know.

Over ten years, the memory had become submerged beneath more current woes, only to reappear now. Again, she had no idea what to do with it. Jack was physically gone from both of their lives. That should be enough, but for Tessa, it no longer was. She wanted to know why Kate and she had each kept this dark thing to themselves. Or at least tried to. It had to have colored their relationship.

"Hey?" Kate waved a hand in front of her face. "Anybody in there?"

Tessa looked up. "Sorry, I was reminiscing."

"Maybe you could do that *after* you finish your ornament? We've got half an hour, at the outside, before they're back."

She tried to smile, but suspected the results were paltry. "Good point."

Self and selfishness. Tessa knew herself better now than she had ten years ago. She also recognized the selfishness in bringing this up with Kate. She would have to do it for her peace of mind, and someday soon, but today was about Isabel and the future. Tessa grimly set back to work on the crèche.

Christmas Eve

Tessa had Isabel by the hand, hauling her down Playa Blanca's sandy sidewalk. She didn't even seem to notice the strange looks they were getting from the people they passed, but Isabel did. She was always conscious of adults looking at her large belly and her young face.

Tessa had said that there was a surprise waiting for her in the village. After the gifts of the Christmas tree, the things for her and the baby, and the songs in English that Tessa had taught her, Isabel couldn't imagine that there were any more surprises left on Earth for her.

They'd parked the van across the street from Margarita's and joined the stream of beachgoers who'd just gotten off the bus from the city. Isabel would have walked slowly in the afternoon sun, but Tessa would have none of it.

"You're less than half my age," Tessa said in Spanish, urging her along.

"But I'm more than twice your size," Isabel said as they crossed the street. She stopped entirely when they reached the curb, and the sun-worshippers moved in a stream around them. "You're taking me to Mila's stand, aren't you?"

"Just come," Tessa urged.

"I told you I wouldn't go there."

"And I've told you to trust me. We'll only be there a minute. I have something I need to discuss with Mila."

Tessa led her through the large covered porch of Margarita's cantina, letting go of her hand only long enough to stop and talk with Javier. Isabel bit back a smile at the way they kissed each other's cheeks, like the French tourists, when it was obvious in their eyes that they wanted to do so much more. All this bother over such a stupid act!

Then on they went, with Isabel no more able to stop what would happen next than she'd been able to avoid any other portion of her fate. As they neared, she worked up her courage, hoping that it would help her to stand tall in the face of failure.

Mila's stall was busy and colorful, and had a blue tarp roof to shade her goods from the sun. But Isabel did notice that something was missing: her paintings.

Mila must not have understood how handing over the canvases had been handing over her heart, with all its small secrets. Mila must not have known, or she would not have thrown out the pictures. And though Isabel couldn't believe that Mila would treat her that way, she was sure that she had.

"Where are my paintings?" she asked, her voice shaking.

"All sold," Mila replied with a shrug.

"All eight?" Tessa asked.

Mila held her empty hands up, palms to the sky. "You think I've hidden them? Of course all eight. Just this morning, a woman arrived and bought one, then came back with her husband and bought three more. Naïve art, she called them."

Isabel wanted to give her arm a sharp pinch. She had to be dreaming this.

"If they went that quickly, you'll need to raise the prices," Tessa said.

Mila reached into the pocket of her baggy yellow skirt and pulled out her cigarettes. "Prices on what? There are no more."

Isabel's blood began to rush. "I will make more. As many as you wish."

It was then that she caught a shared smile between the two older women, and knew that had been their intention all along.

"This will be a business, Isabel," Tessa said. "I'll loan you the money for supplies, but you'll have to pay me back. That means you need to figure out the hours and materials that go into each canvas. Your time has value, and you need to be paid for it."

"But I just want to paint," Isabel blurted.

"You will also want to eat and have a place to live," Mila said in a voice so dry even Isabel felt parched and speechless.

To think that she might one day live off of something she loved doing! It seemed beyond impossible. Money and ugliness had been forever married in her world, and now they stood apart. Something that had been held tight and knotted inside her began to unravel. For too long she had been too angry, too frightened and too sad.

Now, though? She was almost too happy, if such a state could be. Her throat tightened; her eyes grew wet. Soon even her hand over her mouth couldn't hold back the hard sound that pushed its way out of her. She hadn't cried after Luz had beaten her and then left her in Playa Blanca, waiting for death. She hadn't cried those nights when she had lain awake, sick with worry that Hector would find her and drag her back. Now, Isabel cried.

"Oh, no," Tessa said, her hands fluttering like birds seeking the sky. "Please don't cry."

But Isabel couldn't stop, and soon the two older women joined in. Isabel should have felt a fool. Instead she felt like the luckiest girl ever.

"We are scaring the customers," Mila finally said, sounding embarrassed. She took the hem of her shirt and used it to wipe her eyes. Tessa handed Isabel a tissue, then wiped her own eyes with another.

And one day when her grandchildren asked Isabel what had been the happiest day of her life, Isabel would name this one.

Kate figured that even the business of bliss-seizing should get a rest on Christmas Day. Still, she couldn't kick the feeling that her dream of Finca Murkowski was evaporating. Last night, long after everyone else was sleeping, she'd sat at the computer and finished off all the research Tessa had been pushing her to do. The outcome had sucked. She was going to need far more start-up money than she had thought. Buying the land was a stretch; insuring this operation was going to be torture on a Spanish Inquisition rack.

While the bankers she'd met with in Quepos had been polite, she'd sat on the other side of the table long enough to understand their bland smiles and lack of eye contact. They'd sooner light their money afire than give her even the lesser sum she'd thought she would need.

Unfortunately, other than Tessa, who had given her the ten thousand, everyone else seemed to feel that way, too. She'd hit up her siblings for a loan during her Christmas call to them early this morning when she knew everyone would be gathered at Mom's before church, and had been turned down flat. Hell, if the Christmas season couldn't open their wallets, she was a goner. And there hadn't yet been a nibble on her house in Birmingham, either, which was another sign of bad investment karma, since Birmingham was the hottest market in metro Detroit.

Kate wasn't sure what she'd done to invite all this negative response to what seemed to her a very reasonable plan. She'd seen real estate investors use OPM—other people's money—every damn day in the banking business. When the deal turned golden, everyone was happy. When it went south… Well, she wouldn't even consider that.

But big prizes were reserved for the bold. She was going to make her offer, no matter what. And she needed Tessa to make this work, but not just for her money. Kate had always thought of them as two halves of a business whole, although these past weeks of going solo had made Kate realize that the relationship had been closer to a seventy-thirty split. And she needed Tessa's seventy percent of studied decision-making. That was Tessa's forte—picking a deal apart and wringing the numbers until they screamed. First, though, Kate had to achieve that elusive "buy-in."

She'd tried persuasion. She'd shown her the future Finca Murkowski, and Tessa had praised the land. So why wouldn't she get behind this plan, dammit? Kate could think of only one last-ditch approach: the running-with-scissors ploy. If she included Tessa's ten thousand in the good-faith deposit, then crapped out on the final financing, maybe she'd finally get Tessa to sign on as a partner to help her protect that first chunk of cash. She hated to leverage friendship, but would, if forced.

For now, she'd get on with this inevitable business of Christmas. She'd assumed the rest of the household was awake, but when she left her room, she encountered only silence. The mouthwatering smell of roasting beef drew Kate to the kitchen, where she found Mila cutting a mountain of peeled and boiled potatoes into chunks.

"Have you seen Tessa?" she asked the old woman.

"She has taken Isabel to church."

Kate would have been less startled if she'd been told that Tessa had gone cliff-diving. "Church?"

She couldn't recall Tessa even referring to a church since her wedding day.

"Yes. In the village. Isabel insisted. Now get me an egg, then wash your hands. You are about to learn how to make *kartoffelklösse*."

Kate looked at the big pot of water simmering on the stove, then thought of a Christmas roast cooking back in Warren, and the potato dumplings her mother was no doubt starting to fix for her ingrate siblings' post-gift-opening dinner. Kate handed Mila the egg, then said, "My mom calls them *kopytka*, but I can adjust."

With any luck, Tessa would adjust to partnership, too.

Tessa and churches seldom crossed paths, and today was a reminder why. Hearing Mass said in Spanish gave it a music that Tessa had never imagined, yet it had left her sad, somehow.

Perhaps it hadn't been wise to come here with Isabel. She'd made the girl happy, but as Tessa had sat in that church, she'd had time to think about how she'd constructed something like a movie set for a family life. She had all the trappings, but it was illusory. In a matter of weeks Tessa would be gone, and Isabel would be coming to church alone again. And watching unobserved how content Javier was with his large extended family three pews ahead of her had only made Tessa feel more of a fraud. Maybe Don had had a point when he'd been so protective of his cobbled-together family.

Now she stood in the warm midmorning sun as Isabel made a quick trip to the bathroom. She'd said that the baby was pushing on her bladder, and Tessa was willing to take her word for it. While she waited, trying to look as inconspicuous as possible in the crowd, Tessa noted a sea change coming. The wind was curling in off the ocean, and dark clouds were gathering to the west.

"Tessa? It *was* you I saw!"

Using one hand like a hat atop her head to stop her hair from snaking about, she turned and greeted Javier, then wished him a merry Christmas. His family hung back a few steps, and she could feel the curious gazes of those she hadn't yet met.

"I'm here with Isabel," she explained. "I'm sure she'll be along soon…."

"Then, first you must meet the rest of my family."

He took her by the hand and led her to them. After greeting Margarita and Claire, she met brothers, mother, father and a few uncles, aunts and cousins for good measure. Though she made all the expected responses, Tessa still felt odd. Maybe by being here in this churchyard, she was professing to be more a part of the community than she could be. Or maybe she just had a fat case of the Christmas blues.

Javier's mother invited her to join the family for their dinner, and Tessa thanked her, yet declined, saying Mila had a special meal planned. After his family had begun to drift toward their cars, Javier lingered.

"Do you have plans after this dinner of Mila's?" he asked.

"I'd thought about some pool time, but it doesn't look as though the weather wants to cooperate."

He looked to the clouds gaining on them. "It will blow over."

"I hope so," she said, thinking as much of her mood as the approaching rain.

"Do you have time for me this evening?"

"Of course," she said, unable to let this illusion of belonging end.

And that night at Javier's house, after they'd shared wine and made love, Javier left the bed and returned with a small gift-wrapped box in his hand. Her expression must have telegraphed her dismay because he said, "Take it. Please."

"I have nothing for you," she said, wishing she could push the box back at him, but still somehow also wanting to hold on to it for all she was worth.

"A gift doesn't demand one in return."

Tessa smiled, for that was so different from what her relationship with Jack had taught her. Gifts had always required return in powers of ten.

"You're right," she said. "I guess I'm not very well practiced in gracious acceptance."

"Then I hope some man, someday, showers you with gifts until you learn that they're a Contessa's due."

She laughed at that bit of nonsense, then opened her gift.

"Javier, I couldn't accept this," she said as she touched a fingertip to the large, almost teardrop-shaped pearl set in gold and suspended from a delicate chain. It looked to be an old piece and quite valuable, too.

"But if you don't take it, I'll have to stick it in the back of a drawer until I find another Contessa, which of course will never happen."

"It's too valuable," she said.

"It's a gift, Tessa. No strings. No meanings other than what you choose to give it. I saw the necklace in the jeweler's window by my city office and thought of you. It's that simple."

"And that expensive," she said.

He shrugged, and the gesture made her smile at the absurdity of the entire situation. Two naked people arguing over one antique pearl.

"Ah, so the Contessa remembers how to smile. You had worried me tonight. Now let me put this necklace on you and at least see you wear it until you leave Playa Blanca."

"Then you'll take it back when I go?"

"If that's still your wish."

Smart man, Javier Ruiz, leaving her naked and pearl-adorned as she considered her wishes. Did she really ever want to go?

CHAPTER 14

Christmas had passed, and then New Year's, too. As one day flowed into the next, Isabel felt her optimism expanding along with the skin over her huge belly. More paints and canvases had arrived last week, and she'd savored them as though they were her last meal.

Since today Tessa was off somewhere with Javier Ruiz, Isabel had persuaded Kate to drop her in the village on her way to Quepos. Under Isabel's arm were tucked three more paintings, each lovingly wrapped for their travels to Mila's stall. Now that Isabel had slowed and started sleeping more, she had also come to understand the value of her time. She could only pray that Mila's customers would be willing to pay accordingly. Tessa had assured her that sixty dollars for a painting was not outrageous. It still felt that way to Isabel, though.

She smiled at Margarita as she cut past the edge of the cantina, and then gave a nod to the dreadlocked guitarist sitting on the outside ledge of the covered porch, guitar case at his feet to collect the tourists' change. She slipped into

Mila's stall and set out her newest offerings in the open spots on the table that had become devoted to her work.

"Let me take care of these customers, then we'll price your paintings," Mila said. "With this heat, you might as well go wade in the water until then."

"I'll stay here," Isabel replied.

Mila nodded absently, then handed her the cash pouch to hold so that she'd have both hands free to demonstrate sarong-tying to a young girl.

Isabel glanced at the water. Since coming to Playa Blanca, she had worked a quiet truce with the sea. She would observe it from afar, and it would altogether disregard her. She wasn't insulted. The sea was too large, too unknown and too empty on its surface for her to grasp the allure it held for others.

Even this village beach, with its smattering of tourists and the sweet guitar music coming from Margarita's, made her desperate for something to think about other than herself. The doctor whom Tessa had taken her to see again yesterday had told her that the baby was almost due. Isabel would visit the doctor again next week only because Tessa desired it, and not because she had any wish ever to be poked and prodded that way again. She wanted to keep her hard-earned privacy.

Restless, she sought distraction. Now, the overweight old man halfway to the water, *he* interested her. He was a sight, asleep on a lounge chair with a white towel over his head so his bald scalp could grow no pinker. She picked up Mila's notepad and drew a quick sketch of the man.

Just after the sarong-buyer departed, two young women arrived, each slender and with a small butterfly tattoo on her arm. Isabel hung to the edges of the stall as they sorted through the stacks of fabric. Soon, they began to talk with Mila, and quickly switched to their common German. Isabel blocked the sound, as she did that of the ocean. Turning her back on the sea, she faced Margarita's and counted its noontime customers. Twenty-three…a good day for Margarita.

Once she'd examined those of the twenty-three faces she could see, and stored away the details of the most interesting, Isabel let her eyes slip closed and imagined the sloth she'd seen last night, ever so slowly working its way out on a fat tree branch. As she pictured its hooked toes, the guitarist changed tunes, shifting to the quick sort of song that Tessa would make Isabel dance to.

The image of the sloth disappeared, and Isabel found herself thinking of the small lines that traveled from the corners of Tessa's eyes when she smiled. The lines made her beautiful, but she doubted that Tessa would agree.

The guitarist stopped, and Isabel opened her eyes. Once she had, she wished she could close them forever. A twenty-fourth customer was passing through the crowd in the cantina, and Isabel could swear it was the man she wished dead.

Isabel moved closer to Mila, who was still talking with

the German ladies. *Hector,* she tried to whisper, but not even that sound would come out of her tight throat. She tugged on Mila's sleeve, trying to gain her attention.

Mila glanced at her. "In a moment," she said.

Gathering her courage, Isabel looked back to the cantina, and the man who might have been Hector was gone. Her limbs and her stomach watery with fear, she scanned the beach and the sidewalk stretching to either side of the cantina, but didn't see that hulking build or those razor-thin lips.

Had she imagined him? It was possible. The more she painted, the more the real and the imagined blended into one wild jumble in her mind. But she had neither thought of nor dreamed of Hector or Luz in weeks. Still, memories had a way of hiding in her mind, then popping out when least expected. She might have seen Hector simply because her brain was too tired to hide his ghost anymore.

"You wanted something?" Mila asked her.

Isabel hesitated. How could she tell a woman who carried a knife almost the size of a machete—and would use it with pleasure—that she feared a ghost? She gave the crowd one last quick look and saw no sign of Hector, so she said to Mila, "It was nothing."

"Then let us move on to something," Mila said. "How much do you wish to charge for the new paintings?"

Isabel shivered in the heat, worn from the effort of sealing away Hector's ghost.

"They're bigger than the others," she said. "And I used much more paint than on earlier ones, so I was thinking of sixty dollars."

Mila regarded the works with narrowed eyes. "Sixty, you say?"

Isabel's heart sank. Soon she would be paying for a baby's clothing and the doctor's appointments. "Too much?"

"No, too little," Mila said. "You must learn to be as bold with your expectations as you are with your paintings."

Mila had a way of making life sound so simple, and most times it turned out that way, no matter how many monsters Isabel imagined hiding behind the trees.

"Seventy-five, then," she decreed, and kept her nervous hand-wringing in her mind only.

"Much better," Mila said. She pulled a marker and cardboard signs from the canvas bag she kept beneath one of the tables, and drew a large red "$75" that made Isabel's heart beat faster with both worry and hope.

"Are you spending the afternoon with me?" Mila asked.

Isabel looked at the unwelcoming water, then the cantina where a ghost had lingered.

"I think I'll be happier at home," she said.

"Get a bottle of water from Margarita and walk slowly, then," Mila replied. "I don't want you giving birth on the side of the road."

Isabel wrinkled her nose at the thought. She had not

quite reconciled herself to this baby working its way out of her. Then, on impulse, she leaned forward and kissed Mila's leathery cheek.

"Thank you," she said.

"For what?"

Isabel smiled. "For saving me." And with that, she was off.

She'd just left the shade of Mila's stall when the older woman called to her. "Don't think that sweetness will get you out of the dinner dishes!"

Isabel, who knew better, waved, then bought her water from Margarita before beginning the walk home.

The sun sat high in the sky, and the baby within Isabel wriggled and elbowed, as though unhappy with both the heat and slow pace of their travels. Every step she took away from the cantina was a step closer to calm.

She'd rounded the corner from the village, passed Claire Ruiz's souvenir shop, and was within sight of the gate to her home when calm was chased away. Hector, no ghost, slid from a red car parked at the side of the road.

"Your family has been asking after you," he said.

Isabel turned and ran toward the souvenir shop, but in a matter of steps, a hand clamped down hard around her arm. She felt herself being pulled back against Hector's body and drew in a breath to scream even though there was no one to hear her. Something sharply pointed prodded just below her waist, and she let her breath go.

"You aren't happy to see me?" he said into her ear.

"Let me go," she said as her heart tried to pound its way out of her body. "Luz doesn't want me there, and she won't want this baby around."

"But I've decided that maybe I want you around. You'll be worth something again, soon," he said while turning her back toward the red car. "Now be a good girl and get in."

Isabel wished for Mila and her knife, or Tessa who had shown her only good. But all she had was a body too large to do her bidding, and Hector, who would think nothing of hurting her. Isabel got into the car. Maybe in Quepos where there were stoplights and such, she could escape. And if not, one day soon she would. Or die trying.

Tessa stood with Javier on the deck of what, in a matter of weeks, would be the family hotel's new restaurant. In front of them, the blue of the Pacific stretched on to eternity.

"It's hard to believe that when this place opens, I'll be back in the ice and snow," Tessa said.

"How much longer will you be here?"

Her actual departure date had been another subject they'd tiptoed around.

She touched the pearl necklace resting just below the hollow of her throat. "I leave the twentieth of February."

"A month, then," he said, his gazed fixed on the water.

"Plus a few days," Tessa said. She hated the feeling that

time was slipping away from her. Any other vacation she'd ever taken, she'd been more than ready to return to the comforts of home, but this interlude was far different. Instead of feeling excited about rebuilding a life back home, she found herself listing reasons she must do so. And that *must* felt like a lead weight dragging behind her, spoiling these last days of freedom. Or, as Don had so perceptively pointed out, these last days of entanglements entirely of her own making.

Looking out to sea, Javier nervously tapped the rolled-up blueprints he held against the metal rail of the deck, making a hollow, rhythmic sound. Tessa watched with interest, as he wasn't the sort of man who fussed or fidgeted. He was all lean, economical movement; studied to the point that she'd developed a fondness for knocking him off course.

"What's wrong?" she asked.

"I'm debating the wisdom of speech."

She smiled. "Whenever I've done that, I've decided in retrospect that I would have been better off keeping my mouth shut."

"There is that, and yet…"

"Yet, what?"

"There's the regret that comes from not having said what you wanted to. The moment passes and then…" He shrugged. "It's gone, never to come again."

"So we're talking about the lesser of two potential regrets.

Not very optimistic of you, and you're possibly the most positive person I've ever met. Annoying, almost," she teased.

His answering smile was brief, and Tessa felt almost guilty for toying with him.

"Okay," she said. "Spit it out."

He raised his brows at that. "What I'm wondering, Tessa, is whether you've considered staying here a while longer?"

This time, he'd knocked *her* thoroughly off course. "Javier, I—"

"No, wait. You told me to speak, and now you won't let me."

"That's because I've changed my mind. A woman's prerogative and all that."

"Don't panic. Just listen—"

"But—"

"I would like to make you an offer."

"Offer?" She could hear her voice rising in pitch, all the way to shrill. She was a few weeks short of fully and completely unmarried. The last thing she wanted was another relationship. Impermanence in this aspect of life, at least, suited her, though she had to admit that the sex had been stellar.

"An employment offer," he said.

Her feeling of alarm receded, leaving something close to disappointment in its wake. "I see."

"Walk with me," he said. "We can finish talking on the way to the car."

"Okay."

"You see the retail building?" He pointed uphill, where the newly framed-in structure sat.

"Yes."

"We had planned to have Claire in charge of this part of the business. She was pleased to be doing it, until yesterday, when she found out that she and Nick are expecting a baby. She doesn't want to be speeding up when she should be slowing down. She says that her shop in the village will be enough for her to handle."

"Understandable," Tessa said, at least now somewhat grasping where this was heading.

Javier smiled. "I don't begrudge her the baby, but I'd also like not to have to think about these shops. And I decided last night that the wisest thing I could do is make you an offer.... Would you be willing to help me find the proper tenants?"

Tessa hesitated, pausing to slide her sunglasses from her head, down to cover her eyes. The job was a tempting notion, just the sort of thing she was sure she'd enjoy: new people to meet...business proposals to scrutinize... Yet overall it was insanity to even consider it. She started with her smallest objection.

"We have a slight language barrier."

"Your Spanish has improved, and most everyone you'd be dealing with speaks English, in any case."

"But I'm leaving, and there's a good chance I wouldn't have the job done."

"So stay longer. You have no real deadline, no job waiting."

"That's the way to sweet-talk me," she said with more than a hint of sarcasm.

He laughed, and she tried to keep up with his long strides as they climbed the broad stone steps set into the hillside.

"I don't mean to insult you," he said. "I'm just asking if it might not be more in your interests to stay here a while. It's an idea, Tessa, nothing more."

"A complex one. And the thought of working for you doesn't sit right."

"The two of us, we're a separate issue. Officially you would be working for the hotel manager, not me."

Tessa pushed her sunglasses back up her nose. "It's your hotel, though."

"True, but not relevant."

It seemed that he'd rediscovered his calm when she'd lost hers. "What *is* relevant?"

"What's relevant is that we've gone along these past weeks on your terms. I'm comfortable with that, as are you. I don't seek any changes." He hesitated an instant, then gave a shake of his head. "Incredible. My ex-wife always said I could make a declaration of love sound like a contract clause. In that, at least, she was right. Tessa, what I'm trying to say is that I value you.... I value our time together. I'll take your company as often as you choose to give it, and if it were up to me, that would be more often. But I won't push you."

They'd arrived at his car, but Tessa had enough nervous energy that she could have sprinted back to Vee's house. "And the job offer is?"

"From my perspective, two things. It's an incentive for you to stay longer, and a way for me to take care of a business problem. All very convenient for me, no?" When she would have objected, he took her hands in his. "Don't analyze this to death, Tessa. If you want to do it, then do it."

"I don't know what I want," she said.

Except she knew in her heart that this was unsettling only because she saw it as possible. In some ways, she imagined herself far better in this setting than she did in the Midwest.

"Then think about it," Javier said. He opened the car door for her. As she was sliding in, he added, "I'm glad I didn't offer you the gallery space, as I was also considering, or you'd be running for the airport, wouldn't you?"

"Not helpful," she muttered as he crossed around the front of the car and to his door.

Damn, but he was good at planting that seed. And as he'd intimated, he'd also left her very, very scared. North... south...which way lay home? Tessa no longer knew.

The deed was done, and Kate was quite likely one dead dog. She had made her offer on the Finca Murkowski a week before. After a bold counteroffer by the owners, a couple from

San José well aware of the booming land values, she'd ended up putting all her worldly savings—and that chunk of Tessa's—on the line. Today, after a bit more haggling, her counter-counteroffer had been accepted. Torn as she was between joy over ownership and abject terror over the cost of her craziness, she was turning into a poster child for mood swings. Immediately after finding that she was a future *finca* owner, she'd driven to Quepos to engage in one last, desperate round of sucking-up to the bankers she'd met with before Christmas. It had worked no better on them than it had on her, back in the day. She remained a tad short on the financing, but she still had thirty days to pull off a miracle. And she was going to need all thirty.

Now that New Year's had passed, maybe house hunters would reemerge in Michigan, though her agent had said yesterday that the cold snap they were having had slowed business. Realistically, only a cash sale could help her at this point, and that fell into the "when pigs fly" spectrum of possibilities.

No matter which way Kate sliced the numbers, a battle loomed with Tessa. Normally, Kate wouldn't be overly concerned. She usually came out victorious, since Tessa was too wrapped up in the need to simultaneously please everyone to have developed brass balls like Kate's. Of course, that formerly obliging Tessa also would have given her fifty grand, no questions asked. And she hadn't. The times, they definitely were a-changin', and not in Kate's favor.

Kate rounded the sharp bend at the south end of Quepos and slowed for the two-lane bridge that was really more like a one-and-a-half lane. Faced with this bridge, a driver was left with two choices: politely alternate with traffic from the opposite side, or pound the accelerator and go for it. Kate was a go-for-it girl, especially because this van was so big and hideous that anyone with a brain would realize the driver didn't give a damn what she might hit.

Because Kate was a little distracted, she didn't even push forward before the white truck opposing her staked his claim on the road. After that, she took her turn. She was approaching the narrowest part of the rusty bridge when a jerk in a red boat of a car that had been behind the white truck gunned it and ran head-on at her. Kate swerved the van to the side.

"Dickhead!" she yelled at the driver.

Someone else was in the red car. Kate thought maybe the passenger bore a general resemblance to Isabel, but didn't think long about it because she was busy lecturing the driver, who was well by her at this point, about exactly how small his penis was, and how every woman who saw him knew that immediately.

"Great country. Asshole drivers," she said, then left Quepos proper for the road beyond.

As she drove, she kept thinking about Tessa and the money she'd just spent in a chunk, and wondering why guilt was niggling at her over a necessary act. Did the end really justify the means? Kate had lived by that theory, but wasn't so sure anymore. She'd been talking to Don too much, and like Tessa, the guy had an overdeveloped sense of social conscience. Kate hated to think that it was rubbing off on her.

Maybe, like Scarlett, she just needed to return to her personal Tara and hold that warm earth again. To remember what was truly important. The urge strong on her, Kate took a left and headed up the mountainside. She had some major figuring out to do.

On an evening like this, Don could have used a dog with tracking instincts, but Jerry, a complete bum, had instincts only for finding shade and mooching food. The dog was sound asleep while Don was wondering where the hell the women of the house had gotten themselves to.

Part of Don's frustration was his own fault. This morning, it might have made good sense to tell the ladies that he was making his world-famous (in a very small sense) vegetarian chili for dinner, but that would have taken the surprise out of the event. Instead, he'd blown his own timing. Sunset was coming and his chili was turning to mush.

Don stumped his way from the terrace to the kitchen and turned down the flame under the pot. As long as he was by the fridge, he grabbed an Imperial, then returned outside to legal pad number six in what might well be an endless series of notes for his twisted life tale.

In one of her increasingly frequent visits, Kate had volunteered to type everything up for him. But he didn't scribble his notes because he lacked computer skills, he just liked paper. But he also liked the idea of working with Kate, so he'd given her the go-ahead to smack notebook number one—Don, the pretripping years—into a word processing program. Maybe by the time she got to notebook six, he'd have decided if she was utterly screwed up or repairable, and she'd have decided the same about him. He wasn't sure how someone who had grown up in the pack Kate had described had ended up expecting the world to wait on her, but that was his grand mystery to unravel. Once he figured out where everyone was…

About fifteen minutes later, the first to rematerialize was Tessa, with Javier Ruiz in tow.

"Do you like vegetarian chili?" Don asked his neighbor.

"With enough beer, yes," Ruiz answered as a man should.

"Then set yourself a place at the dining room table."

Don grinned as the couple who spent most of their days pretending they weren't a couple retreated into the house.

Next home was Mila, who joined him on the terrace, as she did every night. She pulled a chair away from the patio table, set down her glass of scotch with its customary three ice cubes already vaporized into the Chivas, then lit a cigarette. Don didn't ask her if she wanted his chili; she'd live on that and nicotine, given the chance.

"You must have knocked out Isabel," he said instead, knowing that his favorite teenager had gone into the village to see Mila.

"Knocked out?" Mila hesitated a second, then apparently pinned down the colloquialism. "Why? Is she sleeping?"

"Well, she's not out here to say hi to me." Now he took a second to catch up with the action. "I take it that you don't know where she is?"

"Why should I? She left me just past noon."

Isabel wasn't the sort to disappear for a long stretch. Don worked his way to his feet.

"What?"

"Be right back," he said.

Mila didn't wait. She followed him to double-check Isabel's room.

Don felt a little sick. Isabel and her sketch pad were not far from each other for long. Yet here it sat in the middle of her bed. If she'd been back to the house since noon, it would be with her. But just because he was feeling edgy didn't mean it was time to check the village for a girl in labor. Yet.

"Did she say anything when she left you today?" he asked Mila.

"Just that she was coming back here."

Now he'd share his worry....

"Something is not right," Mila said, beating him to the punch.

"I know."

They left Isabel's room and found Tessa and Ruiz, one floor up, in the living room, sitting on the couch and making out like a couple of horny teenagers.

"Sorry to interrupt," Don said. "I was wondering if you'd seen Isabel?"

"Isabel." Tessa looked around as though she might be hiding behind a chair. "No, not since breakfast. Why?"

"She left Mila's stall at noon, but no one's seen her."

Worry drew Tessa's brows together. "I don't like this," she said.

"Me, either," Don replied.

"It's possible that Kate picked her up again," Mila said. "They might be spending the day together."

Don shook his head. "Possible but not probable. Still, we've got no choice but to kick back and wait for Kate."

"But while we're waiting, I'll call the hospital in Quepos, just in case," Tessa said, then rose. "I don't like thinking of Isabel having that baby alone."

Soon after Tessa had left to make her call, Don went down to the kitchen. He dumped his beer, got a glass of ice water, and returned to join the others in the living room for the duration. Tessa reappeared not long after and said that Isabel was not in the hospital. He had a feeling this was going to be a damn long night—and as the sun slipped into the ocean, he was sure of it.

Kate showed up around nine-thirty. When she saw the group of them in the living room, her smile faded.

"What's up?" she asked. "Gathering of the clan?"

"Minus one," Tessa said. "We were wondering if you've run across Isabel since you dropped her in the village."

"Why?" Kate asked, then tossed the van keys to Don.

"No one's seen her since noon," he said.

Kate frowned. "No, I haven't seen her. I was up at my property, and before that in Quepos, and... *Damn!*"

"What?" Don asked.

"I might have seen her. I can't swear to it, but I'm pretty sure."

"Where?"

"In oncoming traffic," Kate said. "Has she had a boyfriend or male relative visit her since she's been here?"

"No one," Mila said firmly.

"Then maybe this wasn't her," Kate said.

"Or maybe it was," Don replied. Isabel had told him enough of her past that he'd now gone beyond feeling a little sick with worry. "What did this guy look like?"

Kate shrugged. "I don't know... Beefy."

"Beefy?" Tessa echoed. "Can't you do better than beefy?"

"You try describing someone you saw for less than ten seconds, okay? I was a little pissed off. I wasn't paying very close attention."

"Arguing will do no good," Ruiz said as he took Tessa's hand.

Don didn't miss the way Kate's eyes narrowed when she caught that small move. There was too much bad mojo in the air for him to concentrate as he needed to.

"Hector," Mila said to him. "I'm sure it's Hector. No one else would have reason to take her. Luz must have told him that she'd left Isabel in Playa Blanca."

"And who is Hector?" Tessa asked.

Bones and spirit aching, Don slowly came to his feet; he had a drive ahead of him. "Hector is Luz's boyfriend. And I'll guarantee that Isabel didn't ask him to show up here."

Tessa's face had paled. "Where does Luz live?"

"In San José," Don replied. "Where I'm going."

Ruiz stood. "That's easily a two-and-a-half-hour drive."

"No other options available," Don said.

"Two, actually," the lawyer replied. He pulled his cell phone from his pocket. "Tell me what you know, and I'll call friends I have in the city. They can be there before you can. And you won't go alone. I'm coming with you."

"Thanks," Don said, thinking that it was a damn weak word for the gratitude he felt at not making this possibly futile trip on his own. "I really appreciate this."

Ruiz shook his head. "You're welcome, of course, but that's what community is for."

CHAPTER 15

Community.

Javier's one simple word hit Tessa with staggering impact. Long after Don and he had left, she clung to the idea. Curled up on the sofa, with a nervous Mila and a fidgety Kate as company nearby, she considered what her life had been and what it yet might be.

Community… Tessa's marriage had had no community for most of its years. Her job's form of community had centered around the negative…surviving the misery of downsizing. And her relationship with Kate had slipped into a false sense of community. Other than the Midwest National crisis, they had shared nothing of true emotional substance in years. Kate had kept her lovers secret, and Tessa, her doubts about her marriage. And both of them had held tight to their private knowledge of Kate's prior relationship with Jack.

Yet here, in this sun-drenched house, Tessa had found not just family, but community for herself. And most miraculously, she'd done it without being an emotional contortionist, bending her desires to remain always subordinate to others'. Being in Playa Blanca mattered more than what she'd be leaving behind. Here, she could put down roots and—as long as she was dreaming big—maybe even one day get her mother to join her.

All of these hopes would sustain her tonight, while she waited for news of Isabel. And once the news came—*please, God, let it be good*—Tessa would take these hopes and nurture them slowly, in her own way.

She willed herself to relax, to think only positive thoughts for Isabel. Kate, however, was proving a distraction. Seated in a low white armchair opposite Tessa, she had crossed and uncrossed her legs enough times that Tessa was tempted to ask her if she might need to use the facilities. But because Tessa knew she was better off keeping her silence, she rolled the other way, facing the back of the raw silk couch.

"I need to talk to you about my property," Kate said from behind her.

"Not now."

"Why not now? We've got nothing to do but sit around."

Tessa tried to keep the calm she'd been fostering from within, but it was a losing battle. She sat up, facing Kate. "Because *I* don't want to talk about your ranch, even if you do. Ninety percent of my attention is elsewhere, and I want to sit here and…and just *sit*, dammit."

"You heard Javier," Kate said. "It's at least two and a half hours before they even get there. Any news before then is going to be secondhand. You might as well occupy yourself."

Mila sighed, then stood, pulling her cigarettes from her flowered skirt's rectangular patch pocket. "As much as it amazes me to be saying this, Kate is right. We can't sit here and stare at each other for the next two hours. I'm going outside to smoke in peace."

After Mila left, Kate kept giving Tessa an expectant stare that reminded her of a golden retriever awaiting a treat. Tessa finally caved. "All right. What about the property?"

Kate rubbed her hands over her bare knees. "Allrighty, then. Here's my news. I made an offer on it, and after a little…okay, a *lot* of haggling, it's mine!"

Tessa tried to absorb this bit by bit. "You made an offer?"

"I said I was going to."

"But I haven't seen you meet with Javier." And she had been with or near him most of the days he'd been spending in Playa Blanca.

"I decided I didn't need to see him. I'm buying property, Tessa, not setting up a multinational corporation. So aren't you going to congratulate me?"

"Congratulations," she said as politely as she could, considering that she was sure the dreaded other shoe was about to drop with a vengeance. Kate wanted more than congratulations. Guaranteed.

"Thanks, though there's been a slight glitch…. I can't pay you back as quickly as I'd hoped," Kate said apologetically.

It was exactly the shoe Tessa had expected. "Why not?"

"My house hasn't been snapped up as quickly as I'd thought it would be, but the biggest issue of all is that the whole deal is going to cost more than I thought it would. A lot more. But if you'd kick in some more…just another twenty or thirty…I could make you a minority partner and—"

"Kate, I don't want to be a partner. I'm ten thousand in the hole already, and that's a huge amount of money to me. I'm not throwing three times that into something that—A—doesn't interest me in the first place and—B—I know is going to be a long-term investment no matter how much sunshine you blow my way. And I was right in the first place. I *don't* want to talk about this right now!"

"But—"

"I'm not joking, Kate. Not. Now."

Kate stood and began pacing the room. "Tessa, you owe me, goddamn it!"

Kate's words were nearly a slap. "I *owe* you?"

"Hey, I came down to Costa Rica for you."

"And seized your goddamn bliss. I don't see how this makes me owe you."

Kate's blue eyes held an anger that Tessa hadn't seen in seventeen years of friendship. "You just do! You can't just leave me hanging like this. I'm sick of being screwed over."

Screwed over. Jack. Even now, damn Jack. As much as Tessa didn't want to deal with this on top of the night's mounting woes, there was no turning away. She had no excuse of drunkenness, or of fear of shredding the status quo. It was already in tatters.

"You're talking about you and Jack," Tessa said.

Kate stilled in her pacing. Her mouth worked once, then twice before she spoke. "Tell me that you didn't know before you married him."

She had thrown the words as a challenge, so Tessa gave one of her own. "I didn't. And now you can tell me why in ten years you never said a word about this."

Kate sat in the armchair once again and was silent for a few moments.

"So when did you find out?" she eventually asked.

"The Christmas right after Jack and I married, and only because I overheard the two of you arguing. I thought you were just social acquaintances, Kate. That's what Jack led me to believe, and you acted as though you didn't care that we were dating. If I'd known you were involved...or interested in him romantically, I'd never have started seeing him."

Kate's laugh was a dark thing. "We'll never know that for sure, will we?"

And in Kate's bitterness, Tessa began to sense something else...that perhaps all had turned out exactly the way Kate had wanted it to. Tessa's anger grew until she no longer wanted to take care with Kate's feelings.

"No, we'll never know for sure, and that's worked in your favor for a whole lot of years."

"What the hell do you mean by that?"

"It's handy when people owe you, and God knows you can do no better than having Tessa DiPaulo owe you. I'd just come off the worst months of my life when I met Jack. I was busy making up to you for the way I'd screwed up at work after my dad died, and you sure put me through my paces."

"So...*what?* You think I saved up Jack for later leverage?"

"All I'm saying, Kate, is that you thrive on your secret bargaining chips. Look at your relationship with Hank Kyle."

"That's ridiculous! I was with him because I loved him, and I thought he loved me!"

The fire burned strongly in Tessa. All the years she'd tried to be polite, all the years she'd tried to accommodate... Never again.

"First Jack, then Hank. Sorry, but it's entirely too coincidental," she said to Kate. "You know, I didn't think about it until just tonight, but I'll bet it was handy having Jack on the hook. A girl never knows when she might need a favor. But he dumped me, and you lost your ammo against him, so you figured you might as well fling a little guilt my way in exchange for some cash."

"Do you think I *plan* this stuff? That I choose people who I know will treat me like crap?"

"I don't know, Kate. You tell me."

She shook her head. "Christ, Tessa, you're far more calculating than I'll ever be. It scares the shit out of me that you've even come up with this theory."

"It should scare you because, whether you mean to have it happen or not, it does. It's your M.O., Kate. You were born knowing how to manipulate, and the more of us you can get on the hook, the less you have to do for yourself. You're the smartest intentional victim I've ever met."

Kate stood. "You were right. You're in no shape to talk now. Forget we even started."

Tessa was exhausted, both physically and emotionally. "Too late. There's no going back from this one. You can repay me the ten thousand at a thousand a year, no interest. I don't care. But I won't be manipulated into giving you any more. It's time you did something on your own, Kate. And it's time for me to learn to do that, too." She drew a ragged breath, unsure exactly when she'd started crying. "And you want to know the scariest thing of all? Even with all this garbage we've been carrying around, I still love you. I still think of you as my best friend."

"Right." Kate turned heel and walked down the stairway.

A moment later Tessa heard a door slam. She again curled up on the couch, sick for what she'd said, yet relieved, too. She'd burned it all—both the good and the bad. And now that the land was charred and empty, a small green seed might grow. And then they would start again.

Isabel had been reborn, a feat she found quite miraculous for a girl about to give birth. And this birth would happen soon. The pains had started, just one every now and again, as Hector had driven away from Playa Blanca and into the mountains. At first she thought that her wish to die was coming slowly, awfully true. She'd taken it back and prayed to her God for forgiveness. And then she'd calmed enough to sense what was happening to her body.

She'd said nothing to Hector, hiding her pains the best she could. To show him a weakness was to have it used against her. She'd learned that lesson long ago and had no desire to have it repeated. He'd taken her to Luz's house, where she'd been given a hard slap as a greeting. She'd sat in the corner, sullenly nursing her bleeding lower lip and waiting for the next pain to come. It had, but after a few hours, salvation had arrived, too.

When the men came to the door, Isabel had assumed that they were dates for Luz. But these two men were neither dates nor the police. When Luz would have barred the way, they shoved her aside, and one told Isabel that Don had sent them to take her home. Isabel wasn't so kind that she did not enjoy seeing her cousin sprawled on her fat, evil ass, howling like the street bitch she was. Isabel also did not mind seeing the men smash Luz's precious television and all of her dishes as a warning to leave alone those who lived in Playa Blanca. The warning would work, for Isabel had cost Luz and Hector more than she was worth.

And now, hours later, she sat in Don's van, coming closer to her home. She'd learned that the men who'd rescued her were friends of Javier Ruiz, whom she would never underestimate again.

"How much longer until home?" she asked Don, loving that word, *home*.

Don looked back over his seat. "We'll be to Quepos in half an hour, and home right after that." Another pain suddenly gripped her, making her belly harder than the concrete floor in Luz's house. She tried not to make a sound, for she didn't want to frighten Don or Señor Ruiz. But this time the pain was too sharp.

Señor Ruiz, who was driving, didn't look away from the road while asking, "Are you hurt, Isabel?"

"It's nothing. Just a backache," she lied, speaking through clenched teeth. Isabel would do whatever it took to get home, where she had every intention of having her baby. Being born in such a beautiful place would surely bring a child good fortune.

"Turn on the interior lights," Don said to Señor Ruiz, who did as asked. Isabel tried to mask her pain as Don unbuckled his seat belt and came back to join her.

"Truth, kid," he said. "Did you get hurt?"

She could feel sweat popping out on her face, and Don would see it, too. Even if she weren't a panting mess, he would know; Don knew her better than anyone.

"Not hurt," she said. "But the baby is coming."

"Coming *now?*"

"Trying," she said.

"Change of plans," Don said to Señor Ruiz. "We're going to the hospital in Quepos."

He only nodded, but Isabel began to cry.

"I want to have my baby in my own bed," she told Don.

"I don't think that would be very good for the mattress," he said. "Let's go to the hospital."

"No teasing. I want to have my baby at the house. Women do it all the time."

He pushed her hair away from her forehead, which was now damp with sweat. "And there's the difference, kid. You're fifteen and not a woman. I want you where the doctors can help."

She could not argue with him, both because he had only her safety at heart and because her water had just broken.

"My water… I'm all wet," she told Don, and never had she seen a man in a cast move so quickly.

"Drive faster," Don said to Señor Ruiz.

Bracing himself on the seats, Don went to the back of the van, then came back forward with a towel in his hands. Isabel knew it wouldn't be polite to mention that she had last seen him wiping dirt from the van's back window with this particular piece of fabric. She took it and mopped up her legs the best she could. As for the rest, she had a more pressing matter to deal with. Literally.

Tessa had dozed on the couch long after Kate left, but the ringing telephone brought her fully awake. She sprinted to the closest extension and answered.

"Hello?" she said over her pounding heart.

"Tessa, it's Javier." He sounded as exhausted as she felt.

"Is everything okay?"

"It's fine," he said. "We have Isabel, and she would like for you and Mila to come meet us at the hospital in Quepos."

"Hospital? Is she hurt?"

His brief yet genuine laugh was enough to let her relax a little. "She's hurting, since she's in labor," he said. "But she's not hurt."

"Labor! I'll wake Mila, and… Wait, you and Don have the van, don't you? How are we going to get to the hospital?"

"My car is still out front. I left the keys on the driver's side floor since it occurred to me that someone might need to use it. After the drive I've just had, I wish it had been me."

She smiled. Don's Dead Head van was a far sight from Javier's luxury vehicle. "No doubt. Are you at the hospital now?"

"Yes. Don's with Isabel, getting her checked in."

"We'll be there soon," Tessa said, then hung up.

After rousing Mila, Tessa went to Kate's bedroom door. It would be a small step, waking her and inviting her along, but to Tessa's mind, small steps were often those best taken. She knocked, then entered at Kate's invitation.

"Isabel's having the baby," Tessa said. "She's at the hospital in Quepos, and Mila and I are getting ready to leave. I was wondering if you'd like to join us."

Kate didn't answer immediately, and her expression remained shuttered.

"Yes," she finally said. "I think I would."

Tessa nodded and turned back to the door.

"And, Tessa?"

"Yes?" she said as she faced Kate again.

"Thank you for asking."

This could be fixed, Tessa thought as she left the room. But this time she would not take the whole burden on herself. This time, they would get it right. They would be friends as open, sharing equals. No hidden agendas, nothing to make weathering life's course more difficult than it might already be.

But first, it would be Isabel's turn to take another step in life. Tessa, Mila and Kate rushed to the hospital, where Don and Javier waited. At Isabel's insistence, Mila and Tessa joined the girl in her labor room. Six long hours later, when the sun had long ago risen, Tessa became an auntie to a squalling baby girl named Beatriz, who possessed an amazing amount of dark hair. As far as family went, Tessa was sure it got no better than this.

And that, as Kate would put it, sealed the deal....

One week later...

The moment had come for Tessa to make her move. Through a series of phone calls, she had tracked down Vee in Italy. The house was as quiet as it would ever be. Tessa glanced outside. Isabel and Beatriz were both napping under the shade of an umbrella. Kate was nearby, proofing the business prospectus she'd need for upcoming meetings with potential investors to whom Javier had offered to refer her. And Don sat next to Kate, scribbling in yet another writing pad about what he'd told Tessa was going to be a cautionary tale...that of his life.

Tessa drew a deep breath to feed her courage, then dialed. Vee answered on the third ring. When she heard Tessa's voice, she took control of the conversation, as only Vee could.

"It's been killing me not to call you!" Vee said. "But I decided to treat you like you were a monk retreating into a monastery or something."

Tessa laughed at the incongruous image. "That hasn't been quite the deal around here."

"I got your one message, but I figured that Don would be able to help you. He knows that house better than I do. And if something were really wrong, he'd have e-mailed me. But you've been able to relax, right? Maybe think a little?"

"Actually, I decided to live a little."

"Good…*good!*"

There was no time to leap like the present. "Vee, if you and Irv are willing, I'd like to lease your house from you."

"What?"

"I'd like to lease your house," she repeated. "For at least six months. I'd just go out and buy one, except I don't want to be as impetuous as I've accused Kate of being in her local real estate habits."

"Kate's bought a house in Playa Blanca?" Vee asked.

"A small one, along with about half a damn mountain sitting to the northeast of the village. She plans to eventually turn it into a fairly posh base camp for biking treks."

"Not a bad idea," Vee said. "But I want to hear about *you*."

Just for the fun of teasing Vee a bit, Tessa gave half an answer. "I think eventually I'd like something a little south of your location." South would bring her closer to the hotel and the small art gallery she wanted to open eventually. It was in so many ways an ideal plan. She could work with local artists, including Isabel, and perhaps even eventually train Isabel to run the gallery. Tessa had found her small, simple bliss, and she would treat it with care. "I've decided to start a business down here."

"Hang on. I need to sit down and just maybe stick my head between my knees."

Tessa laughed.

"Now…" Vee said. "Why don't you start at the beginning?"

"I am." Smiling, she looked out at the terrace where her patchwork family was gathered. "A brand-new beginning."

And Tessa was sure it would be the last one she would ever need.

Detective Maggie Skerritt is on the case again!

**Maggie Skerritt is investigating a string
of murders while trying to establish her
new business with fiancé Bill Malcolm.
Can she manage to solve the case
while moving on with her life?**

Spring*Break*

by *USA TODAY* bestselling author
CHARLOTTE DOUGLAS

You always want what you don't have

Dinah and Dottie are two sisters who grew up in an imperfect world. Once old enough to make decisions for themselves, they went their separate ways—permanently. Until now. Will their reunion seventeen years later during a series of crises finally help them create a perfect life?

My Perfectly Imperfect Life

Jennifer Archer

HN34
Available March 2006
TheNextNovel.com

REQUEST YOUR FREE BOOKS!

2 FREE NOVELS TO INTRODUCE YOU TO OUR BRAND-NEW LINE!

There's the life you planned. And there's what comes next.

e◆HARLEQUIN.com

The Ultimate Destination for Women's Fiction

For FREE online reading, visit
www.eHarlequin.com now and enjoy:

<u>Online Reads</u>
Read **Daily** and **Weekly** chapters from
our Internet-exclusive stories by your
favorite authors.

<u>Interactive Novels</u>
Cast your vote to help decide how these
stories unfold...then stay tuned!

<u>Quick Reads</u>
For shorter romantic reads, try our
collection of Poems, Toasts, & More!

<u>Online Read Library</u>
Miss one of our online reads?
Come here to catch up!

<u>Reading Groups</u>
Discuss, share and rave with other
community members!

For great reading online,
visit www.eHarlequin.com today!

Since when did life ever tell you where you were going?

Sometimes you just have to dip your oar into the water and start to paddle.

THE
SUNSHINE
COAST
NEWS

KATE AUSTIN

Available February 2006
TheNextNovel.com

HN32

What happens when new friends get together and dig into the past?

Ex's and Oh's
Sandra Steffen

A story about secrets, surprises and relationships.

A forty-something blushing bride?

Neely Mason never expected to walk down the aisle, but it's happening, and now her whole Southern family is in on the event. Can they all get through this wedding without killing each other? Because one thing's for sure, when it comes to sisters, *crazy* is a relative term.

The
GOOD KIND OF CRAZY

TANYA MICHAELS